"...perfectly captures the struggle of a young artist's battle between her dreams and the "real job," all while juggling her responsibilities as an adult, a sister, a daughter, a friend, and the romantic interest.

Reading this novel was like a breath of sweet relief. I kept asking myself, "Was this written about me?" I'm so glad I'm not the only one who feels like this!"

Barbara's honest personality, quirky sense of humor, and passion shine throughout; a thoughtful and inspiring read I'd recommend to any young adult." ~Gabrielle Burke, Pittsburgh artist

"Sweet and smart and goofy and bold, Jadyn is at a financial and professional crossroads when she finally decides she's going after everything women want but are afraid we won't get. Starring an open, giving heroine who has delightfully relatable clay feet, Ms. Brutt's novel is bright and engaging without highlighting its own cleverness, which makes discovering it doubly enjoyable. Set aside some uncommitted hours because you won't want to stop reading as Jadyn figures out that she doesn't have to say yes to anyone but God and herself ...

and to the teal paisley tights." ~*Sandra Byrd, author of Let Them Eat Cake*.

"A lighthearted and fun contemporary debut by Barbara Brutt about the quirky and stormy life of a people pleaser and the desperate journey of her search for the only One who can calm the true storm of her heart. Jadyn's life is full…too full, and from the first page to almost the last, we feel the dizzying impact of her need to say 'yes' to all the demands around her at the expense of her heart and creativity. Brutt displays the exhausting life of a Yes-man…er…woman even through her prose. Teal Paisley Tights is a good reminder that being godly means saying 'no' to what others expect of us and finding God's purpose beneath the flurry for peace." ~*Pepper Basham, author of the Penned in Time and Mitchell's Crossroads series*.

"one of those books you simply can't put down. Whether it be the endearing corkiness of Jadyn Simon, or the relatable concept of dream vs. responsibility, Barbara Brutt has created a book for our time! No matter what stage of life you're currently in, I advise you to open the pages of this book and follow Jadyn on a journey I believe we all, if not most can relate to. I promise you won't be disappointed." ~*Angelea Taylor, Pittsburgh Blogger*

Teal Paisley Tights

*To Raven
of Neverland.
May you always dream big dreams.
Dreams don't always come true,
but they can!*

BARBARA BRUTT

*Thank you for
celebrating
this dream with
me, and enjoy the
dejavu in chapter 2!
Barbara Brutt*

Vinspire Publishing
www.vinspirepublishing.com

ISBN: 978-1-7321348-8-1

Published by Vinspire Publishing, LLC

To Grandmother Betty who flipped my awful sunset painting upside down and revealed a foggy sea scape

Table of Contents

Chapter One

Today would have gone so much better in my paisley tights. If a superpower could be clothing, mine would be teal paisley, and it would make me strong and confident.

Like Superman, I kept those tights hidden away. People weren't ready for them. Definitely not Victoria.

I wriggled out of my tights behind my desk and the privacy of the thin cubicle walls. The air-conditioning units whirred—the loudest noise in the early morning atmosphere. I rubbed my bare legs with my hands as chill air from the vents circled my ankles. But, no use. My freshly shaven legs prickled like a frightened porcupine. I sighed. Straightening my little black dress over my thighs, I stuffed the offending tights into my junk drawer, far from Victoria's scathing gaze.

My boss's words echoed in my head: *Do you have a skin disease today, Miss Simon? Those tights are unprofessional. Remove them.* Even thinking about that moment made my cheeks burn.

What was so wrong with fun, patterned tights anyway?

Coffee. Coffee would take the edge off my fun-deprived morning. I slipped my black heels back on and walked out of my cubicle, only to remember that I needed to mail a client some information packets. Two steps back, and I stood over my desk, rifling through papers. I found the envelopes and scooped them up.

The cubicle wall creaked.

Ethan.

He leaned against the fabric-cladded partitioning, and warmth spread across my face. Forget garden gnomes. I wanted a life-sized marble sculpture of him. I imagined him actually leaning his entire weight against the wall, and how it would buckle underneath his pure muscle.

Smile.

"Just booked our dinner reservations for tonight."

His baritone voice shook me back to reality. Ethan McAlvey. The office hottie had asked *me* on a date! I gulped down a squeal and hid it behind a laugh.

His mint shirt magnified his hazel eyes, and the office lights enticed me to stroke his blond hair. It was the lights. I swear. You can't trust fluorescents. My fingers twitched, and I smashed them between the envelopes I was holding.

I should say something. "What time did we agree on again?" Ethan didn't need to tell me. *Seven* was tattooed on my mind, but I loved hearing his voice.

"I'll pick you up at seven at your place." Ethan glanced at my hand. "Were you headed to the mail room?"

My cheeks warmed again. So glad for light brown skin. Did he know that my envelope-holding hand wanted to fling the papers aside and bury itself in his wheat-colored locks?

"Oh, right." I looked at my hand. "Wanted to thop drese—drop these—off and I need coffee!"

Ethan's eyes twinkled. I resisted the urge to press my hands to my hot cheeks and smiled up at him.

"How about you go get that coffee?" Ethan reached for the envelopes. "And I'll take these for you."

The zap from his fingers brushing mine could have been a caffeine all its own. I wanted to skip down the hallway, singing, "Who needs coffee?" Instead, I swallowed and tried not to grin like a crazy person.

I brushed past Ethan, thrilled at his nearness and breathing in his spicy scent, and stepped onto a magic carpet moving my feet down the hallway. All my nerve endings had transferred themselves to my fingers, and I imagined them glowing. Up ahead, through the glass of Victoria's corner office, a newer employee hunched under a Hurricane Victoria tirade. She was going to need a coffee, too.

Victoria pointed at the door, and my coworker skittered out of the office with folders clasped to her chest. Her straight brown hair curtained her face as she passed, and the tiniest of sniffles escaped. I didn't know her, but maybe a hot cup of liquid comfort would brighten her day, too.

The break room was past Victoria's office. My theory was that Victoria kept tabs on everyone who visited the room for coffee or, perish the thought, took an actual break. I scanned the company bulletin board as I walked by, my eyes lingering on the call for volunteers to work with inner-city teenagers.

With a coffee in each hand, I carried myself straighter, as if I were wearing my paisley tights— or maybe trying not to spill. I set down a cup and perused the creamers. Although an admirer of black coffee, the secret to the ideal cup was the balance of sweet, cream, and bitter. I grabbed two flavored creamers for the road. For a moment, I wasn't sure where to carry the little tubs, but then dropped them into my blouse.

"Excellent. You removed those terrible tights." The coffee cooled in my hand. I glanced over my shoulder at Victoria.

"I need to speak with you."

I followed Victoria back to her office. She gestured to the recently vacated chair with her perfectly French-tipped nails. I breathed deep, sinking into the chair and hoping that Hurricane Victoria wasn't about to strike again. I perched on the edge of the chair with coffees in both hands and two creamers poking the soft flesh of my chest.

"I'm transferring several clients to you. Specifically, Maximillion Louis. We recently stole him from Lines & Designs Etcetera. He's a demanding man who gets what he wants, and I'm determined that he will become one of our permanent clients. I'm reassigning Mr. Louis to you because the previous consultant proved…incapable. Therefore, I let her go. You will also be in charge of all other clients from that consultant."

She sneered down her nose. "There is no room for mistake or failure."

I would need more coffee.

The intern dropped off a box of files on my new clients and handed me a scribbled note from Victoria, instructing me to program Maximillion Louis's assistant's name and phone number into my phone.

I swallowed my frustration. I knew to do that.

Glancing at the overflowing box rooted me to the ground. I exhaled. Sorting the files now would be best so they'd seem less intimidating, but even so, the sheer amount of paper seemed strange when the Internet could easily hold all the information.

I grabbed the fattest folder and flipped it over. Maximillion Louis. Peeling back the cover, I found an 8" x 10" picture I assumed was him. No wallet-sized shots for this guy. The man modeled a pin-striped charcoal suit with a purple satin vest and matching handkerchief. Did I imagine it, or was he wearing eyeliner? His lips were slightly pursed. Not a bad look, but he'd clearly practiced it.

Former model. Entrepreneur. Investor. World traveler. Patron of the arts. CEO of an online male fashion boutique. *He'd like my paisley tights.*

I jumped over to my computer and did what anyone else would do: I searched him online. Only a couple of million hits. I tabbed a bunch of articles on Louis and began some impromptu research.

My cell phone buzzed. I scooped it from the desk before it could cause the cubicle walls to rumble. The lit screen glowed a reminder to stop by the art store to pick up another set of watercolors, but I deleted the reminder. As much as I longed to escape into my beloved hobby, my paid position took precedence. Painting would have to wait.

My ringing cellphone pierced through the quiet of the now empty office. I pushed through stacks of papers and finally found it crammed under a mess of folders that I had been trying to organize. When I saw Mel's name, I hit answer.

"Sister! You picked up! I figured you'd be busy primping."

"Primping?" I shoved my hand through the wiry curls on my head, trying to clear my brain of the clients, ideas, and organization that I'd been stuck with for most of the day. "What are you talking about?"

She exhaled into the phone. "Don't tell me you're still at work."

"Okay. I won't."

"You've got to be kidding me."

One of Mel's favorite rants centered on how Victoria overworked me and how I never told Victoria "no." I knew better. Victoria believed in my ability to do the job right and to put in the necessary effort. She trusted me. My job description probably listed working late in the fine print. All this annoyed my sister but didn't really put a damper on her plans. After all, she had a boyfriend.

A boyfriend. A date. I had a date!

"Pickled cucumbers." I yanked the phone away from my head to check the time on the screen: 6:25. I had thirty-five minutes to get home, clean up, and welcome Ethan into the messy apartment that I promised myself I would clean after work today.

"You say the weirdest things."

"Mel, I have to go." I didn't wait for her reply. I tossed the phone into my purse and gathered the nearest priority files into a pile. Grabbing my work bag, I rose from the floor and stepped toward the cubicle opening. My heel caught on the box and I struggled to stay upright. Three steps out the door, I recalled the paisley tights in my desk drawer. I spun around, skipped over the box, and threw open the drawer to retrieve my tights. No way would I leave without them.

Once on Pittsburgh's subway system, the "T," I crammed the folders into my bag and mentally listed the things I needed to do before Ethan would arrive. Ten minutes later, I lurched into my apartment lobby and hurried into the elevator, swapping places with a UPS man on his way out. The air conditioning wiped away the city's summer heat from my skin—if only it could calm my nerves, too. On floor three, I headed down the hall to my apartment. Two packages stood sentinel outside my door with an envelope with bright red words wedged underneath. Once I managed to open the door, I shoved the two packages inside with my foot while I dropped my bags on the entrance table and kicked the door shut.

I crouched to pick up the envelope and my eyes were drawn to the red words, "Urgent Attention Required." Definitely not an exaggeration for the current state of my apartment. Magazines sprawled across the living room area and dirty dishes populated every flat surface. I checked the glowing digital clock over the television: 6:45. I'd made it in record time. I could do this.

I ripped the envelope open while trying to stack dishes into a pile to carry to the kitchen. Putting the shredded envelope under my arm, I wobbled with two piles of dishes over to the kitchen sink. Then I pulled out the paper.

No.

An overdue rent notice threatened me: Pay up or move out. I had one month. My mind sped through options. I didn't have rent money because my cash flow was shot from the daily expenses: occasional retail therapy, my art hobby, and a slight coffee addiction. My full-time job hadn't lived up to its promises. I worked all the time and still couldn't pay the rent. And night jobs usually involved poles or polos and ball caps.

My eyes wandered the apartment. Heated ceramic floors. Lush carpets. Modern amenities. Those beautiful things had been my downfall. Mel had warned me that I should find a cheaper apartment at first, but I wanted to go big or go home. Now, I might be going home to Mom after all.

I didn't want to live with Mel either. She held too tightly to her things and flung out her know-it-all advice too generously.

Shoot. I still needed to get ready. I ran to the bathroom and checked my face. Pleased to see my makeup intact, I grabbed a mascara wand and ran it over my eyelashes. A dab of lipstick brightened my mouth, and I worked fresh conditioner through my curls, calming the frizz accumulated from work. My curls sprung every which way from my face like an abstract sun, and despite the crazy, I loved it. But after that workday, my under-eyes creased with makeup and my eyeliner blended into my eye shadow rather than a crisp line. Okay, I needed a pick me up.

Paisley! Where had I put those tights? I ran to the bags by the door and pulled the teal paisley hose from the outside pocket of my purse. Had they been hanging out of my purse the entire way from downtown? Oops.

I plopped onto the carpet and began working the tights up my legs, and as I did I remembered Victoria's censure earlier that morning. Would Ethan agree with her assessment?

What Would Mel Do?

My beautiful, stubborn sister. She did what she wanted and had a wonderful fashion sense, but she also hated my obsession with paisley. I think she thought it was too childish or something.

Maybe it was.

I pulled the tights off and hurled them toward my bedroom. I'd stick with my classic black dress and heels. Boring, but acceptable.

I shut my bedroom door against the colorful swirl.

Now to clean. But the open door to my favorite room in the apartment caught my eye. I crossed the threshold, and the muscles in my shoulders relaxed. Stretching out my arms, I wanted to hug the view from the window.

When I'd been apartment hunting, this room had sealed the deal for me. A huge window dominated the room, showcasing a view of the Pittsburgh hills crammed with trees and speckled with houses. What was it about nature that brought God close? Far below, one of the city's three rivers meandered. I still didn't know the name of that river. It could be the Allegheny, the Monongahela, or the Ohio. No matter the name, goodness knew that river struck my desire to paint.

Leaning my back against the window, I stared at the other thing that made this room my favorite. My easel. I'd found it at an antique store downtown and then fixed it up with glue, paint, and love. One of the feet had an empty paint case wedged underneath it to keep the entire thing level. Cups of water, each a different shade of murky brown, crowned the low table where watercolors and brushes crowded. I bent forward and swept my fingers over the brushes, selecting one and dipping it into the water.

My cell phone trumpeted from the other room, playing the chorus of my favorite country song, "Jesus Take the Wheel." Dropping the paintbrush, I made my way to my purse. My heart squeezed when I saw the caller ID, and I chirped a hello.

"I'll be up in a minute, Jadyn." Ethan's voice rumbled in my ear, sending chills down my neck.

"Perfect. See you soon!" I glanced around the apartment, excited to show off its best features, and then imagined how Ethan would view it. My warm fuzzies fizzled.

It looked bad. Real bad.

I scurried stray cups and mugs into the oven, shoved magazines into the couch, and twirled air freshener around the apartment like a floral streamer. I straightened the Joan Miro abstract art book on the coffee table.

A knock sounded on the door.

Hummingbirds drummed against my abdominal muscles, and my feet rooted to the ceramic. I'd forgotten about pre-date nerves.

"Relax, tummy. Deep breath, lungs." I expanded my lungs with cool oxygen. "Shoulders back."

I tiptoed over to the door, straightened my hemline and my smile, swung open the door and froze.

This cannot be happening.

Chapter Two

Travis, not Ethan, stood in my doorway, pizza box in hand. His short, dark hair was propped on end with gel, but his blue eyes wouldn't meet mine. The only time I'd ever seen him in a collared shirt, other than this moment, had been at our high school graduation. But most importantly, what was he doing with a pizza?

My stomach growled. Traitor.

"Jadyn, would you have dinner with me?" The question burst from Travis before a nervous smile quivered on his lips.

"What a surprise." The words tumbled out of my mouth and I thought about Ethan on his way up right this second. *What do I do?*

Travis opened the box and waved his hand over the pizza, wafting the scent toward my face. "I'd be honored if you'd join me for this delicious pizza."

"I have a work thing." I tried to keep a straight face. Travis and I were buddies, which included the occasional pizza nights on Fridays, but usually we planned ahead, and *I* ordered the pizza. Odd. The clothes for one. Our pizza nights always included sweatpants. But then again, maybe he'd come right from work.

Wait. My hand slipped on the doorknob and I banged my shoulder against the door. *No, he couldn't really be asking me out.*

Down the hallway, the elevator pinged, and the hummingbirds took up their thrumming African dance again. Even from this distance, Ethan looked like my own personal blonde fairy tale.

Maybe I can hide Travis? Wild scenarios of drugging Travis, hiding him under a bed or in a closet flew through my head. *Nope, too late.*

Travis, not Ethan, stood in my doorway, pizza box in hand. His short, dark hair was propped on end with gel, but his blue eyes wouldn't meet mine. The only time I'd ever seen him in a collared shirt, other than this moment, had been at our high school graduation. But most importantly, what was he doing with a pizza?

My stomach growled. Traitor.

"Jadyn, would you have dinner with me?" The question burst from Travis before a nervous smile quivered on his lips.

"What a surprise." The words tumbled out of my mouth and I thought about Ethan on his way up right this second. *What do I do?*

Travis opened the box and waved his hand over the pizza, wafting the scent toward my face. "I'd be honored if you'd join me for this delicious pizza."

"I have a work thing." I tried to keep a straight face. Travis and I were buddies, which included the occasional pizza nights on Fridays, but usually we planned ahead, and *I* ordered the pizza. Odd. The clothes for one. Our pizza nights always included sweatpants. But then again, maybe he'd come right from work.

Wait. My hand slipped on the doorknob and I banged my shoulder against the door. *No, he couldn't really be asking me out.*

Down the hallway, the elevator pinged, and the hummingbirds took up their thrumming African dance again. Even from this distance, Ethan looked like my own personal blonde fairy tale.

Maybe I can hide Travis? Wild scenarios of drugging Travis, hiding him under a bed or in a closet flew through my head. *Nope, too late.*

Travis's voice broke through my thoughts. "No, it's cool. I'll knock again."

I imagined his face. It probably had bloomed pink across his cheeks to his ears. After growing up with someone, you tended to know these things.

The knock on the door vibrated through my body, surprising me for some reason. I found myself wondering again, WWMD? *What Would Mel Do?*

I fancied opening the door, grabbing the pizza, and then locking them both out. Pizza for one. A pile of chick flicks and rainbow finger nails. But Mel would never do that. She would open the door, be polite, and get what she wanted in the end. What did I want again?

Ethan.

I peeled myself off the door. Now, I needed to figure out what to do with Travis.

Opening the door an inch, I peered out at the two men and then flung the door open wide. In that instant, I decided that I'd pretend that this was the first time opening that door. Fake the confidence. "Hi, guys! Come on in."

Ethan held out a bouquet of orange tulips and smiled at me, but at my greeting, his eyebrows furrowed. I tried to keep my eyes focused on his face, but I couldn't help but notice that he'd changed into a tan button-up that highlighted his athletic chest and strong core. Yes, I noticed. He'd tucked the tan shirt into a pair of blue jeans and belted them. But it was the smile on his face just for me that made me shiver.

Travis inched past me to walk into the apartment and Ethan followed, his smile disappearing into a frown. I shrugged at Ethan's inquiring gaze and shut the door behind them. Travis stretched across his customary spot on the couch after putting the pizza on the counter in the kitchen, and Ethan stepped toward the armchair.

"So is he your 'work thing?'" Travis hooked his thumb toward Ethan.

I squeezed my eyes shut, trying to imagine Travis's words away. How could he say that?

"I take it you know the pizza guy, then?"

I opened my eyes to find Ethan's lips stiff in a smile and sitting with perfect posture in the arm chair.

I would have taken any super power at this moment, but given the option, I'd claim invisibility. I forced a smile to come across my lips and decided laughing might be well-timed here so I gave a little giggle that sounded more like a whimper. "Ethan from work, this is Travis of pizza nights."

The men eyed each other. My tongue dried into leather. Turning to the kitchen, I asked, "Anyone want a drink? I have water, milk, cold coffee that I can heat up."

"Thanks, I'm fine. So, Travis, how long have you known Jadyn?" Ethan seemed to have regained his professionalism. A good sign.

"We grew up together, so I could tell you all those embarrassing stories that she'd never want you to hear." Travis raised his voice. "Jay, can you grab me a Coke?"

"I don't have any Coke." I didn't like that he called me "Jay" in front of Ethan. Like he was marking his territory, which made me picture a dog watering the plants and I particularly hated the idea of being watered."

"Oh, I think you do."

I carried my glass of water back to the living room with my head tilted slightly in question. Travis grinned at me. He gestured toward my apartment door where the two unopened boxes sat.

"Here. I'll get it." Travis stood and walked to the door. He scooped up the packages and flipped open a pocket knife. In moments, the boxes were open. One held two glass goblets and the other held a liter of coke. Packaging the glasses made total sense, but mailing a liter of coke was plain expensive, not to mention weird.

"Jay, do you have ice?"

I followed him back to the kitchen and opened the freezer. I slid a glance at him as he rinsed one of the goblets. "What are you doing?"

"What do you mean?" He copied my whispering. "I'm washing the glasses before drinking from them."

"No," I pulled the ice tray from the freezer. "What are you doing here? Tonight?"

Travis shrugged, taking the tray from me and shaking two cubes out into one of the glasses. He lifted his head and yelled across the room. "Want some Coke, man?"

"No, I'm fine." Ethan's voice deepened.

Something about the tone of his voice made me eye him. He sat so straight in the chair; the tulips appeared a bit strangled in his hands. For good reason. He showed up to take me out and I had another guy at my place. Talk about two-timing. I walked over to Ethan, hoping my face spelled an apology. I wanted to say something, but I wasn't sure what to say. I opened my mouth, but nothing came out.

"Jadyn, do you still have my PlayStation game? I brought my PlayStation 2. It's in the car. I can go grab it." Travis carried a goblet full of Coke from the kitchen. "Dude, you should stay and play with us."

"Travis, I promised to spend the evening with Ethan."

"Perfect. I love playing three players. I'll go grab my PlayStation."

Now, my eyebrows rose. Travis could be a bit dense, but this was too much.

Before I could say another word, Travis bounded out the door. He might not catch onto social situations quickly, but he sure could move. I reached up to grab a curl and tug on it.

Ethan stood and handed me the flowers. His body was all straight lines; nothing gave. His lips pressed in a thin line and his eyes lacked the smile they had in them earlier in the day. I widened my eyes at him, begging for understanding and hoping he could read my face.

My cell phone cadence broke through the silence that Travis had left behind him. I winced, putting the tulips on the table. "Hold on. It might be work."

Fishing my cell out of my purse again, I checked the screen. Oswald Tumpit. I looked at Ethan and raised my pointer finger. "Jadyn Simon speaking."

"Miss Simon, a pleasure to be speaking with you. This is Oswald Tumpit, personal assistant to Maximillion Louis. Miss Davenport informed me that you would be overseeing Mr. Louis' advertising campaign. I assume that is correct."

My eyes met Ethan's across the room. He had picked the flowers up again.

"If that is the case, you should know that you are required to be at Heinz Hall this evening."

"I'm what?" Professionalism out the window. No one had said anything about attending a performance at Heinz Hall with a client. Normally, that would be no hardship. After all, it was Heinz Hall and I loved the performing arts. But tonight? So not good.

"Heinz Hall. 7:30."

I checked the time. 7:15.

"I have plans." My voice wobbled, sounding pathetic. He'd think I was making it up, but it was true. I had more plans than I could handle. My eyes skidded over the pile of paperwork like a mountain on my table by the door.

"Mr. Louis will not be pleased."

I gulped. This was not the way that I had wanted to start this work relationship. "I'll see what I can do. You want me there when? At what time? Tonight?"

"7:30, Miss Simon." The phone went dead in my hand. Oswald Tumpit had hung up. Anyway, who named their child Oswald Tumpit?

A glass clunked on the kitchen counter. Ethan was placing orange tulips into my only vase. I was amazed that he'd found it, but even more pleased to see the tulips bobbing cheerfully at me. They anchored me. I tossed my phone to my bag and walked across the carpet to him. He stepped back from the tulips. I swear he was admiring his work and I couldn't help but smile. Brushing my fingertips across his sleeve, I came up beside him. "Have you considered becoming a professional flower arranger?"

"You know, that might just be the thing for my spare time, what little I have." Ethan adjusted a larger tulip to be supported by another tulip. "But I don't know if it would work out in my life plan."

"Life plan? Do I make your life plan?" In my head, this is where we would have had that romantic connection that might have ended in a kiss, but instead, my apartment door banged open, announcing Travis' return. Ethan's jaw tightened and twitched. He didn't answer.

I reached for the vase of tulips, trying to distract him, and carried them over to place on the tea table in front of the couch. "Ethan, these are so lovely."

My brain whirled. Ethan. Travis. Heinz Hall. It was too much. I had promised the evening to Ethan, but now Travis seemed to be hijacking the night with his loudness and his games.

"Hey, Jay. Can you give a guy a hand?" Travis balanced his PlayStation between two hands with controllers stacked on top with more game disks teetering under his chin. Things were sliding fast.

I caught the runaway disc cases and set them on the floor near the television. Then I caught sight of Ethan staring at the pizza box. The microwave clock read 7:25. How had things gotten so out of control?

Ethan slid his hands into his pockets and his eyes focused on me, studying me. I bit my lip. If Mel were here, she'd get what she wanted. My shoulders slumped, and the impossibility of it all trampled my little hummingbirds of excitement.

This was not how I had imagined this evening going and suddenly, I just wanted to sleep. Travis talked about something as he hooked the game system to my television, but I didn't hear him.

"Jadyn, I think I'm going to go." Ethan almost marched to the door.

"Let me put on my shoes." I hurried to my heels by the door and jammed my feet into them. Travis could stay at the apartment by himself. He'd be fine.

"No, I don't think that's a good idea." The seriousness in his voice jerked my head up to his face. No smile. "I'll see you at work."

Chapter Three

Two days after Crazy Friday, Mel and I sat in the car, driving to Mom's for Sunday night dinner.

"What are you doing? Turn here." My sister gestured to the road coming up on our right.

I held the steering wheel, but somehow, she managed a little driving, too. *Driving me crazy.* I made the turn that she wanted, following her route to Mom's.

She turned to my personal issues. "You texted me the rundown, but I want to know how you're feeling about the Friday mess."

I let out a long breath.

"Have you talked to Ethan?" Mel tossed a look at me, catching the expression on my face. "Uh-oh. Texted, even?"

"Before we get into this, can you grab me some lip gloss?" As she reached for my bag from the backseat, I remembered that I'd jammed the eviction notice into my purse before leaving, hoping to ask my mom for advice. Mel couldn't see it. "Never mind, I just remembered I don't have any."

Mel pulled some lip balm from her own bag. "No problem. This one's better for your lips, anyway." She opened it and held out the container to me.

I dabbed some on my lips. I checked my rearview mirror as I merged onto the highway, rubbing my lips together.

"If I were you," she said, "I'd be mad at Travis and annoyed with Ethan for not sticking around."

"I'm torn. I want Travis to be happy and I wanted to go out with Ethan. And I want to keep my boss happy." My forehead ached right between my eyebrows. *This commute would be too long to do twice every day, which shot down one post-eviction idea I'd had.*

Mel reached across the car and grabbed my thigh. I jumped. "And the double workload. You need to tell that Victoria if she wants to transfer all that work to you, then you have the right to delegate to interns. Tell her right away."

By the time we pulled into our mother's driveway an hour later, I clicked out of my seatbelt and reached for the car door handle. I loved my sister, but she stated her opinions like law.

"You know, it's almost laughable that all of that happened in one day." She grabbed my purse from the backseat and dropped it into my lap. "You should call Victoria right now. Get it over with. Start Monday fresh."

"Yeah, I should talk with her, but I don't know what I'd say." I opened the car door and stretched my legs.

Before my foot touched the driveway, I heard my mother's voice. "My girls!" She was already out the door with her arms spread wide. With a few quick steps, her arms wrapped around me and I hugged her back. I breathed in Dove soap. Here, my problems disappeared. She'd help me figure out what to do with the eviction notice. Mom released me and hugged Mel. She held on to Mel's arms and stepped back to look at her. "Now, Mel, where is your young man? I hope he knows that he's always welcome in my home."

"Momma, he knows." She pushed a couple of long curls out of her face. Her hair was so like my own except longer right now. Everyone first guessed us as twins, but those people didn't know us.

"I don't know how he could stay away from his favorite girl." She threw a wink at Mel and then turned back to the house, leading the way to the front door. "Oh, dear! I need to check on the sausage!"

She kicked into hyper speed to return to the kitchen.

Mel yelled after her. "What we really should be talking about is how Jadyn had more than her fair share of male attention on Friday night!" My sister threw a grin at me as she walked through the door in front of me. "Two—no, three—men vying for the attention of my baby sister!"

"What is this?" my mom questioned as we joined her in the kitchen. Having checked the sausage and transferred it into the pasta, she began slicing a tomato. Mel dropped her purse on the floor next to the kitchen table and walked to the fridge, pulling out a jar of salsa.

Mel filled Mom in as she unscrewed the salsa and dumped most of it into a bowl. I grabbed the chips and inserted the appropriate "uh-huh" and "yeah" whenever my sister took a breath in her own summary of my drama, ending with, "So now, she hasn't talked to Ethan since he left her apartment and she still has that dragon Victoria breathing down her neck over all these new projects."

I crunched down on another chip, effectively tuning Mel out as she segued into repeating her advice. Sometimes, I wished she'd listen to me and then let me figure out my own problems. But my sister, she loved being in the thick of the action by doling out advice, and honestly, she did give good advice. Most of the time. I swallowed my chip, ready to hear what they were saying when I saw Mom slap down her knife.

"Darling, I just want you to know how proud of you I am!"

I thought she was talking to Mel so I concentrated on the chips.

"Artist types always have trouble staying organized and thriving in a work place."

Now I knew Mom meant me. Mel was a lot of things, but not an artist type. I peeked at Mom and nodded. She'd said that to me so many times while I was growing up. "But your boss must think you can do it! I can hardly believe it. You're grown up—with a great job, a car, a lovely apartment, and guys falling for you."

I nodded again, my very own bobble-head Jadyn. *I may have to scratch one of those things off your list, Mom. But which one?*

She heaved a happy sigh. "My work here is done."

Mom picked up her knife again and began slicing some carrots for the salad.

"Well, she could still stand some improvement communicating with boys and bosses," Mel added as she dipped a tortilla chip into the salsa.

I reached for another chip and snagged the salsa away from her. Seriously, did she ever stop?

"Girls, you're going to ruin your appetites."

"Leftovers are golden, Mom." Mel tapped another chip on the counter. "Do you want some?"

"Dinner's ready." Mom handed the salad bowl to me and opened the fridge to pull out some salad dressing. She headed out onto the back porch.

Feeling annoyed with Mel, I decided to tease her a little bit. I kept my face controlled. "Mel, want to check the front door?"

She started walking toward the front door. "Why am I doing this?"

"Oh, you never know who might show up on the doorstep." I let my cool snap and giggles bubbled as I stepped backwards toward the porch.

My sister spun on her toe and ran for me like a football player. Still holding the salad, I threw my hands over my head. Her eyes flicked to the salad and she slowed her tackle, wrapping her arms around my middle. Now we were both laughing.

"If it had been Travis with his pizza, I would have taken the pizza and ditched the boy."

"Oh, yeah?" I wiggled out of her grip and led the way to the porch. "What if it had been Ethan?"

"The office hottie?" Mel pinched my side. She scooted around me and plopped down in her chair. "Easy. I would have pulled him inside and left the flowers behind."

"Why would you leave the perfectly good flowers behind?" My mom had taken the salad from me and was heaping it in her bowl.

"Come on. We all know the man is more interesting than his gift."

I shook my head. "But isn't the rejection of the man's gift a rejection of him, too?"

Both my mom and Mel stared at me. I should have kept my mouth shut.

"I'll pray for us." I volunteered.

After the prayer, Mom made eye contact with me. "Yesterday, Grandma and I talked about how once we weren't sure if you would ever find a good full-time position anywhere. But you have, and you've held it for two years now!"

I kept my eyes down. I reached for the sausage penne and scooped some onto my plate. "Thanks, Mom."

"And today I was bragging on you to Lillian."

In my head, I pictured the eviction notice crumpled in my purse in the other room.

No way am I telling her about that now.

Monday morning started early. I arrived about an hour before the office would fill so I could look over my priority list. Tapping my pencil against the list, I scooted my computer chair from the desk. *First things first.*

I'd painted a small card for Ethan. I knew it couldn't make up for the Friday craziness but it would be at least a start.

Once in Ethan's department, I passed his office, craning my neck to see if he might be in there.

He wasn't.

I spun around and walked up to his desk.

Everything placed in perfect organization, no piles and no papers scattered about. Everything had a place. It looked ready for a photo shoot, but I didn't understand how anyone could have such a clean desk. Did he even work there?

I glimpsed his business card and slipped one into my dress pocket, placing my little watercolor note right below his computer screen so he would see it but no one who walked by his office would. The bright colors stood out despite being half hidden below the screen; neutrals reigned supreme in his space.

A deep voice that I recognized as Ethan's greeted the department secretary. My heart jumped. I had seconds before he'd turn into the hallway. I scurried out of his cubicle and around the corner to another empty cubicle to hide.

Feeling like a middle schooler, I heard his step pass and listened to him thump his briefcase onto his desk. The computer booted up. Taking a breath, I snuck out of the neighboring cubicle and raced for my department. I breathed in Ethan's cologne and almost allowed it to carry me back to his cubicle, but I steeled myself and returned to my office without running into any other coworkers. What would he think of my gift?

My desk phone rang, causing me to jump and spill my fresh cup of coffee on my navy dress. I set the mug down while reaching for the phone with my other hand. Loud, unkind noises should be universally muted until 10 a.m. I glanced at the clock, confirming the time—just before nine.

"Jadyn Simon, speaking. How may I help you?"

"It's Lana. Maximillion Louis is on his way to see you. Just wanted to give you a head's up." I didn't feel ready for Mr. Louis, especially after babysitting Travis rather than attending the required performance at Heinz Hall. Leaving a guest, even an unwanted one, alone in my home conflicted with all my life training.

"Lana, you're a life saver." Lana worked at the front desk and since starting there, the two of us had bonded over mini-chats at lunch breaks or at the end of the day. She watched out for difficult clients and tried to give me a heads-up when they came in. Dabbing the coffee spill on my dress, I hung up the phone. No one would notice the slightly darker smudge on my dress if I stayed seated.

I turned to my computer and pulled up my documents on Mr. Louis's campaign. I had already spread the previous consultant's files across my desk. I tucked Mr. Louis's client information into a drawer and my mind raced through a mini pep talk. *Breathe. Relax. It'll be fine. You're qualified.*

"It seems that I will perpetually have trouble with consultants." I spun my chair to behold Maximillion Louis poised in the entrance of my cubicle. I jerked to my feet and pasted on what I hoped was a welcoming smile. He scanned me up and down, eyes lingering on the area where I had baptized my dress. He strode into my space with a click of his heels. "I hire them, and then they bail on me."

He ignored my outstretched hand, gesturing to his outfit as though it were an excuse for not shaking my hand. The man checked the chair and then seated himself in it. Louis wore a fitted grey suit accented with a glittering orange bow tie and a handkerchief. Even his dress shoes had a band of orange crossing the toe. He stared at me then and I realized that I still stood with my hand out.

I pulled my hand back and deposited myself into my own chair. "Mr. Louis, it's a pleasure to see you this morning. My apologies for not being able to make it to Heinz Hall on Friday night."

"Miss Simon, allow me to be frank." Mr. Louis leaned back in his chair, watching me through half-shut eyelids.

I wanted to lean forward, but I kept myself sitting straight in my chair.

"I've gone through at least five different consultants in the past couple of months, one at your firm. Victoria has reassured me that my high expectations will be met. I need my consultant to be on call, ready to attend events at a moment's notice. This is how you will best be able to represent my brand, by being present and available."

My mouth fell open. No wonder he'd gone through so many consultants. It seemed humanly impossible, considering we balanced multiple clients and projects on a daily basis, to please such demands.

Mr. Louis caught my eye and pointed his own hand to his mouth, shutting it. I snapped my mouth shut in response.

"All-consuming, I think is how the last consultant for Lines & Designs Etcetera described it before she resigned. At that point, I knew I needed to switch companies, so here I am."

"Well, we're certainly happy to have you, Mr. Louis." I piped up, trying to gain some ground and exude professionalism.

"Max."

I tilted my chin sideways. *Was he telling me to call him by a nickname?* He smiled at me then.

"Max. You can call me Max." He crossed his legs and draped his manicured hands over his legs. "Now, Miss Simon, are you up to this task?"

"Yes, Mr...Max." I swallowed, thinking of all the work I had for other clients and my double workload. There was no way I could do it all. But then, I pictured Victoria firing the other consultant. The eviction notice. My mom's pride in me and my work. I had no choice. "I've been looking over your file and campaign documentation. The notes say that you want to create a fresh social media campaign, something unlike anything you've ever done before?"

Max steepled his fingers, pursing his lips together. "When I said fresh, I wanted not only something that we've never done before, but also something that's never been done anywhere, *ever*."

Max put so much emphasis on the last word that for a moment, I thought he might stand up and strike a pose, but he remained in his seat. He then looked at the papers scattering my desk and frowned. "I hope you're more organized with campaigns than you are with your desk."

I patted one of my stacks of papers, trying to calm my own nerves. "Sometimes creativity works best in a cluttered space."

"I was very disappointed not to see you on Friday. My sponsored cellist inspires just the image that I want for this campaign."

I pressed my lips together in a tight smile and pulled my schedule out from a pile of papers on my desk. "It would be my pleasure to attend any and all of your functions; however, I need more than thirty minutes notice of such an event. Preferably forty-eight hours' notice."

His eyebrows shot up. I took a deep breath and hoped that I hadn't infuriated him. I readied myself for his response.

"Thirty minutes?" His voice shook. His nose turned red. "You'd only been given thirty minutes?" I fought the instinct to sit deeper in my seat. He opened and shut his mouth before finally speaking again. "That is unacceptable. Heads will roll. One head, anyway."

Mine?

Chapter Four

Thursday. Noon already. I shoved away from my desk chair and grabbed my phone from its charger. I clicked over to my favorite shopping app and scrolled through the fun-patterned dresses. I still couldn't shake the fact that the week was almost over. It didn't feel over. My eye lingered on a dress. No. Couldn't buy. I hit the home button.

With a double workload, I either needed an extra twenty-four hours every day or to let some of my accounts and clients slide. Over the past couple of days, I'd managed to touch base with a couple clients who'd felt that their advertising campaigns needed to be set on the backburner.

"I'm sorry, Jadyn, but we've decided to push our campaign back till January." One of my best clients bailing again. I could practically hear Victoria's

French-lacquered nails clacking out another strike against me. Already. Never a good sign for me as a consultant, but it did open up some time to use on my other clients, so I held my sigh of relief in check until I hung up the phone.

My ears picked up on a telltale clip of stilettos walking away from my cubicle. I froze. Had Victoria heard that conversation? *I sure hope not.*

My stomach rumbled.

"Where did I put my purse?" I spun in a circle, hunting for the teal handbag. White papers everywhere. If I squinted, the paper piles almost looked like snow. I shook my head. I couldn't bear the thought of snow, but the weather would soon be changing to autumn.

Finally, I saw a bit of teal peeping from underneath one mountainous stack of papers. I extracted the bag without sending any papers on the floor. Now that was success.

I headed down the hallway toward the exit and my thoughts veered to Ethan. I hadn't actually seen him at all since our failed date. He hadn't stopped by my desk and I hadn't stopped by his except to leave my apology note. In an office with as many departments as this one, you had to plan these casual drop-bys. My steps slowed. Maybe I should go see if he was still in the building.

No. I didn't want to be one of those girls drooling over him. I hated those girls. They seemed so needy. And I was hungry, hungry for lunch.

I started walking again, and I remembered last Friday night—almost a week ago but it still made me cringe. I liked him and wanted him to know it. *Fine. I'll go and talk with him.*

I made an about-face down the hallway and then into the finance department. Most of the cubes were empty and a part of me started to hope that Ethan might not be in his, either. But there he was. Hand shoved into his blonde hair as he bent over some papers on his desk. His other hand tapped a pen against the desk. *Maybe I'll just go.*

Ethan glanced up through his eyelashes. For a moment, I found myself envious of his eyelashes and I looked away. His head came up farther.

I gave a little half wave that didn't reach past my waist. "Hey. I wanted to come over and see how you're doing." *And if you still might like me.*

He sat back from his desk and gave me a small smile. "A bunch of work came in and I wanted to get as much of it done as possible."

"Totally get it. I've been trying to manage more accounts than I usually do." Words dried up in my throat and I wasn't so sure what I should say now. I looked down at my teal bag.

Ethan cleared his throat.

I looked up at him.

"Thanks for—"

"Do you wan—"

We both spoke at the same time. My stomach did backflips, and I threw my hand toward Ethan, "Oh, you go first."

"No, it's fine. You can go."

I watched him pointedly while shaking my head. *Please, please, don't be mad at me for last week still.*

A grin broke across his face. "All right. You win. I was going to thank you for your card."

He pointed to the cubicle wall beside me where I noticed my card tacked. The swirling colors brought a little window of brightness to his neutral office. *He hung it up!*

"I'm sorry about last weekend." I smiled and then decided I could say what I'd wanted to say before. My heart scuttled across my rib cage. "I'm heading out for a short lunch break. Do you want to come?"

He paused, seeming to consider, but shook his head. "I shouldn't. I have a lot of work to complete before tomorrow, but thanks."

"I can get you something." *A sandwich, a drink...maybe a pretty girl—that would be me.*

"Don't worry about it." Ethan straightened the sheets of paper on his desk, avoiding my eyes. "I'll run down to the vending machine or order a sandwich."

48

"Well, I thought I'd offer." Disappointment settled in my tummy; I didn't feel hungry anymore. I pointed to the stack of stamped envelopes on his desk. "I can take those if you'd like. I'm passing the mail room on my way out."

"Thanks for offering, but I need to head down there soon. It gives me a reason to get up from my desk." He lifted the stack up, tapped the sides to bring them in line, and placed them carefully on the edge of his desk.

"Then I'm off." I took a step backwards toward the hallway.

I'd never been so thoroughly rejected for such little tasks before. A part of me wanted to cry. I suppose it was fine, and it probably did serve me right for messing up our date. Doing those extra things for Ethan would have extended my lunch break too long anyway. I neared the front desk where Lana's bent head bobbed. I started to walk away, thinking she wouldn't hear me through the music in her headphones.

"Wow! What's up with the grumpy cat face?"

I stopped mid-step and allowed a smile to quirk across my face. She probably didn't realize how loud she spoke with the music roaring in her ears. But she was right, the zing was out of my step just like a dirty chai latte without espresso.

"Nope. No dodging questions. Why are you all frowny? Did the great and wonderful Louis call you?" She was still yelling.

I walked over to the large circular desk and leaned against the counter. "First take off those headphones and then I'll tell you what's up."

Lana dragged the headphones off her head, allowing them to circle her neck. I could hear the music from where I was standing.

"Dish," Lana commanded.

"Last Friday night." I tapped my cheek with my index finger. "I was supposed to go on a date."

Lana's hands flew up with fingers spread. "I love stories that start with a 'date!'"

"Not this one."

"So who—"

"We were supposed to go out, but then my guy friend showed up at my apartment with a pizza and Guy #1 left. And now, I just tried to chat with him, first to offer lunch and then to take care of his mail. No go. Neither one."

Lana nodded. "Ethan."

After my solo lunch of window shopping and no buying, a metallic click drew me from my brainstorming for Max's campaign. Lifting my head, I saw Victoria, standing in the entrance of my cubicle with her fingernail ticking against the wall.

"I expect a two-minute verbal report from you tomorrow on how things are progressing with Max's campaign. I want to know I've put the right consultant on this job." She moved her fingernail from the wall and pointed it at me. "First thing, tomorrow morning."

"I'll be there." I said to her turning back. I sighed and dropped my head into my hands as I sat back into my chair. The office feared her two-minute verbal reports. I checked the giraffe clock that hung off my only real segment of solid, not cubicle, wall. Five minutes to five. The next ten minutes would get noisy, but after everyone left, the silence of the office would be perfect for formulating my report and then practicing it to myself.

In early. Out late. All week.

As the volume levels escalated, I shuffled papers around my desk, trying to make them neater. Ethan's desk flashed before my eyes. The last time my desk had appeared that neat was certainly before I was hired.

The desk phone buzzed, and I jumped. I lifted the receiver. "Jadyn Simon."

"Travis is waiting for you in the front lobby," Lana said. "Should I walk him back to you?"

I started. *What is Travis doing here?*

"Jadyn?"

"Oh, sorry. Um. I'll come get him." I set the phone down and stood. Coworkers carried their

51

briefcases out of their cubicles. Those with families always left right at five. I pictured going home to a family and couldn't imagine being responsible for other lives. I could hardly keep up with my own life.

I rounded the corner and found Travis leaning over the counter, talking to Lana. She swished her long blonde hair behind her shoulder and laughed at something he said. I frowned. *Could these two work together?*

"Ah, here she is now." Travis lifted a bouquet of flowers from the other side of him. He held them out to me while sending a wink at Lana. She smiled and shook her head, turning back to her computer. Did her smile just turn into a frown?

I peered from the daisies to Travis. "Are those for me?"

"Don't seem so surprised!" He raised an eyebrow and stepped toward me, taking my hand in his and guiding it to take the flowers from him. "Your mom told me that you had a busy week, so I thought I'd drop in and steal you away for a little bit."

"You talked to my mom?"

"Okay, actually, your mom talked to my mom who then told me." He shrugged. "So now you're checking my sources."

Scrambled brains for dinner. I couldn't seem to figure out why Travis had shown up. He knew where I worked?

"I did text you to say I was coming and to let me know if it wouldn't work. I know the last time I made a surprise appearance, I messed with some of your plans, so when you didn't text back I figured we were a go."

When had I last checked my cell? Travis had bought daisies, proving that he had been paying attention when we were children or at least that he'd talked to my mom.

"Come on, Jay. You need a break. Let's go grab your work stuff and then I'll take you out for a nice dinner."

I bit my lip, considering. My to-do list for work threatened to strangle me, but I could probably complete a large portion of it at home, and if I came in early tomorrow, I could finish the last bit. "I've got so much to do."

"Only an hour and a half?" Travis pulled his puppy-dog face.

"Aw, come on, Jadyn. Give the guy a break." Lana stood up and swung her purse over her shoulder as her computer powered down.

Stuck between the two of them, I decided that it wouldn't hurt. I was already super behind on all my tasks anyway.

Sipping my raspberry iced tea, I scanned the crowd of young people around me. Travis had selected Lulu's Noodles on Craig Street. Delicious and affordable. The large pictures on the walls of people and noodles always made me smile. You knew what the place was all about. I leaned back in my chair. Lulu's always reminded me of undergrad. I'd haunted the restaurant back then, but these days, I rarely had time to head into Oakland for a meal. I missed that.

"Travis, I have to ask." I hoped he'd give me the go ahead. I'd been wanting to ask him about Friday night but hadn't wanted to do it by text.

"What's up?" Travis crossed his arms across his chest.

How should I phrase this? One of the aproned waiters came out with two plates in hand. His eyes sought out the table numbers and when he saw ours, he stopped. "Spicy Szechuan?"

"That's me." I lifted my hand and moved my iced tea out of the way. He set the chicken noodle dish in front of me and Travis's pad Thai in front of him.

"You always get the same thing, Travis!" I ripped the paper off my chopsticks and split them in two. "Live a little."

He frowned at me, lifting a noodle between two fingers to hold at mustache level in front of his face. "I know what's good. Why should I try something else and maybe not like it?"

"If you're trying to look like that kid with the noodle hair and beard, you're going to have to try again." I laughed as I pointed to the kid on the wall, but then I remembered my point. "Most times, when I try new things, I find that I really like them."

Travis shrugged at me. "Is that what you wanted to ask me?"

"No." I pushed some noodles into my mouth, spices stinging my tongue. Energy coursed through my veins.

I tried to telepath my excitement to Travis, but his shoulders were slumped forward over his food as he ate. Something was up. "You going to come up for some air?"

Travis straightened his shoulders, reaching for his Coke and taking a long drink. "Sorry, it's work. The hours are insanely long and my coworkers—I don't want to talk about them."

"I thought you enjoyed it being a hospital technician." So this was why he'd been showing up throughout my week. *I'm just a free therapist.* I was glad I hadn't been able to ask him about Friday before the food showed up. Here, clearly, was the answer.

"I did. It seemed like a natural choice since Mom spent so many years as a nurse. I'm familiar with the hospital and all that goes on there."

Even though Travis couldn't hear my thoughts, my lack of compassion niggled me. Thankfully, I didn't have to try hard to come up with a good response. "Well, you're young yet. You could make a career change."

"No. I just—

Travis moved the noodles around on his plate. I watched his Adam's apple bob, and I waited, only breaking my gaze on him for a quick bite of my own spicy noodles.

"Someone died."

I stopped chewing. *Pink potatoes. I didn't see that coming.*

"She was this funny old lady that I worked with once a week. She never had any visitors."

I swallowed, not sure if I wanted Travis to continue this conversation.

"When she died, no one came. No one cared. The coroner came and took her body away. I think the police are doing a search for next of kin, but I don't really know."

"That's terrible." I set the chopsticks down and bunched my hands in my lap. I couldn't imagine dying alone and not having anyone even care that I had left this world for the next.

"No one else at the hospital even seems to care that it happened. I mean we talked about it for the first day, but after that, I'm the only one who seems bothered by it." Travis played with his noodles, pushing them to one side of his plate and then to the other side. He let the chopsticks drop. "I don't want to die alone."

"No one does."

"I'm not going to let that happen to me." His blue eyes darted.

"Exactly. It's a choice." I reached for my yummy drink and grinned. "Anyway, you won't be getting rid of me anytime soon."

His face relaxed into a smile and he attacked his food with relish. I tried to shake a thought that was starting to crawl through my head. *Maybe I shouldn't have said that.*

Chapter Five

The next morning, I thumbed through the files that I'd already read on Max's account. Victoria would be in within minutes and I had to be ready. I rubbed my forehead. Last evening had gone longer than I had intended, especially since exercising my amateur therapist skills, and the weight of the good food, had pulled me right to bed. The next thing I knew my alarm was ringing, leaving me a little unprepared.

"Jadyn, I'm ready for you." Victoria didn't even stop as she clicked by my cubicle. I caught a flash of white and her navy briefcase.

"I'll be right over." I leaped from computer chair, sending it swirling behind me, and picked up a couple of the papers that had the right information on it. *Come on, brain, wake up!*

Before I knew it, I found myself in Victoria's office. I glanced at the clock. 9:00 a.m. I had till 9:02 to impress her. Victoria sat at her desk, leaning back in her chair with a view of the city spread out behind her through the windows. Her long blonde hair was pulled into a sleek ponytail. White button-up blouse. White pencil skirt. White stilettos. *Where did she find a white pencil skirt?*

"Mr. Louis and I have met once so far to discuss some of the previous branding and marketing strategies he has used for his separate companies," I began. "They all featured minimalist designs and simple but bright color choices. He no longer wants that."

Victoria held up her hand. "You did tell him that this style is in."

Although not a question exactly, the tone of her voice suggested a response. I tilted my head to the side, feeling my curls bounce around my ears. It made me feel like a little girl.

"Continue."

"Um." I shuffled through my papers, hoping that something would leap out at me. Nothing did. I decided to pretend that was the end of the report and to hope she'd let me go. "We plan to meet again in the near future to discuss themes for branding his company. Mr. Louis stated that he'll want me to attend some of the musicians' shows as well."

Victoria pressed her lips together and stretched her neck, peering at me through thin eyes. The way she'd drawn her eyeliner on reminded me of a cougar, watching its prey before pouncing. *Stop it.*

"Tell me about the other companies and what they've done for him."

"Of course." I frowned. I only remembered what he'd said about the other consultants failing him. "He's had five other consultants before me and not one of them has pleased him."

"Yes, but the campaigns."

I stood in an oven that was gradually heating. I wanted to wipe my lip where I could feel perspiration beading. Who'd turned up the heat? *I don't know, but I can't say that.*

A tap at the door to the office distracted Victoria's eyes from me.

"I'm sorry, Victoria, but I wanted to let Jadyn know that her 9:00 a.m. appointment is here." Lana stood only partially in the doorway. I could only see half of her blue vintage dress.

"Thank you, Lana. Would you mind letting…" I couldn't remember who I was meeting with.

"Mr. Serafina." She offered me the name quietly. Her eyes bore an apology and she bit her inner cheek.

I gave her a smile. "Right. Let him know I'll be right over."

Lana backed out of the office. I stepped toward the door.

"Jadyn, I noticed on the internal network that a few of your clients have paused their campaigns."

My mouth dried. I forced a smile and shook my head. "It's quite unfortunate. Through no controllable factors of my own, they've decided to maintain their current strategies so they can focus on some specific work themselves. They've all slated dates for re-opening their work with us."

"That might be the case, but you are meant to continue the work of their campaign even if they are unable to work with you for a time. They suspend their campaign; they suspend their payments."

I bit my lip. I knew this was true, but when three of the clients had suggested postponing their campaigns, I had no energy to fight them on the point. "Yes, ma'am. I'll try to be better about that."

"No, you will do it." Victoria glanced at the clock. "Go to your appointment. I'm disappointed that you can't remember my client's name when you're about to go work with him."

I swear she nearly snarled.

"What was your client's name?" There was no teasing in her voice.

"Serafina."

I checked my phone in between my 11:00 client and my 11:30 client. A missed call from Mel and a text from Ethan. For a moment, I considered ignoring the text from him. I don't know why— maybe I was nervous. But then, I had to open it. The morning had flashed by in a whirl of not having anything prepared. I needed something good. *Maybe he'll ask for lunch?*

Checked the budget for one of your clients. Something's not adding up. Come over when you can. -Ethan

No. Not lunch. *I don't have time for lunch anyway or eating ever again, actually. Or my art...* I thought longingly of my paint shirt and the fresh watercolors I still hadn't picked up.

I sent off a quick text, promising to come later in the afternoon between clients. I half-hated myself for scheduling my day full of clients but what had been the alternative? It was convenient to gear up for the meetings all in one day, but I couldn't seem to catch up.

A tap on the cubicle wall signaled my next meeting. I glanced up and didn't recognize my client. I spoke anyway. "Good to see you again! Allow me to grab your folder and then we'll move to Meeting Room C."

I pushed papers aside, trying to force myself to remember who this appointment was for. My schedule couldn't be found in this short couple of seconds. My cheeks heated, and the warmth worked its way down my neck. *WWMD?*

"Pardon me, Miss. But we haven't actually met yet." I glanced up in surprise to see that my client had stepped farther into my cubicle. I now noticed his dapper bow tie and slim suit that had a European flair to it. As did his accent. He stuck out his right hand to me. "Oswald Tumpit at your service."

I straightened and accepted his hand. We shook. If I had viewed my schedule for today, I would have known that I was meeting with Oswald. *Pickled cucumbers.* I had just pretended to know him. And now he knew that. "Oh, you remind me of someone else."

I hoped that covered for my earlier assumption. I couldn't remember his accent from our telephone conversation last week. My eyebrows drew together. "We spoke on the phone once, but I don't remember hearing your accent."

Oswald gave a small smile. "British. My accent is not as posh as some. I've lived here for too long."

"That explains it. I couldn't quite place the vowels." I grabbed up a notepad and found my folder on Max's campaign. "Let's move over to the meeting room."

I led the way. We sat on either side of the long conference table that could easily fit eight and a few more if needed.

Now I saw that Oswald carried a briefcase. He lifted it onto the table in front of us and clicked it open. I couldn't see what was inside, but he pulled out a laptop, paper, pen, and his smart phone.

A part of me wanted to honestly admit that I hadn't taken the time to examine the campaign notes again before meeting because I was so stretched for time. *Not professional.*

Who or what was Max trying to sell again? *Not good.*

I straightened my pad of paper and wrote the date across the top of it. Oswald booted his computer up. I patted my hips, wondering if I had brought my cell phone with me. Somehow, I'd managed to stick it in my pocket although I couldn't remember having done it.

"Right." Oswald clicked something and then faced me. He lifted some brochures out of his briefcase and passed them to me. "These are the papers we have right now representing some of the other brands that Mr. Louis has founded."

I picked up the first brochure and admired the quality paper with its simple design and readable font. Basic, but perfect. The next was similar. "Simplicity first in design. Push the envelope and you can lose credibility unless it's amazing."

"That's why Mr. Louis hired you—to create something that pushes the envelope and is amazing. But which retains his credibility."

As Oswald spoke, I began to recall that the brand had to do with music. I still couldn't remember the specific campaign, though. I remembered the folder in front of me and flipped it opened. The quick fact sheet was empty. I hadn't filled it out yet.

He clicked on his computer and inspected me over the screen. "I also have a list of performance dates for you that you need to take utmost care to be present for in the upcoming weeks."

"Of course." I grabbed my pen and poised it over the paper. "Hit me with those dates."

"Better yet. Give me your email address."

In moments, the dates were in my email inbox. I needed to take some charge in this meeting to prove that I was on top of this job. I decided to take a stab. "To better brand the campaign, we might consider visiting some music schools for inspiration."

Oswald gazed at me with a wrinkle on his forehead. The silence started to feel uncomfortable, so I kept talking. "We could poll children about what they love in learning music. Talk to music teachers. Maybe even take a lesson ourselves."

He was still staring at me.

I scribbled those notes on my pad of paper. When I finished, Oswald hadn't moved. My stomach twisted.

"Miss Simon, you do recall that Mr. Louis wants to unearth a brand that will sell two performers: a cellist and a pianist, correct?" Oswald tilted the laptop screen down so he had a better view of me and leaned forward.

My face fired red lava, but my body iced over. I'd obviously messed up big time with guessing at the campaign when I couldn't remember. *How do I fix this?*

I took a deep breath and tried to smile calmly at Oswald. "Of course, but I thought we might resource these music schools as potential venues to inspire children and their teachers."

I wanted to pat myself on the back. Where had that sentence of finesse come from?

Oswald lifted his head up slowly and then let it drop down. *He's not buying it.*

"Maybe for artists geared toward children that would be a good idea, but Mr. Louis wants these two to start a classical music revolution." Oswald messed with his bow tie. It seemed to be too tight by the way he pulled at it.

"Ah, but why not start with children? They are some of the most honest responders you will find." I didn't know why I was still fighting for this idea. Oswald had a point, but it was too late now. If I had been better prepared, I wouldn't be in this scrambling position of seat-pants-flyer. "Children are also the next generation of music artists. You win the children; you often win the parents as well."

The papers stacked in front of me made me want to bang my head against the table. The idea of selling professional artists to children was a terrible idea—maybe one day long ago, it would have worked; but these days, parents bought their children goofy little nursery rhyme songs.

My phone screen lit up. I quickly made the screen go dark, but not before I saw that it was another text from Ethan. The dumb part of me hoped that it might be a non-work-related text, but it probably wouldn't be. *I want to open it now.*

Oswald was saying something. His lips moved, and I forced my ears to hear what he was saying. "—a meet and greet for the musicians. It's black-tie so Mr. Louis will provide an on-loan outfit for you if need be."

I think my ears perked up. I definitely looked away from the phone.

Later that afternoon, I crossed my ankles and relaxed into the park bench. I had hoped for a quiet place to think after the day had so thoroughly gone askew, but no, there was some sort of summer festival happening. Food trucks lined the curbs and pedestrians strolled the sidewalks, stopping at booths along the way.

I shut my eyes. So many things had gone wrong today. *So not good.*

My phone vibrated in my pocket. I slid it out and unlocked it. Two texts. Ethan's from earlier and the one that had just come in was from Oswald. I checked Oswald's first. It gave information for where to pick up a gown for the black-tie event. I loved this idea, but was I forgetting something?

I opened Ethan's text. My heart did a somersault. "When are you coming over to assess that account?"

I sighed. Another thing that I'd forgotten and messed up already.

Smells of roasting potato and cheese wafted through the air. My mouth watered. Had I eaten lunch? *Nope, but now, in the middle of the afternoon, I will.*

I headed toward the pierogi food truck, a Pittsburgh favorite. I ordered the six-piece potato and cheese pierogi combo. Although well-priced for takeout, I probably should have been packing my meals and not eating out.

Maybe I should just let Ethan go. While I waited for my pierogis, I stared down at my phone, rereading the text. He hadn't even used a smiley emoji in the message.

The girl in the truck plopped my pierogi plate in front of me. The food reminded me of Travis. He loved street food. I recalled the way he had looked at me at Lulu's Noodles. No, he only wanted to chat—nothing more.

I carried my pierogis back to my bench and sat down. Biting into the first pierogi flooded my mouth with savory cheese. I liked Travis, but not like that. I could never date him.

Why not? the voice in my head questioned.

"Well, for one thing, he's still obsessed with video games," I told my pierogi but then jerked my head up to see if anyone had noticed that I was talking to my food like a loony person. No one was nearby, so I continued my reasoning. "I can't imagine it. He's like…a brother."

It seemed like a good enough reason. My thoughts returned to the office hottie on my third pierogi. Even thinking about going to his office to talk about work soon made my stomach want to fly away. I tingled from top to toe, and I wondered if I could fly on this feeling. *Stay here, stomach.*

"What would Mel do?" I asked my last pierogi. It didn't respond.

"She'd go after what she wants," I informed the empty plate as I threw it into the nearby trash can and then strode back to the office to reconnect with Ethan.

Chapter Six

I rounded the corner into Finance and forced myself to slow my steps. I had practically run all the way here so as not to lose my nerve. As I steadied my breathing, I heard a lilting laugh followed by a deep voice. I recognized both: Lana's laugh and Ethan's voice. The workday was almost over so I couldn't leave and come back later.

I stopped cold. Lana sat on the edge of a chair, leaning as close to Ethan's desk as possible. I took in his straight back and animated face. My heart squeezed. Mel would march in, but I wasn't quite ready to do that, so instead, I tapped my finger nail against the aluminum of the cubicle.

Their heads swiveled toward me. Ethan blushed while Lana grinned at me and stood. I smiled at her as she left, hips swinging behind her. I suddenly wished for curvy hips while also wondering what to make of my friend camping out in there.

"I lost track of the time." I approached Ethan's desk but didn't want to sit in the chair that Lana had vacated. "You texted me about an account budget?"

"Right." His cheeks were still flushed. He flipped open his tablet to pull up some files. "If you'd like, take a seat."

I adjusted the chair so I would have an easier view of Ethan's tablet and sat. My mind raced. How could I show him that I wanted to give us another try? Was it too late?

He spun the screen toward me and pointed at some numbers. "According to the budget we drew up with Jones at the beginning of the year, they wanted twenty-five percent toward social media, twenty-five toward billboards, and the final fifty toward television. However, the numbers have been coming back differently. You seem to be targeting more social media and less billboards and paper advertisements."

"A lot of our clients are making that switch," I said, wondering why he needed me on this point, but I couldn't complain because I liked being near him.

Ethan shut his tablet case. "Actually, I was hoping that I could talk to you about something else."

Conversation whiplash. I shifted in my seat. I hated when people started a new topic with that type of preface.

"Yeah," I cut in right as Ethan took a big breath to speak, thinking I could change the direction of the conversation. "I actually wanted to talk to you, too."

A small smile flickered at the corner of his mouth, so I stuck my right hand out across the desk. "Can we start over? Hi, I'm Jadyn Simon, Account

Services Consultant. I interact with clients on a number of levels, specifically campaign brainstorming, presenting, and all the details of executing their advertising campaigns."

Ethan took my hand in his, and we shook. I tried to pull my hand away, but he tightened his hold. His pressure on my hand was like a direct connection to my heart, sending it into a spasms of flutters. "Actually I'd prefer if we skip the introductions and get right to the good part. Would you consider leaving early and having dinner with me?"

All of me wanted to say yes and I think my head even nodded a little bit, but my spontaneous dinner date from last night had totally thrown my day into a downward spiral. Of course, things were looking up at the moment—"up" kind of looked like a blond-haired, hazel-eyed guy. I sighed, slightly frustrated to have to say no, but decided to change it into a joke. "Wow, Mr. Spontaneous. I need to stay late tonight, but what about Saturday?"

"No can do for me." He drew circles on the back of my hand with his thumb. *Does he know he's doing that?* I couldn't concentrate. I either needed to take back my hand, or I could chop it off and let him keep it. *At least then I could think.*

"Ethan, I need to talk with you." Victoria swung around the corner of the office and I yanked my hand back. Her eyes flew between the two of us, but she held her ground and waited.

"Rain check?" Ethan raised his eyebrows.

I couldn't shut off my smile, even smiled at Victoria, and exited the space.

You bet I was going to redeem that rain check.

Saturday, my stomach grumbled, pulling me out of my art zone. What time was it anyway? At least I knew it was still Saturday, but most of the day could have passed. Time should never intrude on art, and I wasn't quite ready to face reality. The box of sunshine on the carpet made me guess afternoon. I needed to enjoy my big painting space while I had it.

I gazed at the paper in front of me. Greens and blues spiraled across half the page, coming to a point where they collided with reds and yellows, zigzagging the rest of the paper. *What happened here?*

Me. I happened here. That point where all the cools and hot colors slammed together in the middle of the paper was me. *A war within.*

"And outside." I thought of all the things I needed to do and heaved a sigh. "Jesus, give me strength."

Minutes later, having discovered it to be late afternoon, I sat by the front door, my mail stack in front of me, looking for an official-looking envelope from the apartment management about my upcoming eviction. *I hate that word.* Instead, I discovered a small card with actual handwriting on the envelope.

Slitting the envelope open with a finger, I drew out a note card with "Thank You" scrawled across it in script. I flipped the card open.

"Dear Jadyn, I wanted to personally thank you for assisting the youth group in their Spring Retreat this year. I know it's been months since then, but I've now just gotten around to writing. The girls loved you and you connected with them so quickly. We'd love to have you join us for our weekly meetings…"

I grinned. It had been a good weekend even though I hadn't wanted to do the retreat at first. I remembered the late-night talks of boys and periods. Those girls wanted someone to admire, but in my head, I still pictured myself at age thirteen sometimes. *But I would do it again in a heartbeat.*

A knock thumped against my apartment door. My heart skittered in my chest. I leaped to my feet. *I'm not expecting anyone.*

I peeked out the peephole and recognized Travis. What was he doing there again? I didn't want to let him in. Maybe he would go away. *Jadyn, that's not nice.*

Squeezing my eyes shut, I rubbed the back of my head with my hand. I'm sure my curls stretched afro-crazy and I hadn't put on a bra yet for the day. It almost seemed too late in the day to give in to the structure of a bra.

He rapped a staccato on the door.

Be nice and open the door. But I don't want to.

Angel Jadyn won out and I unbolted the door. Travis's face broke into a grin and his eyes glued to my hair. I crossed one arm over my chest, hoping to mask my bra-less state. Travis's eyes slid over the rest of me and then returned to my face.

"Sleep well?"

I didn't want to talk to him, but I forced myself to give a response. "Leave me alone. It's Saturday."

He shrugged. "Can I come in?"

I couldn't keep a frown from creasing my face. This was supposed to be *my* day. But this was Travis, my childhood friend.

"Sure." I waved him through the door and locked it back up behind him. I turned around to see him surveying the mess.

"What happened to cleaning? My management would evict me if my place looked like this."

Sore point. Crossing my arms, I tried to keep in a retort, but I couldn't. "That's why I *didn't* call you."

"Wow, Suzie Sarcasm, chill out." Travis pretended to roll up his sleeves and walked over to the stack of dishes on the end of the low table in front of the couch. For a moment, I thought he

75

might help me out and my frustration ebbed. He moved the stack an inch, then flopped back into the couch and kicked his feet up to rest on the place where the plates had been.

I'd handle this better with a bra on.

Spinning on my toe, I strode to my bedroom and shut the door behind me. The firm slam surprised me. I checked my feelings. Anger.

I jerked open my top dresser drawer and lifted out a sports bra. If he wanted a therapy session, he had another thing coming. Why had I opened that door?

Pulling my t-shirt back on over my head, I stalked out of my room to tell Travis to leave. What I saw flickered my anger into a low, intense burn. In the minutes that I had been in my room, Travis had reconnected his Play Station 2 to my television and was in the middle of a game. *I still have the PS2?*

I clamped my teeth together. My mind flipped to Ethan, imagining him doing this same thing, but I couldn't. He'd probably played video games as a boy, but I doubted that he played them often anymore. At some point, grown men were supposed to be finished with these silly games. *Don't compare Ethan and Travis. They're two different men.*

Walking into the living room, intent on clearing out the dishes, I began to stack the ones nearest the low table.

"Jay! You have to play with me." Travis didn't even look at me as his thumbs twitched, his arms jerking this way and that. I had a glass in one hand and a stack of plates in the other.

Something cracked in me. I plunked the dishware against the table and then walked over to the television and shut it off.

"I was winning!" Travis cried. He searched the couch for the remote control, but he didn't find it. A messy room had its benefits.

"Shouldn't you be done with video games?" My hands found my hips. "You're twenty-five. Aren't you supposed to put childish things behind you when you become a man?"

Travis's face dropped.

My mouth continued speaking even as my brain scrounged for the brakes. "But maybe you aren't a man, yet."

As soon as the words left my lips, horror spilled through me. My hands jerked to my mouth. "Travis…"

"No." He held up a hand. "I think you've said enough."

Travis stood and moved toward me. And like magnets of the same polarity, I moved away from him. Even now the horror of my words struck me, but the relief of finally saying them mattered, too. Game Over.

Travis left.

An hour later, after washing the dishes from the last week, I went back to the living room to grab a glass I'd missed off the television stand. I reached for it and remembered Travis reaching in the same way for the power button of the television.

I chewed my lip. I hadn't been kind to him.

But I wasn't actually sorry for what I had said. *Maybe for the way I said it.*

"Yeah, he didn't deserve that." I agreed with myself as I carried the glass back to the kitchen and set it down next to the sink. "I need to apologize to him."

My mind replayed what I had said, especially the part about putting childish things behind you. I frowned. That portion came from 1 Corinthians 13, I thought. I walked to my bedroom and took my Bible off the nightstand, flipping to the passage. I skimmed through all the things that love should be and shouldn't be. There it was, right after all the loves.

A thought pinched my heart. "Love is patient, love is kind…"

I can't do anything right. Not work. Not my apartment. Not my love life. Not my friendships. I dropped my chin to my sternum. Where had my love for Travis been?

My eyes sought out the page again. "It does not dishonor others…it is not easily angered."

Oh, Jesus, I keep messing up.

That evening, I stood in front of the cream-colored, sequined dress in my closet—one surprising perk of working with such a style-savvy client and attending his black-tie event. I wanted to buy new shoes to wear with it even though the dress was only on loan. *There's a reason you have an eviction notice.*

I still needed to figure out how to handle that problem, too. I had time. Didn't I?

My eyes came back to the dress. I would love for Ethan to see me in a gown that highlighted the brown tones in my skin so well. What if I took a plus-one to this event? *You can't do that.*

"Well, why not?" I imagined him seeing me in this dress.

The event is for your job and you don't know if Max would allow it.

That voice in my head was getting annoying. What did I have to lose anyway? The likelihood of Ethan being free that evening was small, but I remembered him holding my hand and knew I had to ask. If he said no, I wouldn't be dogged by regret for not asking and if he said yes, I'd deal with getting Max's permission then.

I ran for my phone in the kitchen before my courage faded with the first attack of doubt. I opened a text message and typed Ethan's name.

Then, I thought better of it, pulled up his details, and dialed.

Time to redeem that rain check.

Breathing deep, I prepared to leave a message. Time, day, place, event, dress code. *I've got this.*

He answered. "Hi, Jadyn."

My thoughts skedaddled away. I leaned hard against the counter. *I don't got this. Say something.* "Oh, hi, Ethan, I didn't expect you to actually pick up."

His chuckle reminded me of faraway thunder. "I can hang up, and you can call again."

I laughed. It was nice to have gotten over that Crazy Friday rough spot. My heart lifted. "I was hoping to redeem my rain check. I have a black-tie event for one of my clients, and I wondered if you'd come with me."

I'd said it. I wanted to pat myself on the back for actually getting the words out, but then I realized he hadn't answered. I held my breath.

"When is it?"

Air rushed out of my mouth, blowing into the phone. No way he didn't hear that. "It's next Sunday evening."

That's what I had been forgetting. *I'll call Mom after this.*

"Sure, I can do that."

I clamped back my scream of excitement, but ended up squeaking, "Awesome! Do you want to meet there?"

We finalized the details and hung up. I slid the phone down to the counter that I still leaned against. He'd said yes. *Rain checks are the best.*

I flung out my arms and spun around the kitchen. My fingertips brushed a glass, and it wobbled. I quit my spin to steady it. Nothing could shatter this moment.

Chapter Seven

Just a quick week later, Magical Sunday Evening had arrived. Grandmother's vintage silver clutch hung around my wrist as I exited my blue car. Streetlights glinted off clutch and sequined dress. I couldn't help but feel like Cinderella; thankfully, no glass slippers cramped my toes. I gazed down the sidewalk. I didn't see Ethan anywhere, so I snapped my clutch open and checked my phone for missed calls or texts. Nothing.

Inside the Andy Warhol Museum, we had planned to meet in the room with the silver floating pillows, but a part of me hoped to run into him on the sidewalk. As I walked the block toward the museum, I caught other pedestrians staring at me in my lovely attire. I'd tamed my curls into a loose French twist and my clicking heels echoed down the street. On a night like tonight, I had no need for fairy dust.

Max strode up the sidewalk with his assistant a step behind. Oswald wore a grey satin bow tie while Max sported an unusually conservative black suit with vest. His main ornamentation included both a gold cello lapel pin and a silver piano lapel pin.

I dipped my head toward each man as we took the last few steps to enter building. "You clean up well."

I winced on the inside. I hadn't yet seen either of them anything less than dressed up. Neither one blinked at my statement. Max came to me with his hands outstretched so I put my hands in his.

"My dear, you are radiant in this dress. I knew Tezma would find you the loveliest of dresses for this event. She charged the borrow fee to my account, correct?" Max spun me slowly, releasing one of my hands to tuck a curl into my twist. "Who did your hair? It's stunning. I'd better warn the straight boys that I've hired a heartbreaker for a consultant."

Movement caught my eye and I saw Ethan. *There's no way he didn't see Max touch my hair.*

I laughed and drew my hand back from him. My hot date was only steps away. That's when I remembered that I had never asked Max's permission to bring a date. My heart dipped a little. I'd totally forgotten.

Max eyed me. "You laugh, but I'm serious."

"I don't think you need to worry, sir." Oswald cut in to our conversation. "Seems like she's already got someone."

Oswald nodded to Ethan who had his eyes fixed on me. I shot a look back at Oswald who smiled small across his lips. If he weren't so smug all the time, I'd probably think him attractive. Few girls could resist a European man, but perhaps I was one such girl.

"My heavens." Max scooted next to my side so he could watch Ethan reach us. He whispered to me. "I love a man in a tux, too."

Boy, was I glad the dim lighting hid blushing.

Ethan stepped into our circle. I loved how he was bold enough to insert himself into new situations. I smiled at him and glanced down and then back up through my eyelashes. All dressed up like this, shyness tugged at me. I pushed away the feeling. "Max and Oswald, this is Ethan."

For a moment, I had wanted to introduce Ethan as my date for the night, but I chickened out. Max and Ethan shook hands. As Oswald reached to shake hands with Ethan, he brought his left hand across his waist and I noticed a wedding band on his ring finger. *Do all single women look for them, everywhere?* I blinked back to the situation at hand.

"So how do you know this scrumptious thing?" Max asked aloud. I couldn't figure out who he was talking to and was beginning to wonder if he'd had too many glasses of red wine at dinner.

"I kno—"

"We—"

"Sir, we need to check the decor before the night truly begins." Oswald won the clash to respond to the question and guided him away from us. *Maybe Oswald isn't so bad.*

"Want to head to the floating pillows room?" I said as I took in his suit with a black skinny tie. Forget the car. He'd probably walked right out of a magazine to join me at the museum.

"Excuse me." Max was back. "Jadyn, I would like you to meet my pianist, Lionel, and my cellist, Sophia."

I squeezed Ethan's arm before letting go to shake hands with the duo that made up the main focus of the advertising campaign. Lionel stood tall and boyish alongside Max's shorter frame. Glasses perched on his nose and his suit fit flawlessly. His eyes watched Max with a sort of awe. Meanwhile, Sophia held broad shoulders back, a small frown on her face. Her navy dress hugged her plump body, showing off her sumptuous curves. These two were far from happy symmetry, but opposites could create a versatile campaign.

Seeing them in person, I knew immediately that an advertising campaign focused on children had been a misstep.

"Since we'll be working together to create advertising that will draw you lifelong fans, did either of you have any ideas on how to best sell yourselves?" Some of my coworkers never liked to ask their clients about their ideas, but I had found the easiest way to please clients was to ask them. It made them feel more a part of the process even if you didn't end up using their thoughts.

Sophia squinted at me. "Although we're a duo, I'd like to be seen as a quality soloist as well. If we can create something that sells us together and separately, that would be ideal."

"I have this fantasy of a photo taken with Sophia playing her cello on top of a grand piano as I play." Lionel obviously had a nerd streak.

Mentally, I began to create a list of what types of questions to ask my different music sources. Lionel kept speaking.

"Or maybe we can have the cello on top of a piano, kind of like Marilyn Monroe in curvy instrument form."

Sophia glared at Lionel. He seemed like an overeager puppy whereas Sophia held herself like a self-aware feline. I'd have to keep their interesting relationship in mind.

"The trick is to convince your audience that you can give them something that no one else can. You achieve that, and you score a fan who will share you with their friends and family." I broke into Lionel's downward spiral of advertising ideas.

Sophia's eyes flashed with interest. "Is it really that simple?"

"In theory. But it still requires a lot of brainstorming to create a campaign that accurately represents what you want to be to your audience." I took a breath and shot a look at Ethan. His eyes focused on me and I was happy that he hadn't wandered away. I met Lionel's eye. "We'll have to discuss what makes you different from everyone else out there. And then brand you."

Lionel's eyebrows scrunched together, reminding me of a large caterpillar. "I'm a really tall pianist?"

We have work to do. I glanced at Sophia and caught her rolling her eyes to the ceiling.

"Do you know what makes you different as a musician?" I posed the question to Sophia.

She rested her hand on her hip. "There are a couple of ways that you can go with this. Lionel's tall. I'm plus-sized. I funded my music career almost completely solo because my mom was unable to help me. I embody the American Dream."

My brain zeroed in on one word: mom. I had forgotten to call my mom to tell her that I'd miss our usual family dinner tonight. I curled my toes in my shoes. But now was not the time.

"We play music for every man, not just the people that know their classical music." Sophia continued her thought. "We're not too proud to play at weddings or in somebody's back room. Of course, we'd prefer Heinz Hall."

We all chuckled at that admission.

"Well now, these two must greet other guests and then play some music if you two would head to the auditorium." Max hurried the musicians away from me and Ethan, but he still talked to me over his shoulder. "I expect brilliant campaign ideas after tonight!"

Ethan offered his arm to me as we walked. "I reserve the word 'scrumptious' for use on food, but I can think of a fair amount of other adjectives to describe you."

I slipped my hand around his bicep and all other thoughts fell away. Not quite sure how to respond, I settled on a simple and light. "Oh?"

"I think 'lovely' fits the bill or maybe intelligent, personable, thoughtful."

I smiled at him and found Ethan grinning down at me. His hazel eyes sparkled and that was all the magic I needed. My tongue remained still.

We entered the auditorium, and I saw the grand piano.

That's when I reminded myself, no matter his sweet comments, this was work, not Cinderella's ball. But his nearness made it hard to think.

"I called you five times last night." My mom's voice jumped through the phone during my lunch break on Monday.

"I saw your five missed calls when I got home. Late."

"Didn't you think about how your mom would worry when you didn't show up for Sunday night dinner?"

"Mom, I'm sorry. I meant to call you this past week." I sighed and relaxed into a park bench near the food trucks. There was someone else that I had meant to call, but I couldn't remember. "It's been pretty crazy the last couple of weeks."

"You didn't even tell Mel about it. She tried to pick you up at your apartment."

"It slipped my mind." I rubbed my forehead. I could feel a headache coming on, and I wanted to curl up underneath a blanket in my bedroom. "I need to go eat some lunch. I love you."

I hadn't even darkened the screen of my cell phone before another incoming call brightened it. Apartment management. *This can't be good.*

"Jadyn Simon speaking," I answered.

"Miss Simon, your outstanding rental payments have not been paid; therefore, your eviction notice is final. You must be out of your apartment three weeks from today."

"I've had no notice of this final date." I pictured all the mail sitting by my door that I hadn't sorted.

"Unfortunately, you have, ma'am. We've sent you both warnings and payment options through the regular post and to your door. We would appreciate your compliance in this matter."

"Fine, I'll be out." My patience was up. Nothing like an eviction to slash your dignity.

My politeness kicked back in right before I hung up the phone. "Thank you for the call."

I slid my phone back into my purse and pulled my legs up onto the bench so I could curl up right there. People could think whatever they liked.

"Mommy, look!" A little voice called out nearby. My eyes popped open, thinking that she was probably talking about me. The little girl with a large purple elephant on her shirt held her mother's hand and was pointing toward the food trucks. A young man wearing an octopus hat on his head juggled colored balls. He was adding more and more balls to the bunch that he juggled. His hands moved faster and faster. The juggler nodded to someone and another ball flew toward him. He caught it and continued to entertain the bystanders. *That's like me.*

One of the balls fell from his hands and he reached to swoop it back up into the group but missed. Suddenly, all the balls thumped across the sidewalk with people rushing to collect them. *Ball drop #1: apartment payments.*

What was next? Boss? Clients? Family? Friends? Ethan? I couldn't afford to drop any of them, but I felt them slipping as my hands moved faster and faster. What was I going to do?

I made it back to my office and tapped my pen against my desk. Three weeks. I had three weeks to find a new place to live. On top of creating a stellar campaign for Max, managing my other clients, pursuing a relationship with Ethan, and trying to paint in the spare moments.

Lana popped her head into my cube. "Are you trying to bore a hole to China through your desk?"

I dropped the pen. My mind tossed the image of Lana flirting with Ethan before my eyes. I frowned. "Sorry. Lots of things on my mind."

"Let me guess." Lana placed a hand on her hip and raised an eyebrow. "Ethan."

"What?" was my brilliant response.

"I heard you guys went to Mr. Louis's event." Her smile looked a tad strained. Lana waved her hand at me. "Don't worry about it. He's cute, but I'm going on a date with a guy I met online."

Why would she even think I'd be worried? She must have some interest, because that came out of the blue. She wiggled her fingers at me and left me by myself again. Lana made goo-goo eyes at any male that would look at her twice. Her rule of thumb was "say yes."

Serial dating Lana-style sounded so exhausting.

I shrugged and stared at the list of possible apartments that I had scribbled out on a notepaper. Mom's house was out because of the lengthy commute. Ethan's was out since our relationship was way too young to consider sharing anything other than a meal once or twice a week. All my other girlfriends were crammed together in apartments and had no space for a new roommate. Lana's revolving boy toys would not create a good living situation. My mom would have a canary if I moved in with Travis, and I didn't feel like rocking the boat that much.

The only name that remained on my list as a practical option? Mel.

Good commute. She had an extra room, too, though she thought she had a right to know everything I did and how I did it, but that was my only con.

Crossing my arms, I leaned back into my chair. I definitely didn't want to tell her why I had to leave my apartment, but maybe I could say this move-in would only be temporary. *Because it will be.*

I reached for my phone and speed dialed my sister's number. It rang for a while, and she picked up.

"Hey. How would you feel about having a roommate for a month?"

She didn't say a word.

"Mel?"

"Who are you asking for?"

"Me. Can I stay with you?" I asked again, feeling kind of queasy. She wouldn't say no to her own flesh and blood. Would she?

"No, I don't think so." She took a breath. "I need to go. Sorry, Jadyn."

Chapter Eight

I rushed into work on Tuesday morning, clutching my half-full double espresso Chai latte close. Sleep and work completion tussled for attention these days, but the results remained—not enough time for either. Lana sat at her desk with headphones tucked into her ears. She waved me over.

"Did you hear?" Her perfectly shaped eyebrows came together.

I grinned. "Your music?"

Lana rolled her eyes and shook her head. "No, did you hear about Ethan Alvey?"

Ethan's name worked faster than caffeine on my body and suddenly, I woke right up. Sunday night had been like a dream from my little girl fantasies. We'd texted a bit since Sunday, but I hadn't seen him. He hadn't told me anything special. I hated to admit that I didn't know what Lana was referring to. *Be cool.*

My curiosity got the better of me. "I didn't. What's going on?"

Lana knew everything about everyone, so I wondered what kind of news she might have about Ethan. A polygamist? A closet shoe collector? *The second isn't so bad.*

"Oh, honey." She pushed a hand through her blonde hair, tucking some behind her ears again. "Apparently, he got hit by a truck yesterday."

I resisted the urge to drop my latte and instead, placed it on the front desk. My heart seemed to have stopped beating. *Is he dead?* "Is he okay?"

"Yes, if you count having emergency surgery to remove your spleen small potatoes."

"But he's alive." Breath rushed back into my lungs. When had I started holding my breath?

"I think I'm going to organize an office dinner support system. A bachelor like Ethan will need someone to take care of him during recovery; after all, his family is hours away."

She was right, but I didn't want Lana being so domestically wonderful to him. *She's just being nice.*

But I still didn't trust her motives. Lana's southern sweetness attracted most males and her blonde beauty and curves didn't hurt anything. Since beginning to work at Davenport, I had witnessed Lana's ways. She took up and discarded men like one uses a napkin to dab her mouth at dinner. And she did it so sweetly.

A question tingled in my mind. I picked up my latte but had to ask. "Do you know if we can visit him?"

"He's in the ICU for monitoring, but I think he can have visitors. I bet you can call the hospital to find out."

"Thanks. How did you learn all this?" I tugged on one of my curls. "Also, you can put me down on your list."

"Eh, the news gets around. Ethan's boss told me."

So Ethan hadn't told her! If I had hips, they would have been swinging as I walked to my cube.

As soon as I entered my little office space, I placed my latte down and reached for my cell phone. I doubted that Ethan would pick up, but on the off chance, I decided to try. The phone rang three times.

"Hello?" A groggy voice sounded through the space connecting our phones.

"Run over by a truck? Isn't that code for hungover?" I opted for trying to make him laugh. It was a good way to deal with difficult things.

I heard a snort come through the speaker. "My days of joking about feeling like a truck ran over me are over. Or maybe, it's the perfect time to be making that joke."

"I'd run with it."

"No running for me any time soon, especially after ice cream trucks." His voice sounded tired.

"I was wondering—wait, did you say 'ice cream truck'?"

"An off-duty ice cream truck wasn't playing its tunes."

I grinned. I couldn't help it. The guy I liked had been hospitalized by a freak run-in with an ice cream truck. "But the question is, did you get a lifetime supply of ice cream?"

"Snap. I didn't think to ask for that while I was laying flat on my back in the middle of the asphalt."

"Next time. You'd better ask for that and make sure to include ice cream for a second person." I giggled and knew that I sounded flirty. I glanced up to see Victoria looking into my cubicle before spinning back to the hallway. Time to finish this conversation and get to work. "But hey, I was actually calling to ask if I could come see who fared better in this ice cream duel."

Ethan didn't say anything for a little bit; then I heard him clear his throat. "I look pretty bad, Jadyn. I haven't seen myself in a mirror, but I can see all the wires and gauze."

"I'm a tough cookie, which is a perfect topping for any ice cream scenario. Anyway, it will help distract you while you're cooped up."

I waited for Ethan's response.

"All right. I'll sign the release form for your visitation, but no laughing at my new head gear."

"I swear." I said, placing my hand over my heart and then realizing that he couldn't see me. "It sounds like you could be the next big super hero."

Lunch on the run included no breaks unless you counted waiting for the light to change, but I had no choice today and I wanted to stop in to see Ethan. So a long lunch break it would be. What better way to show my interest in him? Entering the Allegheny General Hospital, I noticed that most people coming in carried gifts with them. I hadn't even thought of that and now I had already passed all the street vendors, but I didn't have any extra money to spend at the moment. What could I do?

I glanced around the waiting room and noted magazine stacks and health pamphlets. Nothing I could use there. "Silly girl, you love to draw."

A lady eyed me. I grinned, deciding to explain myself. "Sometimes I talk to myself."

She returned to her magazine.

Finding an empty chair away from other people, I pulled out my planner and hunted till I found an empty page in the back. Everyone said switching to a phone planner that connected everything to your computer was practical, but I liked my paper. I also kept a few pens in my purse for this very reason of needing to create on the spot. A brilliant design began to bloom in front of my eyes across the piece of paper. Within ten minutes, the dandy doodle was ready to be presented to its recipient. The sketch depicted a girl holding crutches while letting the boy lean on her. The girl had my crazy curls. Would he like it?

I approached the receptionist, who wore a pair of lavender scrubs. She popped a piece of gum into her mouth and asked, "What can I do for you, ma'am?"

"I'm here to see Ethan Alvey in ICU."

"Name?"

"Jadyn Simon."

She checked her computer. "All right. You're on the approved list. He'll be in Unit 4C."

Five minutes later, I stood outside his room. I needed some sort of opening line. I knew he was expecting me and we had less than an hour for visiting. My feet propelled me forward and I entered the room. One bed, a chair, and a muted television made up the bulk of the furniture. Ethan lay in the bed, wires splayed out from his chest near his heart and from his hands. Bandages wrapped his abdomen, making his wound appear quite a lot larger than an emergency removal of a spleen. An oxygen tube wound away from his nose. Ethan was watching me. Despite his joke of head gear earlier, only his hair stuck out crazily.

He looked pretty bad.

"I'm thinking the truck must look worse than you," I joked. "And where's your walk-in freezer of free ice cream?"

Ethan winced. "Don't make me laugh."

"Oops. I shall pause all jokes at the expense of others and myself until you don't look like someone cut you in half and then glued you back together." A hand flew up to my mouth. Too far. I had said that. The urge to melt into a puddle came over me.

"This is why you were the right person to come visit."

I smiled, and he smiled in return. I caught him up on office news, and he told me about a new client he had just been assigned in Chicago. Ethan asked about Max and the brainstorming.

Reaching into my purse, I yanked out my recent creation, holding it up and then offering it to him. "I made this for you, speaking of brainstorming."

He accepted my piece of paper and gazed at it. "You always bring brightness with you wherever you go."

I knew the generally accepted response to compliments was supposed to be a simple thank you, but I ignored it. I pointed at Ethan's new nose accessory. "Do you feel like Darth Vader in that nose get-up?"

He faked wheezing and gasped out in a deep voice. "Luke, I am your father."

"I sure hope not."

I jumped.

A male nurse breezed in with a notepad and pen in hand. "I'm Luke, and your friend here is a bit too young to be my dad. Brothers, maybe."

Luke finished up his paperwork and then headed back out of the room.

I glanced at the clock and realized that time was passing faster than I wanted. Searching my mind for new information to talk about, I remembered my earlier conversation with Lana.

"People at work are putting together a meal squad for you." People referred to Lana, but I didn't want her getting any more brownie points with Ethan. I pulled the one chair closer to the bed. I quelled an urge to lean against the mattress that Ethan lay on.

He frowned but didn't speak.

"What? You don't like free food?"

"It's not that." The skin under his hazel eyes stretched thin. "I have a hard time accepting help, even from my family. Anyway, they're in Chicago."

"But you're not going to be able to recover well without help from someone. Can you even move right now?"

Ethan shook his head.

"Exactly. Here's the thing, if you refuse our help, you steal our joy of caring for you. We might have grown up in a culture that lauds independence, but we still need community."

He pressed his lips together. "I see what you're saying, but I want to be self-sufficient without anyone else taking care of me."

For some reason, this declaration pinched my heart. It hurt.

"What if someone wants to care for you?" The question seemed almost too transparent, and I could feel my cheeks heating like a furnace.

Ethan looked out the window and I glanced at the clock. Time to go. I stood and touched his shoulder. "Visiting hour is over."

I wanted to offer to help him out, but he had just rejected that kind of help. I withdrew my hand from his shoulder and threw him a quick smile. "See you later, handsome."

Four days later, Mel picked me up to volunteer with a teen night at the church. I couldn't keep my foot still, tapping it constantly as I thought about hanging out with teens. We both wore jeans and my big sister had her curls pulled back into a ponytail. My curls were too short to pull off a sophisticated ponytail. It reminded me of a pom-pom on the back of my head; curls made ponytails look hilarious.

According to the phone call on Monday, I only had two weeks now before I needed to be out. I could have asked Mom for money, but she'd complained to me about having to cut back her budget because of a car repair. Even though she'd said no, Mel was still my best option—after all, I was her little sister. It was easy enough to pretend that something had happened at the building, forcing all of us to leave. My mom and sister didn't know any of my neighbors, so they couldn't check up with them. It was only a twist from truthfulness, and I didn't want them to freak out.

Mel's voice broke into my thoughts. "Anthony said something to me today that's been bothering me."

"What?"

Mel's most recent boyfriend, Anthony, often challenged her way of thinking. They'd only been together for a few months, but he seemed to be good for her. Other guys she'd dated had been cowed by her strength of opinion and sense of what she wanted, but Anthony spoke up. He never seemed to do it out of spite or a desire to knock her down a peg or two either.

"He asked me straight out this morning if I ever got tired of giving out advice to people!"

"Anthony said that?" If Mel had been telling me this on the phone and not in person, I probably would have done a happy dance right there. Leave it to Anthony to ask the question.

"Yes, he did. Right after I told our server at the pancake place how to pursue her dream career with community college classes and to dump her boyfriend who was totally creeping on her from two booths away and would hardly allow her to wait on her tables. Seriously, what a jerk."

Although hearing Mel, I was starting to think about my eviction notice again. And words popped out of my mouth before I was ready to actually speak. "Speaking of advice, I have a problem."

"He's so frustrating. I can't believe he thinks I would ever tire of giving people sound advice." She jerked the car into the left hand turning lane and jolted to a stop. "It might be my calling."

"I got a call from my apartment management the other day." I started again.

"He's such a great guy on so many levels." With her foot on the brake, Mel took her hands off the steering wheel and began to tick off her fingers. "He's supportive of my dreams. He's not intimidated by me. He's attractive. He goes to church. He's never afraid to challenge me."

"They need me to move out for a while."

She continued her thoughts. "Maybe I like him best because he does challenge me, but I think advising is one of my best qualities."

"I thought maybe I could move in with you for a bit so the management could get the—"

"I already told you I can't have you." Mel hit the gas as the light changed to green and made the turn.

I should have started with that little fact. "Yeah, I know, but I have no other options. They're doing a mandatory cleaning on my apartment and it will take a couple of weeks."

"That's odd. I've never heard of anything like that." She signaled and parallel parked with quick efficiency.

My mind rushed for a logical explanation and I recalled some reading I'd come across. "Didn't you hear about that bedbug outbreak?"

"What! You have bedbugs?" She grimaced at me sitting on her car seat. "Why didn't you say anything? Oh, my gosh. You should be sitting on plastic."

"It's no big deal." I tried to calm her down.

"No big deal! There's a reason that bedbugs become such an infestation." She gasped. "I hugged you."

"I'm pretty sure my apartment doesn't have them. I haven't seen any, but the management wants to shut down the building for thorough cleaning anyway."

"That seems like a lot of effort for no solid evidence." She reached for her purse from the back seat and checked her phone.

"Well, maybe it's that someone else has bedbugs." My skin dewed in sweat. Keeping up with this story would be tricky, but there was no way I could tell her that my move came from not being able to keep up with rent.

"When do you need to move out?" Mel selected something on her smart phone. I guessed her calendar.

"Um, two Sundays from now."

"Fine. But don't bring anything to my apartment that hasn't been thoroughly washed. Better yet, we can store all of your things."

Relief should have flowed at this news. But I couldn't afford a storage unit. Worse yet, I knew I had just given up my paints, brushes, and easel since I likely wouldn't have space to paint at Mel's. And then, my poked me about having lied to my own sister.

Chapter Nine

Wednesday night was the best night to start moving some of my stuff into Mel's apartment, so I started packing. I'd found boxes pretty easily near the copier and had brought some home. Now, cozy next to my television, I stacked my collection of movies and placed them in boxes. Sandwiched in the videos, I pulled out a PS2 game. I flipped it in my hands. "Travis Bulrick" was written in fat marker on the back. I hadn't seen or heard from him in a while.

I'd forgotten to call him to apologize.

Checking the time on my phone, I calculated that I could stop by Travis's work and apologize before heading to my sister's. Maybe I could even slip in a quick visit to Ethan? I threw some pots and pans into another box and carried them out to the car.

A few minutes later, I was outside the hospital in a ten-minute parking spot. Ten minutes was far too short for squeezing in a visit to Ethan—it would be like a drive-by hello. I locked the car and ran in. An older woman sat behind the desk. I'd met her once before when I had been with Travis.

"Adelaide, is Travis around?"

She lifted her silver head and smiled.

"Yes, he is, honey. You can find him somewhere along that hallway there."

I followed her pointing hand and hurried down the hallway. I quieted my breathing, hoping to catch the sound of Travis's voice. A man in light blue scrubs walked out of a room and instantly, I recognized him.

"Travis!"

Did I imagine it or did his shoulders tense? Serious eyes met mine. I had hurt him.

I closed the yards between us as he came to a stop. I decided to skip preamble; after all, I had less than ten minutes. "I owe you an apology. I should have talked to you sooner."

His eyebrows drew together. I held up a finger, pausing any response he might venture and reached into my purse, pulling out the PS2 game. "I found this and remembered how I spoke so cruelly to you. I forget how comforting childhood games can be."

I paused and gathered my next thoughts. "I was frustrated because I wanted to see you happy and succeeding, not wasting your time on these games. But that's no excuse."

I took a deep breath, checking Travis's face. I could tell that he was tracking with me. I handed the game to him. "Will you forgive me?"

That question was always the hardest for me to voice because it found me at the mercy of the person that I had wronged. A precarious position, basically offering your throat to their rejection. I tried not to hold my breath.

"Yeah, I'll forgive you. I have to admit that it hurt a lot."

I took a deep breath. "I challenge you to a Mario Kart tournament. Winner buys the pizza."

Travis grinned, raising his hands. "Wow. Why should the winner buy the pizza?"

"We both know, I stink at all video games and I don't want to buy the pizza." *Also, I don't have the money to buy anything out of budget.*

"Why don't you make some pizza? Oh, right, because last time you made pizza, it resembled dried lava." Travis grabbed for his throat.

"What can I say?" I pretended to think while watching Travis's dramatic performance. "I'm gifted."

Thirty minutes later, I knocked on my sister's apartment door. I heard the lock slide and then the door opened.

"I'll take that." Mel lifted the top box out of my arms.

I followed her into the apartment. She led the way to the extra bedroom. I visualized my stuff occupying the empty space. Was there room for my art supplies?

I placed my box in the middle of the cream carpet. "I didn't bring much this trip, but it's a start. Do you want me to store my television or bring it because it is newer than yours?"

"Store it." My sister flipped the lid off one of the boxes. "You said this move was temporary anyway. Only bring the necessities. I have pots and pans. Besides, my lease is up in three months, so I'll be looking for somewhere."

I swallowed. I didn't like lying to Mel.

"Oh, I wanted to ask you about something that I found on your door the other day." She said as she pulled movies out of my box. I bent quickly and opened the other box. My heart hammered, and I was certain that Mel's proclamation couldn't be good.

Her phone rang. She leaped to her feet and followed the noise. I heard the music silence and then her voice answering. *Saved by the ringtone.*

The only thing that I could think was that Mel might have found an eviction notice, but I could hope that she found a love note from the hot neighbor or something. I piled my favorite pots and pans near some mugs that I'd brought over.

I heard Mel's speaking. "Oh, yes. That was my sister I brought to volunteer with me."

I folded the boxes back together while trying not to listen to my sister talking about me, but I couldn't help it.

"Jadyn does dabble in art."

Dabble. Frowning, I lay down across the bed. I hated that she said it as though I were an amateur even though I had studied it for years in high school and then college. I forced myself to relax and breathe deeply. *She didn't mean anything by it.*

I tuned back into their conversation. "She is good with teens, but I'll have to ask her. Hold on a sec."

The floor creaked under her steps as she walked across her apartment to what was to be my room. She stuck her head in the doorway as I sat up. "So, this is Nancy on the phone from the teen night that I took you to."

I tilted my head.

"She wants to know if you'd be interested in teaching an art class once a week, starting in two weeks. Apparently, Nancy saw your art degree on your volunteer application, and the teacher who was going to do it totally bailed on them. They've already advertised to the kids. They've got five signed up so far." Mel had her hand pressed over the phone.

My brain raced. I mean, I had studied art and it would be a great way to work on my own painting, too.

You don't have time. But it would only be one night out of the week. I could commit to that, even with my busy schedule. And I liked teens and painting. "Do you know how long the class goes for?"

Mel whipped the phone to her ear, asking my question and then listening. She made a face. "The commitment is for an *entire* school year? Till *June*?"

Her eyes sought my face. Air caught in my lungs. That was a long time. She took the phone away from her head and raised her eyebrows at me.

"I need to think about it." As much as "yes" was on the tip of my tongue, I wasn't so sure I had anything to offer these kids. "Would you mind asking her if I could have a few days?"

Mel finished off the call, promising to make sure that I got back to Nancy. She handed me her cell phone and instructed me, "Program her number in your phone."

As I added Nancy's number to my contacts, my sister talked at me.

"I love teen nights. I think you'd make a pretty good art instructor, but you've never done it before. And you're so busy."

In a minute, if I waited, she'd tell me exactly what she thought I should do.

"—turn her down because your schedule is crazy and you'll be moving back to your place, too. You don't have time for another commitment."

This time, her advice had an opposite effect on me. I had already been leaning toward saying yes, but now I wanted to do it just to show Mel that I could handle all of it.

It was one more thing to do, but I could handle it, right?

On Sunday morning, I walked to church in my paisley tights. It was church, right? Like a total no-judge zone. *If only that were true.*

The day was still cool enough that tights at the end of summer wasn't such a bad idea and I knew the church would be freezing.

A little bit later, I slid into a hard wood pew and opened my bulletin. Mel and Anthony joined me as the music began. I loved attending the same church as my sister. It felt right. Church was meant to be about family and community.

The sermon began. I tried to keep my mind present and listening to the pastor. I pulled out my Bible. My brain kept shooting off to consider the tasks that I needed to complete before the workweek truly began. At the top of it all, should I volunteer as the art instructor?

"Have you ever noticed how long people lived in Genesis, chapter five?" The pastor's voice cut through my mental to-do list. "We've got men having children as old as five hundred years old! The youngest had children at sixty-five!"

I flipped to Genesis five in my own Bible to read the chapter. My eyes snagged on the verses about a man named Enoch. One read, "Enoch walked with God, and he was not for God took him."

The pastor rapped his fist against the wood podium in front of him. "Enoch pleased God. In a time where his society was becoming more and more evil, he still chose to walk faithfully with God. If you read at the end of the chapter, Genesis introduces Noah, who, with his family, was the only sample of humanity that God spared during the Great Flood because of the sin of humans."

I itched to raise my hand to ask the obvious question. *How do you please God like Enoch?*

"Turn to Hebrews 11:5. 'By faith Enoch was taken up so that he should not see death, and he was not found, because God had taken him. Now before he was taken he was commended as having pleased God.'"

Wow. It was like my pastor had heard my silent question.

Why didn't the writers spend more time on Enoch? I reread the Bible verse, trying to map out in my mind how Enoch had lived a life that allowed him to escape death.

"But don't stop there!" Pastor Morey's voice pricked through my thoughts. "And without faith it is impossible to please him. God rewards those who seek him!"

I crossed my arms in front of my chest and leaned back into my chair, ready to listen. I wanted the pastor to outline specific steps as to how to please God. For a friend, of course.

"Now, this is only me speaking." Pastor Morey explained before continuing his thought. "I think the reason that the Bible doesn't explain more about Enoch is because if his life was laid out before us, we would turn his life into rules. Christianity is often based on rules, but it's meant to be guided by a deep relationship with the loving God of the Universe."

But I like rules. Uncrossing my arms, I straightened the hem of my skirt and considered the pastor's words. Rules seemed easier than relationship. But I wanted relationship and more importantly, I wanted to please God. So, then, I couldn't do without faith. I wasn't sure how I felt about that faith thing. It seemed like a lot of work and I wasn't sure exactly what faith looked like in my day-to-day life. But I did know about relationships with friends, so I could probably do that with an invisible God, too. *Maybe.*

After church, we were walking slowly through the Cultural District, but sweat still slicked my legs.

"What a cute little art gallery." Mel pointed to a storefront that I hadn't noticed before.

We stopped in front of the window and stared in at the walls created for hanging paintings. Lovely paintings. I wanted to go in to the store, but I knew my sister and her boyfriend were hungry. A poster hung in the window announcing a grand opening artist contest. I repeated the website name in my mind.

"Oh, look! A contest." My sister stood next to me, reading the poster. "If you were serious about your art, you could do that."

I gulped back my frustration. I was serious about my art. Why didn't anyone else see it?

It didn't seem to be a part of my schedule. I stayed silent and gazed at the poster, wishing to enter. I had paintings already, but the poster asked for a canvas accompanied by ten snapshots of other works. The deadline was in a week. My sister and her boyfriend were already walking away so I hurried to catch up with them.

At a nearby Mexican restaurant, we were seated at a nice table outside underneath an awning. Nearby, two other ladies sat, working through a basket of chips and salsa. Anthony and Mel discussed an event they were attending later in the week while I daydreamed about entering the art contest. I shuffled through all my paintings in my mind. I had a few good ones that might stand a chance.

A voice from behind me interrupted my thoughts. "I don't know how you young women find any men these days."

I pretended to crack my back so I could see the speaker. A white-haired lady sat directly behind me, talking at a pretty brunette. I turned back around, but the lady's voice carried over to us. "It's my opinion that you young people should hire a matchmaker, and that online dating is a finicky thing. How are you supposed to trust anything about the other person without knowing the people in their lives?"

I met Mel's eyes, which were wide. Anthony reached for the water that had magically appeared in the last couple of moments. We were all eavesdropping.

"My advice to you, dear, is to look around and grab the closest man."

I couldn't hold back my gasp. Mel laced her fingers through Anthony's. He squeezed as though he knew she was thinking that he was the nearest man at the moment. We were all thinking it, I'm pretty sure.

Until the old lady and her young friend left, we made stilted conversation. Once they were out of sight, my sister freaked out. "What kind of advice was that! I have never heard such terrible advice and so uncaringly shared."

I raised my eyebrows at her. "I'm sure the lady was well-meaning."

"That did not sound well-meaning to me. Advice should be wise, thoughtful, and kind."

"Huh." I said. "Maybe you should take your own advice."

Mel's eyes snapped to me and stayed. I fought the urge to squirm. I didn't feel bad for saying that. Someone needed to tell her.

"Are you saying that I'm like that lady?" She jabbed her thumb over her shoulder in the direction that the women had walked. "Because I'm not."

"What I'm saying—"

"I'll be back." Anthony stood up. "Bathroom."

Smart man. As he went, I noticed that his head followed every pretty girl he passed before he finally reached the building. That was weird. I refocused and started my thought again. "What I'm saying is that you could very well become that way."

"How could you say that?" Mel's eyes watered around the edges and the corners of her mouth turned down. "I don't want to be like that."

"I know you don't, but you give advice out a lot without the person first actually asking to hear it."

"I do not."

118

"You do." I sighed and selected a chip from our almost-empty basket and tried to scoop up the little bit of my lunch still on my plate.

"Well, I think I have a good perspective on the world and other people need to know good ways to handle these things."

"I'm sure that's what that lady thinks, too."

I bit into the chip only to find Mel glaring at me. She whipped her napkin off her lap and threw it at the table. It floated to a resting place on the ground as she flew to her feet, striding to the front of the restaurant where the bathrooms were. She met Anthony on the way and they talked briefly before he returned.

"I think we're going to head out now." He cleared his throat and handed me forty dollars. "Can you close out the bill?"

I stared at the money in my hand and watched him walk away to join my sister.

So this is what I get to look forward to while living with my sister.

Chapter Ten

A couple mornings before I was supposed to move out of my apartment, I lugged my favorite canvas to the office. My paintings were the last things I took off the walls. They made my space home, and all of them would be moved to storage while I was at Mel's. She was adamant that my stuff should go into storage. She didn't want her space crowded. *I guess I understand.*

I leaned the painting up against the only real wall in my cubicle and settled in, preparing for my meeting later in the day with Max. His advertising campaign had been slowly progressing. The production team had incorporated many ideas to create actual advertisements. We'd taken a common advertising concept and flipped the entire thing on its head, trying to make something that would grab the attention of our music audience, reaching them in new ways. I wondered if this would be original enough for Max, but he'd okayed all the plans so far.

My desk phone rang.

"Jadyn Simon speaking."

"Good morning, Jadyn. Mr. Louis looks dressed to kill."

"Hopefully not me!" I joked back. "Thanks, Lana!"

I set the receiver of the phone down as Max clicked his heels outside my cubicle. I waved him in. Lana couldn't have been more right. My most eccentric client wore an all-black outfit—even his collared shirt, vest, tie, and handkerchief were black. The only thing that stood out in all the black was a pink waist watch. Max reached for that pièce de résistance and checked the hour.

"Oswald will be here in minutes." He lowered himself into the chair across my desk and brought his leg across his knee. His eyes scanned my office and landed on my lone painting. He stood and moved swiftly toward it. "May I?"

My heart began a rapid beat. I bit back an apology of my work being amateur painting; I'd learned that art needed first to be appreciated without any preface or explanation. "Sure, go ahead."

I twisted away from Max because I couldn't bear to watch him and see what he might think of my most beloved painting. I loved it because of the power of the colors and the contrast of them across the canvas. Flipping through my notes on the campaign, I stacked them in preparation for moving into a meeting room once Oswald arrived. I checked the pocket where I had already placed my memory stick with a slide show. It was still there. I opened a drawer and pulled out a new blank pad of lined paper and a pen. Technology definitely kept things organized, but I still loved the solidity of paper.

Max mumbled to himself and I shot a quick glance at him, wondering if he was still looking at my work.

A rustle sounded on the aluminum siding of my cube and Oswald stepped into view, framed by my cubicle's walls. In his hand, he balanced a coffee carrier with three paper cups. He opened his mouth to speak, but before he could get a word out, Max spoke. "Put those down and come over here."

Oswald placed the carrier on my desk and approached Max who held the painting. "Have you seen work like this before?"

It was getting crowded in there. I wanted to turn away from them looking at my painting, but I knew that I needed to stay present. I steeled myself for whatever they might say.

Oswald lifted a canvas out of Max's grip and held it up. "It's definitely a unique style." Somehow, he managed a bored sneer.

"The colors clash, and the brush strokes run against each other. It makes me feel like someone brushing my hair in the wrong direction." Max sniffed.

"I don't know where to focus. The entire thing is far too distracting."

Their words speared my heart like needles. I tried to keep myself like stone rather than soft sponge. I didn't want to suck up these comments. The two men shook their heads, frowning.

Oswald spoke again. "I don't like it. Whoever did this should never touch a paintbrush ever again."

I gasped. Never touch a paintbrush again? That would kill my soul, but his comment left my soul dangling from a thread. I wanted to flee, tail between my legs, and never return. *Maybe he is right.*

"Who's the artist?" Max asked, eyeing me over his shoulder.

I swallowed like a schoolgirl caught doing something wrong. "Me."

His eyebrows shot up. He looked at the canvas he had in his hands and then to me. I could see him running through everything that he and Oswald had spoken aloud in front of me. "I'm a bit of an art connoisseur so I know my artwork. You mix art styles in a way that I have not seen yet."

His voice sounded tinged with apology, and yet, certainty in his own ability to know art. I considered that any compliment from Max, who dressed like a super model, should probably be noted.

"You need to watch how your colors bleed together. Watercolor can be a difficult medium, but you need to learn how to channel its weaknesses into strengths." Max continued his review of my work. "At the same time, don't forget to utilize the transparency of the color that comes with watercolors. It's a strength that can become a muddy mess of a weakness."

He pointed to a spot on the canvas, drawing an imaginary line with his pinky finger, while Oswald held it. "Right along this area, you've allowed the white of the canvas to show. I think that's unique, but it seems to have no purpose here. Art is definitely appreciated differently by every person, yet you can guide your viewers with a surer hand. Oswald, do you have anything to add?"

The way Max spoke to him sounded less of a question and more of an expectation. Oswald set the painting on the floor. He crossed his arms, challenging me with his eyes. "My wife played with painting for years. I think she is talented, but she's never done anything with it."

Oswald cleared his throat and frowned. "You have raw talent, but you can't let it sit in the corner of your office like this."

A raw talent? I didn't want to hear anything that he could say; after all, he had said that the artist should never pick up a brush again. That artist was me. Just remembering his words cut like a scalpel. I tried to focus on his words rather than how to toss him from my office.

"You already combine different painting techniques within your work. Have you considered mixed media work?" Oswald's voice broke into my thoughts.

I frowned. "The last time I did mixed media work I think I was in my college freshman Intro class."

"He's right!" Max interrupted. He rested his chin on his hand as he stared at the painting. "Mixed media will bring your paintings to life. Then, I think you could make a name for yourself in this art world. Your watercolor work has potential, but the additional dimension of other types of media will push you into a new category."

I mumbled under my breath. "Right. Like entering an art contest."

"That's it!" Max straightened his suit jacket and spun toward Oswald. "Look up art contests in the area."

Oswald nodded but reached for the coffees still sitting on my desk and passed the cups out to each of us. I reached for mine gratefully and took a sip. I needed some comfort after that harrowing scrutiny. The bitterness of the coffee combined with creamy hazelnut flavoring soothed me. I'd never expected to come to work with my favorite painting and have it so thoroughly picked apart. It hurt to have them critique so much, but those tiny compliments I wanted to trust as genuine.

"Yes." Oswald had his smart phone out of his pocket as he quickly worked across the screen. "La Rosa Galleria is hosting a grand opening art contest for new and unknown artists. If you win, you gain a full art show in their gallery, plus some prize money."

"You must enter," Max said. Was that an order? Or encouragement?

The contest that I had seen on Sunday, with Mel. The gallery came back to my mind's eye and I imagined seeing my work displayed behind those big glass windows in the middle of Pittsburgh's Cultural District. *Just a dream.*

But Max wouldn't tell me to enter unless he meant it, right?

I wanted to. *I'm going to.*

After they left, I relaxed into my chair while gazing at my canvas. *Jesus, you gave me this talent for a reason, and it pleases you when we use our talents. This must be your will.*

I knew I'd win. Wasn't this like Enoch? Pleasing God and myself.

"Hey, Jadyn." Lana flew into my office in a sky blue flowing top that accentuated her curves in an ethereal way. "I found out Ethan's back at home now. I sent the first meal over to him and he informed Sherry that he didn't want any more meals from us. What a way to greet the very first meal!"

I shook my head. It didn't surprise me after my conversation with Ethan earlier.

Lana dropped into a chair across from me. "You know him better than the rest of us. Tell him to let us take care of him."

I leaned back, wondering how to get out of this sticky situation. Lana waited for me to say something with her arms crossed and her lips pouted. Maybe I needed to do some public relations work for Ethan here.

"Lana, I'm sure that he appreciates the effort put into organizing this, but he is fiercely independent. In this case, I'm pretty sure it's not you, it's him."

Wow. That had just sounded like I was giving an after-break-up pep talk. Lana let out a little snort and crossed her arms more tightly. "Do you think I should keep up the meals?"

"That's a tough one." I frowned, trying to think about how to proceed carefully. Knowing Ethan, I'd stop, but I wouldn't mind if Lana completely wore out her welcome with him. *Not nice.* "You know, I'd stop the meals if I were you."

"I don't want him to starve."

"He won't. He's a grown man." But a little part of me doubted that he'd be able to get out on his own. Illness tended to make men act like babies.

I found myself wondering if Ethan would make a good boyfriend. One of the joys of being the girlfriend was caring for your boyfriend. What if he refused to be cared for?

A couple of evenings later, I fielded texts from both Ethan and Travis at the same time. Travis wanted to schedule our video game tournament, and Ethan seemed bored because he hadn't left his apartment for a while. His food situation was probably down to a last frozen pizza, considering his mother lived states away. He had no one to actually take care of him.

I grabbed my purse and ran out of my apartment that looked less and less like my own. I didn't like spending time there anymore.

At the grocery store, I bought all the staples and planned out my go-to dinner recipe that I could make. I pushed the cart to the checkout. As the numbers rang in to the cash register, my temperature rose. Food cost so much. Somehow, I had selected sixty dollars' worth of food.

Technically, I didn't have the money to spend, but this was not for me. I could justify spending money on a friend in need. Reaching into my wallet, I pulled out my credit card and handed it over to the cashier. *Thank goodness for minimum payments.*

Fifteen minutes later, I parked my car outside Ethan's apartment building. I hadn't texted him or called him since earlier, but I knew he was there. Hauling the plastic bags of food up to the door, I buzzed his apartment.

"Yeah?" Ethan's deep voice came through the speaker.

"Grocery delivery." I replied in a chipper high voice.

"I'm not expecting anything." The static shut off and I knew that he had disconnected us. I buzzed him again. When he didn't respond, I buzzed again. Nothing. I hit the buzzer again.

"I don't need anything." Ethan's voice sounded grumpy.

"It's Jadyn." I normalized my voice and fought down my annoyance. Of course, I was the one who had showed up unannounced.

"Oh. Come on up." The door unlocked.

Within minutes, I stood outside his apartment door. I'd never been there before, but I had been able to get the address from Lana's failed dinner crew.

I knocked on the door.

Ethan swung it open.

I held up the bags and moved to pass him, but he took the bags out of my right hand, then lead the way to his kitchen.

"What's all this?" Ethan peeked into the bags that he dropped on his kitchen counter. I took in the kitchen. Not one dish stood dirty in the sink. Everything was spotless.

"Do you even use this kitchen?"

"You answer my question first." He placed a hand on his side, winced, and then moved his hand lower.

"Fine." I pulled a half gallon of milk out of one of the bags, opened the refrigerator, and placed the carton on an empty shelf. The fridge sparkled. "These are your emergency get-better-soon supplies."

I searched out the other cold items from the bags and put them into the fridge. His immaculate fridge. I circled around to look at Ethan who stared at me. "So are you going to answer my question?"

"Oh, I use this kitchen. But not super often."

"What do you eat?" My eyes looked him over, seeing that he'd lost weight and his shirt bunched around where a bandage covered his wound.

"I'm not hungry right now." He gestured to his side. "I think the medication that I'm on dampens my hunger."

"Well, you must eat." Ethan watched as I began to open and close his cupboards, taking stock of the types of tools that I had to use to make some dinner. "Have you eaten today?"

"Cereal, at breakfast. Lunch consisted of some crackers."

"Crackers shmackers! And then, you canceled the company's meal service that Lana arranged. Free food to your door every night." I shook my head. Ethan still looked good despite his ill pallor. His shirt brought out the color of his eyes, and I'd never seen him in sweatpants before. I quite liked him with sweatpants on. *Maybe I can suggest a new dress code to the CEO.* "I know your independence runs deep, but can you imagine someone wanting to take care of you?"

I found a bowl and yanked it from the cupboard. Sausage penne would be a quick meal to make and had lots of good healthy fats. Ethan stepped toward me. I reached for the penne noodles, but his hand got there first. He wrapped his hand around mine, which somehow managed to draw my eyes to his face.

He hesitated but finally spoke. "When I was young, my mom often struggled with illness so I took care of everyone. I'm used to fending for myself." His free hand came up and tugged on a curl. He touched my cheek, and I held my breath. I wanted to speak, but I found that I couldn't move. Ethan's eyes were inches from my own.

"Would you do that for me?" I whispered, referring to how he cared for everyone. The question squeezed out between shallow breaths. Our noses almost touched, and I could feel his breath rushing in and out. He released my hand and slid his arms around me. I moved to do the same. My hand knocked at his bandage, and Ethan inhaled sharply.

I gasped. "I'm so sorry."

He winced but still managed a grin. I had taken a few steps back, but Ethan closed the space between us. He lifted my arms to his shoulders and then slid his arms around my waist. Again, our noses almost touched.

"It would be an honor to take care of you if you needed it."

"Then you should let me do the same."

Ethan didn't speak, but he pulled back a tiny bit and looked me deeply in the eye. "May I?"

I couldn't figure out if the question was meant for caring for me or for kissing me, but I loved the gentleness in his tone. My voice caught in my throat. I moved my head up and down, willing myself to shine my answer of yes from every pore of my body.

Our lips touched.

Chapter Eleven

The next day, Max stormed into my office like a gray thundercloud with yellow accents. I checked his cuff links to make sure they weren't shaped like lightning bolts. He looked ready to strike something, so I gestured to the seat across from me in my cubicle and kept myself low, knowing that lightning seeks height.

He dropped his phone on the desk across from me. "Have you seen this?"

An online advertisement glowed at me, and it looked like one of ours. I enlarged the picture to take a closer look. The advertisement made our original idea for the campaign seem not so original. In fact, it looked like we were copying. I hadn't seen the ad so I shook my head.

"This cannot happen." Max grabbed his phone from my hand and stood up. He paced around my office with the phone in front of his face, and I suspected that he might need glasses of some kind. "I need to walk. Come with me."

His voice left no room for argument. I grabbed my lovely, new yellow purse that I probably shouldn't have purchased and followed Max through the building and into the street.

Max waved the phone in front of us as he speed-walked down the sidewalk. "You need to do something about this. I can provide the funds for you to buy this advertising campaign out or get the company to pull that ad."

I bit my lip as I tried to keep up with Max's fast pace. "Unfortunately, that's impossible. Since the advertisement is already live on social media, it cannot be recalled. News these days does not work like the paper news."

"You need to fix this." Max pointed his finger at me, stopping abruptly in the middle of the sidewalk and causing me to backpedal so I wouldn't slam into his finger. "This is why I hired you. From now on, I expect you to take my artists' suggestions seriously. If they offer an idea, I want it to be a part of the campaign. They are, after all, creative professionals, specializing in their field."

I cringed recalling Lionel's ideas. Sophia's "I am the American Dream" statement wasn't so bad, but it could turn people away from her by offending her audience as if she were the only American Dream. Once Max relaxed a little bit I would speak up, but he needed to get it all out.

Max led me down a road, and I kept trying to keep up with his quick step. "You and Oswald will need to work together to plan some events to really cause some actual social buzz about Lionel and Sophia. I want you to come up with a look for the two of them. I think we should have weekly music nights. Maybe I should rent one night a week at a coffeehouse for them. I expect their careers to soar—and my investment with it."

"Why not just buy a coffeehouse?" I whispered to myself.

"That's not a bad idea." Max responded, proving that his hearing was sharp indeed, as he opened the door of a small coffee shop called Daisy's. The shop oozed creativity with brilliant colors spiraling the walls and white daisies patterning the edges of the room. One corner of the room stowed a treasure trove of paints, books, and easels. You could tell that this place wanted to be a creative hotspot.

Max's voice interrupted my observations of my surroundings. "Also, I want all the newspapers throughout the country to have a story on my two musicians. How many reporters do you think you can get here to interview them?"

"Usually, I don't work the reporters." I replied to his question before I had figured out if he actually wanted a response. We stood in front of the coffee counter. The guy standing at the register had dark skin and gray-laced dreads.

"Now you do." Max snapped his fingers at me and refocused on the man behind the counter. "I'd like an Americano. Large."

I swallowed. I wasn't this man's personal secretary or even his personal assistant. Where was Oswald?

Max rubbed his hand across his forehead. Fatigue settled in circles under his eyes. "Do you want something, Miss Simon?"

Not a good sign if he'd switched to using my last name. "Uh, no, I'm fine."

Max's Americano arrived, and I had to hold a sigh in because I actually did want a coffee. I followed him to a nearby table, where he sat heavily. "The truth is that I'm tired of being a patron to new artists. Nothing seems to go right, and they all have their crazy personalities."

"Sounds a bit like burnout."

Max's head snapped up, and he glared at me. My eyes widened.

"Burnout is for personal assistants and consultants, not for men like me. I don't have time for it." He straightened his back and pulled himself together, taking a long sip of his coffee. "Speaking of which, you aren't planning on burning out on me, are you?"

"Nope, I'm fine." I raised my hands up. "I'm a chronic people pleaser." The worst I could do was learn how to say no.

"Good to hear. So you'll take care of it?" Max stood as he asked, looking like he was ready to leave now that he had dumped on me.

I frowned. I might be a people pleaser, but my job description didn't include his demands for event planning. I had no personal time, so I would have to do this on company time. I couldn't do that without speaking with Victoria. Already, I suspected I knew her response.

Max gave me a salute, expecting my acquiescence, answered his ringing cell phone, and left.

Standing outside Victoria's office, I screwed up the courage to knock. She hummed, and I guessed that she meant "enter." I creaked open the door. She stood at her window, a perfect picture of poise and fashion. Were all bosses like her?

"Good morning, Jadyn. I heard Mr. Louis paid you an impromptu visit this morning."

I nodded, clutching my paper list, ready to share Max's demands. She eyed my posture. I pulled my shoulders back, feeling shabby, like I had walked out of a thrift store. *I like thrift stores.* "He had a couple of requests that I wanted to run past you before agreeing to them."

I read off Max's list of demands with my stomach in knots.

Victoria just stared out the window.

"Victoria, I'm afraid that I can't handle my other clients and all Mr. Louis's requests."

Victoria eyed me, and I wanted to slide under the desk for even having voiced my work concerns. "Mr. Louis is one of our star clients. We can't lose him, and you know our policy on transferring clients to other consultants. We only do that if the original consultant is...terminated. Figure out something. Make him happy."

My stomach dropped. How would I ever survive, especially since I wanted to teach that art class, pursue my own art, and do my work well? I wouldn't have time to find a new apartment. What would it be like to live in a cardboard box?

Back in my cubicle, I frowned down at my phone. I needed to call Nancy about volunteer teaching. With so many other responsibilities, I wanted to pass this ball off to another juggler. Maybe I should turn down the opportunity. The Enoch sermon came back to mind, and how he had pleased God. Wasn't pursuing my own gifts and talents something that would please God since he'd given them to me in the first place? I hugged my arms around myself, knowing that teaching art would fill me in a way that nothing else would. *Father, give me strength to balance all these activities and set my priorities in a way that honors you.*

I dialed the number for Nancy. Volunteering with this teen club would feed my soul, not only with art, but also with the chance to serve the kids. The phone rang and then she picked up.

"Nancy, this is Jadyn Simon." I took a breath. This decision would definitely complicate my already crazy life, but I couldn't run away from the fact that this seemed right. Calmness flowed to my fingertips when I considered adding this to my busy schedule. "I do want to teach your art class."

Like you could ever teach art. I hated that voice in my head and tried to push away the remembrance of Oswald's piercing censure of my work.

"Oh, my heavens. You are a lifesaver!" Nancy gushed through the phone.

"What time on Thursday nights?" I drew my notepad and pen across my desk.

"Seven. For an hour, from September until June. We do have holidays, and you can plan your own syllabus as well."

I jotted the information down.

"Honey, I'll also need you to make up that syllabus this week so I can get it approved by our head committee. They like to keep an eye on all the programs that we offer to the young people."

I hadn't seen a syllabus since college. How long would it take me to brainstorm an entire year's worth of art classes? I'd probably need more than a week.

"Nancy, do you think there's any way that I could have two weeks to make up the syllabus?" I hated to ask, but I did want to sleep this week. More and more, sleep deprivation and I seemed meant for each other.

Her silence hung heavy. I bit back my desire to rush in and promise to give her the syllabus tomorrow. I opened my mouth to apologize for my request when Nancy spoke. "You know, since this is a special circumstance, I'm sure I can get you approved for the extra time."

Relief flooded through me.

"Jadyn, if you'll give me your email address, I'll send you all the information."

I gave Nancy my email address and then heard a beep in my ear. I checked my phone and saw Oswald's name on the screen. I didn't want to pick up. "Nancy, I have another call coming in. I'll talk to you later."

Tapping the screen, I switched the phone over to Oswald's call.

"Hello, Oswald." I tried to keep my voice light even though I found myself feeling bitter toward him.

"Jadyn." He paused. "Max is uncertain about your ability to carry this campaign through to success."

Oswald's matter-of-fact statement punched me in the gut. His blunt ways were getting frustrating. I thought I had handled Max and his demands this morning, but now Max was telling his assistant something else. I swallowed, keeping my feelings at bay.

"I'm sorry he feels that way, but I have carried every one of my campaigns through to the finish with exceptional success."

Oswald ignored me. "On top of that, Lionel is threatening to leave the duo. He feels that he would have better success as a solo artist."

I wanted to hit my head against my desk, but instead, I rolled my shoulders back, feeling knots in my muscles. I really wanted some coffee. Or a massage.

"How can I help you in this situation?" I asked Oswald instead of hanging up the phone and burying myself under the mounds of paperwork that piled on my desk.

"First of all, you cannot fail this advertising campaign. Secondly, I think if you call Lionel and tell him all your campaign plans we'll have success in keeping him on. Max, Sophia, and I have all already talked to him."

Scratch the coffee and massage. I needed a vacation. "Sure, I can give him a call."

"No, that's not good enough. If we lose Lionel, we'll have lost a great deal of money, not to mention Sophia as well, since she's loyal to the guy."

I gulped back a retort, realizing that losing Lionel would mean losing Max's business on this campaign, which would infuriate Victoria. "Do you have a better idea?"

"Max is providing tickets to a symphony performance at Heinz Hall. We want you to take Lionel there and revive his dreams for this campaign."

"Exactly how is a symphony going to revive his dreams?"

"Lionel spent years in a symphony as a teenager and he never wants to be in one again; however, that's where an artist will spend his time because it pays the bills."

I sighed. Paying bills or chasing dreams. Did it always have to come down to that?

"Let me think about it. I think I have his number on file."

I hung up and sank my head into my hands; I needed to do some digging. This day had gone from fast to faster.

The sun was setting as I crossed the street to my apartment building. I didn't have many nights left there, and I worried about finding a new place to live in my price range that would meet my picky standards. I ran up the stairs instead of using the elevator. Outside my apartment door, a man sat. Travis.

"What are you doing here?" I pulled my key from my purse and gave him a one-sided hug as he stood.

"I figured I'd drop in for our video game tournament." He shrugged and smiled shyly. At his feet sat a bag and I didn't need X-ray vision to know that it contained all his gaming stuff. "Your television is better than mine."

I swung open my apartment door, instantly glad that I hadn't stored my television yet, but also, simultaneously remembering that I'd never told Travis I would be moving. A couple of months ago, he would have been the first person I told. But these days, I found myself gravitating toward Ethan or even Mel more than Travis. Our friendship was changing, and I wasn't totally certain why. But he had been acting weird too.

"When I said you should clean up, I didn't mean you should throw away all your stuff!" His voice was teasing, but Travis looked worried as he circled the room. All the things that I could move by myself were already in storage. Only the larger items remained.

"I'm moving out." I sighed and dropped my three work bags. Three seemed like overkill, but with the amount of work that I had to do, I needed them.

Travis began to set up his gaming system. "Can you order the pizza?"

"Sure. Same thing?" I grabbed my phone from my purse.

"You know it."

I pulled up the app and tapped in our usual order of pepperoni pizza with breadsticks. "They'll deliver in about a half an hour."

Travis leaned against the couch. "So, what's with this moving thing?"

"Actually, I'm being—" I caught myself before I said the dreaded word. If I told one person the truth, it could get back to my sister and my mom. People talked. "Temporarily moved because of a bug problem in another apartment."

"That's hilarious. You're kidding, right?"

I kept my face serious, hoping he wouldn't see through my lie. Travis studied me and then slouched.

"You know, I have heard of some cities having bug infestations. Should I be worried?"

"The only bug here is probably you."

He tossed a pillow at me. "Oh, I don't know about that."

I giggled and launched the pillow back at him. That's when he jumped at me with two in both hands.

I squirmed away as Travis attacked me. Laughter bubbled through me, knocking aside the stress I'd been clinging to. I stuck my fingers at Travis's side, wiggling them. As ticklish as when he was a kid.

He heaved and moved his limbs, trying to push me away.

I dodged his flailing arms.

Suddenly, Travis changed tactics and lunged for me. He wrapped his arms around me, pulling me close. Our breath rushed in and out of our lungs. Travis didn't release me.

I pushed away from him gently, but he held me tightly. Confused, I pulled my head up to look at him and found him staring intently at me.

He leaned forward with his lips pointed at my own. I gasped and turned my cheek, almost cringing to feel his lips brush my cheek. His lips didn't touch me. I pushed back again, and he released me.

Chapter Twelve

"Travis has been your friend for your whole life." Mel dropped a box of cereal into the cart that I pushed behind her. "Experts say that's a great foundation for romantic relationship."

My sister insisted that I meet her at the grocery store so we could meal plan since we'd be living together in only a few days. And I had updated her on my work and love life.

"Do you like Greek yogurt?" I held the grocery list in my hand and was trying to keep us on task even as she wandered through the store.

"But on the other hand, you obviously feel a thrill with Ethan, and a part of me wants to say don't ignore the pull of attraction."

Mel led us to the cooler section of the store where she selected Greek yogurt, milk, and butter. She placed each item in the cart. "You know, a rule of thumb that I try to stick with when dealing with men is to never shut the door on a possible relationship."

My mouth dropped. This did not sound like my sister who always seemed to do what she wanted. Her advice chafed me.

Mel read my expression. "You've got it wrong. There are ways to say no without actually saying the word."

"But wouldn't it be easier to say no right out?" I tried to focus on the grocery list in front of me again, but her advice still bothered me. *What happened to "no" means "no?"*

"Try it." Mel jutted her chin out at me.

It seemed like odd advice, but what did I stand to lose?

I returned to my empty apartment after stopping briefly at my—Mel's—storage unit to retrieve my paint supplies. If I intended to enter this art contest, I needed to actually have some mature art to enter. I had been able to unearth some older canvases to take snapshots for my entry, but I'd been unhappy with most of what I had found. Quantity I had, but I wanted quality. So I only needed two more paintings to showcase my growth as an artist. At this time of night, I'd usually be headed to bed, but tonight I had a mission.

The echoing space around me created my favorite type of studio.

Around three in the morning, I finally laid down my paintbrush with two beautiful paintings to show. Chaotic splashes that reminded me of Jackson Pollock layered over impressionism inspired by Renoir. I smiled. I didn't bother to move to bed, but let my body relax across the carpet. I forced my eyelids open to gaze at my work. As much as Oswald's and Max's criticism had hurt, their advice—even Oswald's—had improved my work. Adding artist pen and acrylics to the canvas brought my watercolor alive like it had never been before.

Maybe I had a chance to win this contest!

On my way to the office the next morning, I dropped off my entry to La Rosa Galleria and picked up a "Shot in the Dark," a large coffee with a shot of espresso. After only a couple of hours of sleep, I needed all the caffeine I could stand. I still needed to coax Lionel back into the partnership, fix Max's campaign, and stay ahead of all my other clients.

First things first, I dialed Lionel's number. He picked up on the fifth ring and answered in a groggy voice. Instantly, I realized that he'd probably been sleeping.

"Lionel, it's Jadyn."

He grunted. This grumpy Lionel did nothing to remind me of the chipper string-bean guy whom I had met at The Warhol a couple of weeks ago. I continued with my plan.

"I have tickets for a show at Heinz Hall. I thought it might be something you'd enjoy." I gulped, knowing that he'd most likely not enjoy the show if what Oswald had told me was true.

"Fine. When is it?"

"Tonight at 7:30."

"I'll meet you inside the front doors." Lionel spoke and then hung up the phone. I found myself wondering if he might struggle with depression or something similar.

I think the caffeine from the espresso helped me stay hyper-focused throughout the day because I managed to formulate a new plan, taking all of Sophia's, Lionel's, and Max's previous ideas into consideration. Through a series of meetings, I had a new campaign rolling forward. The intersection of art and people. I even somehow made time to complete a heavy chunk of work in some other priority campaigns as well. During my lunch break, I started my art class synopsis. Honestly, I'd hit my groove despite lack of sleep.

My mind wandered to the art contest. I had entered on the last day; judging would occur within the week. The grand prize winner won a gallery show and profit on any pieces sold. It also came with a $2,000 cash prize. I found myself already mentally spending that money. If I had won something like this two months ago, I could have stayed in my apartment longer. Or maybe quit my job and pursued art. That thought surprised me. I wondered what it would be like to pursue art rather than rushing around trying to create successful advertisement campaigns—selling others' art.

My mind came back to the present immediately as Victoria clicked into my cubicle. She crossed her arms over her chest and stared at me. "I wanted to check on how Mr. Louis's campaign was progressing."

"I've pushed a new plan through based on Mr. Louis's demands. We should be seeing new images within the next few days."

"Actually, I saw the plans. You need to return to the drawing board. The ideas are so ill-focused that no one would ever understand what you're trying to sell. We need minimalism. Clean lines and a certain thread."

My heart flew to my throat and tears burned at my eyeballs. Victoria exuded calmness as she tapped her fingers absently on her arm.

"I'm not sure how to meet Mr. Louis's requests without creating a crowded image. This seems to be the type of thing that he'd appreciate." I tried to keep my voice even.

"I've already recalled the project. You'll need to run it through again." Victoria checked the jeweled watch on her wrist. "It looks like you still have an hour before the day ends. If you work fast, you can catch all the people you'll need to chat with. I'm beginning to question your ability to follow through on this campaign."

I had no words. I gulped and tried to keep my tears in check, wishing that Victoria would leave.

She stared me down. "Nothing goes out the door with my name on it if it doesn't meet the standards of Davenport Cities Consulting."

After this proclamation, Victoria finally exited my office space. My tears seemed to know that she had left, and they spilled down my cheeks to my chin. I took deep breaths, trying to gain my composure and not make sobbing noises for all my cubicle mates to hear. *No crying at work.* I sniffled, brushing my fingertips underneath each eye to wipe away the mascara trails from my face.

Lana floated by my office with a stack of files, following after Victoria. I thought I heard my name in their conversation, but I couldn't be sure. I strained my ears. Their laughs intermingled before the door shut out the happy sounds. How could the two of them get along so well? They seemed to grow closer every day. Lana worked well with everyone, but a part of me wondered if I ought to be worried about their friendship. Shaking my head, I refocused on the work ahead.

I had a lot to do in the next hour before dinner and then Heinz Hall.

A little before seven, I stood within Heinz Hall's doors. All I really wanted was to curl up in bed after my day, but responsibility was responsibility. Although the original plan had been the symphony, I'd come up with an alternative that I thought would work better for Lionel. Earlier digging had helped me find some of his favorite artists and connections. I checked my watch, hoping that Lionel wouldn't bail on me since I'd then have a lot of apologies to make.

People grouped around the little lobby in light jackets. Summer slid into chilly evenings. I scanned the crowd again. Lionel was so tall that I fully expected to see him heads above the others. While I waited, I figured I'd send Ethan a text as he traveled home from Chicago. Due to his injury, he had decided to drive there and back; driving promised a smooth ride rather than the uncertain turbulence in the air.

A moment after I sent my text, my cell phone rang. I glanced at the screen and saw Ethan's name. I searched the growing crowd for Lionel, but I didn't see him, so I picked up the call.

"I was thinking of you when your text came through. I figured I'd just call."

My stomach dipped in pleasure. "Oh, I like that."

"I'll be in Pittsburgh in an hour or so; could we meet up maybe after the concert?"

I took stock of all the things I needed to do and how much I had already done this day. Bed was all I wanted. Mel's advice came back to me like a brick—did I dare say "no?" Maybe she was right that if I shut the door anywhere, at any time, Ethan would drop me for someone else.

"Sure," I said. "I could be there at 10:30."

"I look forward to it."

At that moment, I caught sight of Lionel standing in a corner of the lobby. "Ethan, I need to go. I'll see you later."

I ended the call and wove through the crowded space to Lionel. His hair reached for the ceiling on one side of his head while the other side stuck so close to his skull that at first glance you guessed it to be a bad haircut—not bedhead. Wrinkles across his clothing shattered any ideas of being recently ironed, and the orange-tinged stain in the middle of his shirt trumpeted that laundry hadn't been done for a while. Honestly, he needed some cheering up.

"Hi, Lionel." His hunched shoulders cut his height almost in half. "I'm glad you could make it tonight. Do you mind if we deviate from our original plans?"

Lionel stuffed his hands into his jean pockets. "Okay."

"Follow me." I hailed a cab. It would be quicker even though we could walk to the location I had in mind. Going to Daisy's with Max the other day had inspired this deviation.

"The corner of Craig Street and Fifth," I told the taxi driver as Lionel and I climbed into the back seat. I tried to think of possible conversation topics, but finally settled into the silence. A part of me wanted Lionel to be curious and to ask.

The taxi stopped, and I paid the driver with some cash from selling our symphony tickets. I led the way to Daisy's. Warm light welcomed every individual, and brewing coffee filtered through the air. In the treasure trove corner of art, three men sat with different projects spread around them. Lionel's first piano teacher, Bernard. Max's most recent protégé, Alex. And William, a little-known piano player who had been most difficult to track down but was Lionel's first music inspiration. I ushered Lionel into the group of men and I returned to the counter to order coffees all around.

When I'd contacted the men, I'd already gotten their orders. Professionalism meant thinking ahead. I ordered from the dreadlocked man, wondering what kind of hours he worked. I heard a guitar chord strum through the shop and I peeked over my shoulder. A musician perched on a stool in the corner with his guitar. Three girls hunched behind laptop screens, typing away. Everyone had something that they were working on.

I drew my eyes to the group of men in the corner, wondering how things were progressing. I didn't know whether I should stick around or sneak out after delivering their coffees.

The coffees came and with the help of the dreadlocked barista, we carried them over to the group.

"Max gave me my big break," Alex shared with the group. Each man had selected different mediums and were working on doodles in front of them. "I think he always wanted to be a musician himself but lacked the necessary training when he was young."

"Does anyone want this black marker? It creates some beautiful bold lines." Bernard scrawled lines across his sheet of paper. "It's important to not allow your artistic inspiration to begin and end with your specialization. Branch out into hobby arts so you can be refreshed."

William nodded at me, accepting the coffee that I handed him. "Lionel, what's making you step back from this opportunity? Mr. Louis has a reputation for taking his artists to the top."

I decided to stick around and see how the evening would unfold. Lionel had started to smile while bobbing his head in response to the comments from these men. I pulled up a chair and sat on the edge of their circle.

Lionel cleared his throat and lifted his piece of paper. One word stood out in the middle of the page: Fear. "I'm terrified of screwing it all up, letting Max and Sophia down."

I watched as the men exchanged glances. None of them seemed surprised by Lionel's confession. I shook my head. Why did it come back to fear?

"Lionel, I'll call you in the morning." I stood and smiled at the group. "It was a pleasure to meet all you gentlemen. If you order anything else, please keep the receipt and send it to me. I'll reimburse you."

I walked out of Daisy's drinking my Caramel Steamer, warm milk with a flavor shot, and feeling rather proud of myself. I'd diverted immediate disaster and would even make it to Ethan's earlier than planned.

I texted Ethan, letting him know I'd be there soon. But I regretted foregoing an espresso shot. I pushed away the siren song of my bed.

Thirty minutes later, I stood outside Ethan's apartment building, hitting the buzzer. I heard the door click open. Apparently, he just trusted it was me. I dragged my feet up the stairs. Although I'd arrived an hour earlier than I thought, I'd give my week's coffee money to be home and preparing for sleep.

I lifted my hand to knock on the door, but it swung open before I got a chance. In two strides, Ethan had me in his arms. The hug warmed my entire being and I relaxed. The tired me wanted to stay here for the rest of the night—in his arms. He pulled back and gazed at me. "I've missed seeing you! I love Chicago, but the one thing it's missing is you."

A smile pushed across my face and I forced my eyelids open. "I am one of a kind."

"I'd say so." Ethan wrapped one arm around me and drew me into his apartment.

I relished the feel of his arm around me and snuggled in.

"You move in with your sister soon, don't you?"

I nodded, allowing my head to drop onto his shoulder. His apartment was perfectly neat despite the fact that he had been gone for a couple of days. I didn't know how he could manage that.

"Do you want something to drink?"

"I'm fine." I cuddled closer to him even though we were standing. "But do you have a bed?"

He chuckled, and the vibrations of his laughter traveled through me. That's when I realized what I had said. I pulled back. "That's not—I—sorry. I'm so tired. I stayed up late last night preparing my artwork to enter a contest, and it's been such a long day."

My eyelids slid shut. Ethan's hand cupped my chin. "You entered an art contest? And if you were so tired, you didn't need to come over."

His quiet voice sounded like a lullaby. I tried to shake my drowsiness. "I did enter an art contest, and I wanted to see you."

"I could have waited till tomorrow." Ethan kissed me on the forehead. "Let's get you home. I don't trust you by yourself."

He was as good as his word. Taking care of me.

Chapter Thirteen

Friday morning came way too quickly. A zing traveled through me—today I would find out the results of the contest. If I heard back by 6:00 p.m., I'd made the top five. If I didn't, then I had to go pick up my paintings. Butterflies erupted in my tummy. I had to win, but a little voice in my head whispered doubts.

I looked at the small amount of clothing still in my apartment. It had been so long since I'd worn my paisley tights; with the cooling fall temperatures, tights were about to become a fashion necessity. Right? I frowned. I'd probably be seeing both Victoria and Mel. They both hated those tights.

"What kind of adult am I if I can't even wear the tights that I like?" I shoved my thoughts and the tights into my take-to-Mel's pile, hoping that I'd find a good time to wear them again. I tried to convince myself that I didn't want to make waves at work or at home with the tights.

Instead, I chose a navy cardigan with a white blouse, black pants, and comfy flats. Practical and professional. Both my boss and sister would approve. I guessed I could wear my secret hope—winning the art contest—in my heart. That would add the bounce to my step, if not the paisley tights.

Grabbing my three work bags, I scanned the list that I had somehow managed to write up after Ethan had dropped me off the night before. I needed to call Lionel. I checked the time on my phone, noticing three texts from Travis at varying hours during the night. Each text offered a different activity to do together some time in the next week. I rubbed my head. First things first, call Lionel.

I dialed as I locked my apartment door behind me. Lionel picked up with a groggy voice.

"Hey, Lionel. I wanted to check in and see how the rest of the night went."

In my mind, I could picture him rubbing the sleep from his eyes. He cleared his throat. "Thanks. It was cool. Good talking to all those guys again."

"Can I do anything else to help your creative process?"

"Probably let me sleep some more."

I laughed. "Sorry, I didn't mean to interrupt inspiration."

"I'll give you a call in a couple of hours. I've got a few ideas to discuss with you, Max, and Sophia."

"I look forward to it." I grinned and dropped my phone in my purse. His voice sounded more hopeful than I'd ever heard it.

"I have news!" Lana waltzed into my cubicle with a grin across her face that same day. "Victoria has decided to promote me."

I bit the inside of my cheek. Was Lana to be my replacement? I tried to banish the thought of the girl who'd come before me and had been fired for not meeting Victoria's expectations. I'd been keeping up with my workload, especially by working every available moment. Hadn't I? I had a pang of guilt for spending that one night working on my art, but I pushed the feeling away, knowing that the art fed my soul and my hope. *When would there be more time for my art?*

"Oh, congratulations. When will this happen and...to what job?" I asked just as my phone vibrated. I flipped it over and checked the screen. Travis was calling. I stopped the vibrating and watched Lana expectantly. She wore a white pencil skirt with a black sleeveless shirt. *Is that Victoria's pencil skirt?*

"I'm going to be a consultant! Like you!"

I forced a grin. "That's great." She *was* after my job!

"Victoria's going to assign me to shadow someone for a while and then we'll go from there. I guess it's kind of like an internship of sorts. Learning the ropes and then taking over."

Lana usually looked like she was floating, but she must have had wings on her feet this time. Meanwhile, someone had just doused me with a bucket of ice water. Did Victoria mean to threaten me with Lana? Taking over? What did that mean?

I still have my art. Hope bubbled up in me as I considered possibly winning the art contest. With the prize money, I could work part-time and pursue my art. I pulled a piece of paper off the nearest stack, flipped it to the clean side, and started to consider my finances. I really needed to cut back on coffee, online shopping, and…everything.

I scribbled in my desired expenses and began to do the math. Even living with Mel for the next couple of months didn't help with the finances that much. I cut the imagined expenses down wherever I could, but things still didn't line up in a way that would allow me to live alone, pursue art, and eat. I bit my lip.

Who was I kidding? All that prize money needed to go to my landlord to cover my outstanding rent anyway.

My heart longed to discard all this busy work and delve into painting. Paper and paint made my fingers tingle. Placing the sheet aside, I decided to concentrate on brainstorming Max's campaign. Obviously, I couldn't quit my job any time soon, so Victoria and Max needed to know that I was the best person for this job.

My cell ring tone played a piano ballad. I recognized it as Lionel's number and picked up.

"Lionel, good morning once again."

"Right. Can we schedule a time to meet with Sophia, and Max as well, within the next week to discuss the campaign? As I mentioned, I have a couple of ideas."

Lionel and I discussed times to meet. Armed with a set of available times, I hung up with Lionel and called Oswald to schedule a time with Max and then Sophia.

"Oswald Tumpit speaking."

"Oswald, I need to schedule a time to meet with Max in the next couple of days. Does he have any available times?"

"I'm sure he does, but I am not able to make any of those appointments for him." Oswald's voice sounded frustrated. I wondered what was causing him to be so uppity today.

"Well, when do you think is a good time for him? I have a list of times."

"Frankly, Jadyn. I don't have time for this." The phone beeped in my ear, and I took the phone away from my head and stared at the blinking screen. *Did he hang up on me?*

And what did he mean by saying that he didn't have time for this? This was his job. He should be making time for Max's scheduling. I crossed my arms, considering who I should call to set this up for Max. I settled on sending Max a quick, cheerful text with the available times for meeting. That could possibly do the trick.

Late afternoon, Victoria called my cubicle phone. "Jadyn, can you meet with me in thirty minutes?"

I eyed my planner, mentally shuffling through my tasks, knowing that there was only one answer to Victoria's request. "Sure, that would be fine."

"I'm going for my afternoon speed walk around the block so if you have tennis shoes with you, I suggest you wear them."

She hung up. Thank goodness for my broken-in flats. Speed-walking would be fine in those, although I'd probably miss having socks.

Thirty minutes passed quickly, especially while worrying over what Victoria would want to discuss with me. I knew she took afternoon walks, but she'd never invited me before. Maybe I should be honored, but I only worried.

A couple of minutes early, I waited outside of Victoria's office. She came out the door, gave me the onceover, shrugged, and then sped down the hallway, expecting me to follow. She wore a white designer workout suit with fancy tennis shoes. I tried to imagine her wearing any thrift store item. She'd hardly be recognizable without her brand-name clothing.

Victoria stayed quiet until our feet touched the sidewalk. She propelled herself forward at a superhuman speed. I found myself jogging to keep up with her walking pace.

"Jadyn, I've decided to promote Lana to consultant. She has no experience, but she has been a quick learner in other things. I want you to train her. Show her your accounts, how you handle them, how you come up with ideas, that kind of thing."

Victoria was never anything but blunt. If she ever beat around the bush about anything, I'd turn in my teal paisley tights. I wanted to stop jogging to keep up with her and ask the sky how I kept finding more and more things to fill my time.

"You realize that I'm already swamped with work, right?" A part of me froze. I couldn't believe that I had just said this to my boss. *I blame lack of sleep, stress, and needing to find a new apartment.*

Then I remembered the art class that I needed to prepare for. With my mile-long to-do list for work,

I didn't think I could be so excited for this class, but I was. *I need to write a class syllabus.*

Victoria spun on her toe and speed-walked backwards while looking at me. I found myself worrying that she might run into someone, but somehow, the oncoming pedestrians were able to scatter in time. Her aura of authority traveled before her even backwards.

"Davenport Consulting believes in hiring from within and equipping our employees with the necessary skills to succeed in their career life. When you signed your contract with us, you agreed to this as well."

I swallowed but pushed forward. "I think it's a great company belief, but I'm already working the load of two consultants plus Max's campaign, which has been the most consuming work that I've had in months."

"This should be perfect then." Victoria faced forward once again. "Lana can take over a portion of your work."

"In theory, that sounds great. But you know that training someone makes doing simple jobs take twice as long." I tried to hold onto my earlier morning hope, but it was slipping. I exhaled, saying quietly, "You don't pay me enough for this."

Victoria's ponytail cracked around like a whip. Her eyes cut through me. "What did you say?"

"I didn't say anything." I pursed my lips and tried to still my rapidly beating heart. I wanted to fling my hands over my mouth. When had I become so gutsy? "Sorry. I'm not used to talking while jogging."

"I find it refreshing."

We'd come around the block, and I could see our building in front of us. I could hardly wait to be back at the safety of my own desk. As we entered the building, I glanced at Victoria. Somehow, she seemed perfectly pristine.

"Lana starts with you immediately, and then, soon…I suspect the firm will want to promote you to our Chicago branch. But first, retain Max and finish his campaign, then we'll discuss your future."

"Wait. I'm being promoted?" This possible promotion could solve my financial troubles. "Would it come with a pay raise?"

"Definitely. We'll discuss this after Max's campaign succeeds." Her voice marked the end of the discussion.

My mind brimmed with questions. I didn't even know that they were considering me for promotion. That meant more money—that was good. It also meant moving cities and states, which meant more art opportunities for me, but then again, it would also mean continuing to promote other peoples' arts rather than my own. I refocused, realizing that I needed to ask Victoria some of these questions. A small clump of other employees surrounded her. Each seemed to have papers for her to sign. Lana entered the clump with her own pile of papers. She gave me a little wave, and I remembered that Victoria wanted me to train her. *Starting immediately.*

I held in a groan. I liked Lana, but I didn't like this situation.

I pulled my phone out and quickly checked email, hoping to see something from the La Rosa Galleria.

Nothing.

On my way back to my office, I decided to stop by Ethan's cubicle. As I neared his workspace, his voice rumbled as he talked to himself. I didn't know how his cube-mates could even concentrate when he did that, but no one seemed to be bothered. Thankfully, we weren't in the same department; the sound of his voice might distract me for hours on end.

Standing in the entryway of his cubicle, I admired his profile. I could hardly wait for his gaze to turn to me so I tapped the side of the cubicle. Ethan looked up from his work, and his eyes crinkled around the corners. His look of tenderness suddenly made breathing difficult; I forced my eyes away and moved toward the desk to sit across from him.

"I had the strangest conversation with Victoria. She told me that after satisfying Max's campaign,

I'd be promoted to a job in Chicago. I'm not sure what to think. I'm shocked, actually." I gazed at my fingernails, nervous about what I might see in Ethan's face if I looked at him.

He was quiet, so I raised my eyes. I shrugged at him and he cleared his throat. "My gut reaction is that you shouldn't take the job. It's selfish, though, because I want you close to me. Besides, you won't know anyone out there."

I blinked. "Victoria also is promoting Lana to consultant."

"Really?" Ethan's tone caused me to study him. He leaned back in his chair as though he were considering something.

"What's up?"

"From a financial standpoint, Pittsburgh's office only can afford four consultants at a time."

I counted in my head. Me. Alysha. Sabrina. Kelsey.

I loaded a stack of cardigans in my car. Over the past couple of weeks, I'd managed to store all my furniture, kitchen accessories, painting supplies, and surplus clothing. Tonight, I'd put all the small things in my car.

The only things left in my apartment were my work bags, laptop, sleeping bag, pillow, and a toothbrush. I'd leave in the morning. I could have moved right away, but I wanted to have my own apartment for this last night. I needed to start apartment hunting, but I hadn't had time.

My cell phone sang, "Sisters. Sisters. There were never such devoted sisters." Mel.

"Hey. What's going on?" I lay down on the floor and stared at the white ceiling.

"Aren't you coming over tonight?"

I paused. Hadn't I told her that I wouldn't be moving in till tomorrow? "I wasn't planning on it. I figured I'd stay here for the last night."

"You don't have a bed there!" She sounded like Mom. "And besides, you'll be back in like a month, right?"

"I know, but I do have a sleeping bag." I still hated not telling my sister the truth, but in this case, I only withheld the truth. Hiding this huge change and the embarrassment of an eviction tore me up. Honestly, I wanted someone to mourn this with me. But I was an adult. I could take care of these things myself.

"Well, I think you…" Mel trailed off.

"You think what?" I prodded her. She usually didn't hold back her opinions.

"No, you don't want to actually know." Her voice sounded a bit gravely. "I'll see you tomorrow morning. Are you having breakfast here?"

I frowned trying to figure out what had gotten into Mel. "I was hoping to."

"Simon Sisters Specialty breakfast. See you tomorrow."

No advice? No sage wisdom? I shrugged and flipped the phone away from me.

Art Contest. *Maybe I'd missed the email!*

Opening my laptop and booting it up, I tapped my finger against my leg. Finally, it loaded. I signed into my email and scanned through the inbox. Lots of coupon offers and one personal email. The corners of my mouth turned down. My eyes darted to the time on the screen. I should have heard by now.

Maybe the Spam folder. I navigated to that page and ran through the listed senders. Nothing from the La Rosa Galleria. My hopes slid into my stomach. I clicked back to my inbox and noticed a "Thank You" email from a Christopher Johns. Curious, I opened the email and read.

Dear Miss Simon,

Thank you for entering your artwork in our Grand Opening Art Contest at La Rosa Galleria. Please come at two in the afternoon tomorrow to pick up your works.

Christopher

Chicken liver. Lord, I don't understand. I thought it pleased you when we used our talents.

Eyes tingling, I set my laptop aside and walked to my empty art room to stare out the window. Maybe it was time to leave my art dreams behind. Just like this room. I would miss this view. Sky stretched far, reaching to all the tree-covered hills. City lights obliterated star lights. Even through the night lighting, I could see that the leaves on the trees were changing from green to all shades of fire. Things were dying.

I returned to my computer and started to search apartment rentals in Pittsburgh. Fatigue crept in as I scrolled past apartment after apartment.

I shut my laptop and clung to my pillow.

Chapter Fourteen

Mel slammed the trunk of my car while balancing a box on her hip. "I must admit I'm impressed that you packed up your stuff so efficiently."

"You haven't seen my storage unit."

"You mean 'my' storage unit. And you're right, I don't want to see it."

"Right. Sorry." I held the apartment door open as she maneuvered past me. We dropped our loads into the middle of my new room. Mel headed to the kitchen. Right now, I pretty much owed her everything. I needed to get on my feet again. Since I'd completely moved out, I was free from my high rent payments, other than the tiny matter of $4,000 overdue rent. There was no way that I could afford the overdue rent plus a deposit on a new apartment. I'd already received a notice warning that if I didn't pay up within a month of moving out, the management would file a claim against me. I couldn't afford that. My heart dropped to my toes. I stood in the middle of my new bedroom in Mel's apartment with all my things piled around me, listening to her banging around in the kitchen. Cooking, she called it. I gulped. Everything would be okay, right? I found myself longing to run to my big sister and ask for advice. *Maybe I should.*

My phone buzzed in my pocket, but I ignored it. Whoever it was could wait. *Probably Travis.*

I let my knees give and I flung myself across the bed. It caught me and bounced me once before allowing the comforter to engulf me. Couldn't I just stay here until this all worked itself out? The job promotion would help the money problem, but I had committed to a year-long art program. My family was here. I loved Pittsburgh. But I needed the money, and my mom would be so proud of me for getting a promotion. Warm fuzzies filled me when she bragged on me to her friends. I wanted to make her proud.

From the kitchen, I heard breakfast sizzling and knew that my new roommate was making pancakes, bacon, and eggs. I wouldn't have to eat for the rest of the day after this first meal. I jerked my body to the other side and grabbed a pillow to cuddle. Wanting retail therapy, I reached for my phone and then stopped myself. I couldn't risk spending money now. I was in debt. I didn't know where I'd get the money. Mel would probably lend it to me if I asked but then I would have to confess my lie. Strapped for funds, Mom couldn't help me even if she wanted to. And I definitely didn't want to be beholden to Ethan or Travis. *I'll ask Mel.*

Taking a deep breath, I pulled myself up off the bed and headed into the kitchen. My sister glanced up at me and smiled as she shoveled fresh pancakes onto her growing stack.

"Perfect timing! Breakfast is almost ready." Mel poured the last bit of batter into the pan. "Can you grab some milk? I've also decided that you can store your separate groceries on the bottom shelf of the fridge. I've allocated space in the bathroom for your stuff, too."

"Sounds great." I headed toward the refrigerator. "So one of my friends is struggling to pay rent. Do you have any ideas of how she could earn some extra money pretty fast?"

"You mean something other than stripping?" Mel giggled as she flipped the pancakes on the frying pan and then checked on the eggs cooking on the stove top.

I couldn't help but laugh as I reached for plates, glasses, and silverware. "Yeah, what kind of advice would you give her?"

"I'm out of the advice business." Her laughter disappeared. I thought over my question. It hadn't been offensive. Why was she clamming up?

"What's up with you?" I asked as I lifted a pancake onto a plate.

"I'm fine."

Never trust anyone who says they're fine when they're obviously not. I decided to let it go this time. I wondered if my comment to her about over-advice-giving had sunk in at the restaurant the other day. Just when I needed her help.

I stood across from La Rosa Galleria later that same afternoon, wishing that I didn't have to pick up my paintings. Honestly, I didn't want to show my face since I wasn't there to accept the prize. *Get in, get out, cry at home.*

Checking the oncoming traffic, I marched across the street, trying to steel myself for the coming interactions. I pushed through the door of the gallery and took in the lovely paintings hung on the walls. My heart plummeted to my feet, and I tried not to step on it more than I had to. I so wanted my paintings hanging on those walls. If people saw them, maybe I would sell some.

"Welcome and Bienvenidos a La Rosa Galleria." A lovely Hispanic girl spoke from behind a counter. Her dark hair was piled atop her head and she wore all black. Kohl-rimmed eyes took me in. "Are you looking for something in particular?"

I wished I could pretend that I was coming in to buy a painting, but I also wanted my work back. My gaze took in the entirety of the minimalist studio with hanging canvases, and this time, I noted the paintings of varying sizes on the floor leaning against the wall with stacks of photographs in front of each one. I scanned them until I found my own. My eyes came back to the girl. "I'm here to pick up my artwork from the contest."

She pressed her lips together. A flash of compassion shot through her eyes. "Sure. Go grab your stuff and check it out with me."

A well-dressed couple lingered over the different entries, and they were approaching mine. The woman stopped in front of my canvas and stared at it, pulling her male companion to a halt with a hand on his arm. She pointed to my painting. "Dear, I like this one. It draws me, but the colors feel off. Or maybe they're exactly as they ought to be."

I resisted the urge to rush my baby away from their critical eyes. I took a deep breath and allowed my curiosity to win out. Taking a step toward a nearby canvas entry, I tried to pretend that I was studying it rather than eavesdropping. This was when I began to note that all the paintings tended to have some sort of Latin or Spanish theme. My artwork did not match the style of work shown here. I wanted to kick myself for not thoroughly researching the gallery. No wonder I hadn't won.

Her husband bent down and lifted up the photographs of my other paintings. He flipped through them while his wife stood by his side. "It reminds me of Andy Warhol, and he's barely an artist. I could do this."

My fingers clenched. That guy had no concept of the time it took to come up with each idea, and then transfer it to paper. He probably thought artists were people who didn't know how to work.

The woman saved me from interjecting. She placed a hand on his cheek. "You could do this, but you *didn't*."

That small statement settled the dust storm in my head.

The man grunted and wrapped his arm around the lady's waist. "I suppose you have a point."

They moved on through the other entries, allowing me to scoot in and pick up my pieces.

Once I was at the counter, I lifted them up for the girl to see. A big smile came over her face. She blinked. "Ohh. So you're Jadyn Simon."

I tilted my chin, trying to understand what she meant by that. I waited for her to explain. Still stinging from the man's criticism, even though I sometimes agreed with his opinion of Warhol, the receptionist's interest in me and my entries caught me off guard, especially since they obviously hadn't won the competition.

She kept her small smile and made a note on her paper. Pulling a business card from a drawer nearby, she handed it to me. "Christopher will be back soon, but you may want to keep this for later."

I eyed the card. Christopher W. Johns, proprietor and owner of La Rosa Galleria and m1x3d. Hope trickled into my dried-out veins. I had received the email from this man, but it must be a good thing if he wanted to talk to me even after I lost his contest.

As I read the business card, the door's bells tinkled. I slid the card in my back pocket and picked up my things to move out of the way. The girl behind the counter put her hand up. "Wait a minute."

I watched as she hurried over to a man who had just walked in. He wore jeans and a solid blue shirt. The girl spoke to him quietly and his eyes landed on me. I pulled my eyes away, trying to pretend that I was enthralled by the way the ceiling attached to the wall. The whispers silenced, and I wanted to peek, but I kept my eyes from them.

"Ma'am?"

Turning, I found the blue-shirted man beside me. Surprisingly, we were about the same height. He put out his hand to shake and I slipped my hand into his. "Jadyn, I'm Chris. Rosa told me that you came in to pick up your paintings."

I smiled. Words not coming to mind.

"If you'd come back to my office, I'd like to chat with you." Chris's statement brooked no disagreement, especially as he placed a hand on my elbow and guided me to a plush chair in a back corner of the gallery. He sat across from me and lifted my painting from my hands, setting it between us on the low table.

"You have a lovely gallery," I piped up, trying to regain my speaking abilities.

"Jadyn, as I'm sure you recognize, art is my specialty and I pride myself in showing original and creative art." Chris crossed his legs and leaned forward. "This painting doesn't fit the tone of La Rosa, but it's completely unique with its range of colors and use of art tools. When I look at this picture, I feel energy. I regret that my judges couldn't choose it to win this art contest."

"It's fine," I broke in, exercising my stiff upper lip. I didn't want him to know how much I needed this break for my career but more for my broken piggy bank.

"Throughout the contest, we left the artwork lining the studio as you saw it when you came in. A number of different clients have strolled through and asked if your piece was for sale. At the time, I had to decline since we didn't allow our contestants to sell their pieces."

My heart jumped into a fast rhythm. I couldn't believe it. Surely, this was a dream. I wanted to ask Chris if he'd pinch me so I'd know that I was indeed awake, but I kept that to myself. He was still speaking.

"Based on the interest in your work, I'm wondering if you might consider showing some of your pieces at my m1x3d gallery in the Strip District."

I swallowed. Jumping Giraffes. There was no way I could say no.

Tuesday lunch, I sat with Max, Oswald, Lionel, and Sophia at a cute Italian restaurant near my firm. Oswald had his tablet ready to take notes while I wielded my trusty pen with a notepad.

"We speak on collaboration all the time." Lionel leaned forward while spreading his arms out. "We talk about community—our need for others and their ideas and companionship, but then in the art world, the competition is ruthless. Community holds you back. If it hadn't been for Jadyn and her coffee shop this past week, I wouldn't have realized this gap in our music community."

Lionel's praise for my idea rimmed my world in a golden glow. But Sophia studied the tablecloth and tapped her temple. Max seemed to be checking his fingernails while Oswald glared at me over his tablet. The glow dimmed. I kept my smile trained on Lionel, hoping that he'd continue despite his seemingly uninterested audience.

"So what if we stress collaboration as part of our campaign? We can work with artists of all types, not only musicians, but also dancers, sculptors, painters! It wins us potentially new fans through the fans of these other artists; therefore, further emphasizing the importance of community."

"Max, if it hadn't been for Jadyn, I'd never would have thought of this. I was struggling with my music, my dreams, and my responsibility to my craft. And to you. She took me to a coffee shop where she'd arranged for me to meet an old teacher, my favorite small-time musician, and Alex. Once again, I know we can do this."

Lionel sank back into his chair as the waitress arrived with bread and spiced oil. Immediately, everyone seemed to snap to attention. We all reached for the bread. I was beginning to think that Lionel should have probably made his big collaboration announcement after we had eaten rather than as the food was coming, but I could still try to bring the conversation back around. "What if we build on that idea even more, allowing those different artists to incorporate any of their students in the collaboration process as well? In that way, you open the door to more potential fans and you create a great educational process."

Sophia groaned. "You are always trying to educate people."

"How else do we improve on the things that we're already interested in?" I waved a slice of bread. "Someone teaches you. You teach someone else."

"Is that what you were doing when you sabotaged my Heinz Hall plan?" Oswald hissed at me from across the table.

My mouth hung open, and I set my bread onto my plate. My mind raced to understand what Oswald was referring to. I shook my head at him. Before I could fully reply or even come up with words to say something, Max clinked his knife against his water glass. "Wait, you mean you didn't attend the concert as planned at Heinz Hall?"

I swallowed. I hadn't thought to clear the change of plans with Max or Oswald. My eyes flicked between the two men. Oswald seemed like his calm was about to break while Max seemed puzzled.

"I'm glad she didn't take me to a symphony." Lionel broke the uncomfortable silence.

Now, Max and Oswald stared at him, not at me. I found that I could breathe again. Max eyed me, seemed to come to some conclusion, and then gave a little shrug as though dismissing the issue.

"I love it! Collaboration! Can we change the campaign to focus on that?" Max seemed ready to jump out of his seat. "Let's make this a huge event, inviting as many collaborators as possible. Do we know how to select the right people for this type of endeavor? A venue?"

I shared a grin with Lionel as Max continued to jitter in his seat, waving his hands but then bringing them back to rest behind his head.

My "change of plans" gamble had paid off.

Max pointed at Oswald. "Oswald, you and Jadyn need to put your heads together."

Oswald looked almost purple now.

Max was still speaking. "Oswald, make a note of tracking down some celebrities to work with us. I bet we could get Justin, Sarah, or Katy. Is it possible to do something huge—like the music awards, but without the awards? Everyone bringing their own community and fans?"

Max seemed to become more and more wound up while Oswald reminded me of a blueberry. I wondered if he was holding his breath. He ignored his tablet and stared at Max. Eventually, Max's words came to a stop as he caught sight of Oswald. "Why aren't you taking notes? We have a lot of work to do."

Oswald opened his mouth and then shut it. Then, in a whisper, he spoke, making the rest of us lean in to hear him. "You promised me a vacation after this, but there are no vacations working for you. Besides, if Jadyn is so perfect, she can handle this. I quit."

"What?" Max jumped to his feet. The entire restaurant silenced and seemed to swivel to watch our table. "You cannot quit."

"I hereby terminate our business relationship." Oswald stood and packed his tablet away. "I'll email you my notes. Good luck." Oswald gave Max a curt nod and the rest of us a small smile. He didn't meet my eyes.

Chapter Fifteen

Over the course of a busy work month, Ethan and I had gone from texting, to weekly telephone conversations, to meals shared together, on top of the moments stolen together at work. Sitting in his car one night after dinner, I slipped my hand into his.

We were headed to my mom's house for Sunday dinner. We'd left earlier than Mel and Anthony who were driving separately so we could have some couple time before spending a few hours all together. A part of me wanted to stay in the car forever with Ethan. To keep driving down the road until we ran out of gas or discovered some interesting tourist location.

I smiled at his profile. He glanced at me out of the corner of his eye. He rubbed his thumb over the back of my hand, sending trills through my skin. "Can we stay in this moment forever? I feel perfectly content right here."

A smile spread across his face and he lifted my hand to his lips, kissing it. My cell phone rang, singing Mario's theme song and successfully breaking the moment. Assigning ringtones to each contact had been a good idea at one point, but there was nothing like a video game song to ruin a romantic moment. I reached down into my purse with my free hand and tried to retrieve my phone. Not finding it, I loosened my hold on Ethan to use both my hands to look for the obnoxious phone. I finally found it and pulled it from my purse.

"Sorry, Ethan. I'm going to take this." I jabbed the answer button. "Travis, what's going on?"

I really tried to make my voice sound nice, but a tinge of annoyance trickled into my words because Ethan glanced at me. I gave him a shrug.

"Hey, Jadyn. I was wondering if I could crash your mom's Sunday dinner today."

I squeezed my eyes shut, rubbing my temple with my free hand. Options raced through my head. I could say yes, but that would make for some awkward times with Ethan and Travis in the same vicinity. I'd also been hoping to let Mom get to know Ethan better. This was, after all, the first time I'd be bringing him home. But Mom did like Travis a lot and we had grown up together.

"You still there?" Travis's voice came through the phone into my ear again.

"Yeah, I'm here." I took a breath and let it out slowly. Ethan was sending me a lot of concerned glances. "Listen, Travis. This week isn't good. Mom loves you a lot, but the notice is too short to add another person."

I held my breath, waiting for his response.

"What? I've come right before dinner, and I've never been turned away." He took a breath. "I should have shown up."

I dropped my head into my hand. "Travis, I appreciate that you did call this time to ask because this week isn't good for extra guests."

"I thought we were better friends than this."

"This is exactly why I should feel safe being honest with you." The back of my throat burned, and I wanted this conversation to be over.

"Fine."

I heard the phone click in my ear. First Oswald, now Travis. I was beginning to wonder if I sent out a vibe of hang-up-the-phone-on-me. Dropping the phone into my purse, I sighed and wove my fingers through Ethan's again.

"That sounded like a difficult conversation."

"It was." I heaved a sigh. "I want Travis to be happy, but I can't help him on this occasion so now I feel kind of sick to my stomach."

"I didn't realize that making other people happy could cause such a strong physical reaction." Ethan squeezed my hand.

"Not always, but it definitely does." I looked out the window, recognizing that we were almost to Mom's. Our turn was coming quickly. I pointed. "You need to make a right at the next street, but can we drive around the block once?"

"It's good not to always please people." He flicked on the turning signal and then made the indicated turn. "When you become the "yes" person, people tend to take advantage of you."

"I know, but it's easier to smooth things over. It's not usually difficult to do what they want, and it doesn't cost anything." I caught sight of my mom's house. "It's that tan house with the flamingo flag."

Ethan smiled and drove past the house. He rubbed his thumb across my hand as we took in the scenery of suburbia. Fifteen minutes later, we pulled the car into the driveway next to Anthony's car. My sister and her boyfriend had managed to beat us despite our different departure times. I reached for the door handle, but Ethan tugged on my hand. He leaned forward and brushed his lips across mine. "I'm proud of you for standing up to Travis right there, just so you know."

"I like making people happy, especially you." I tried to minimize the situation and grinned at him, thinking that my stomach now jolted with electricity rather than nausea.

Once inside the house, my mom enveloped us both in our own hugs. Anthony stood over the oven stirring something on the stove while Mel worked on a salad.

"Wow, Mom. You run a tight kitchen over here."

"You bet I do. You figure out the drinks." She winked at me and pointed at the fridge. Then she threw a look at Ethan. "And you, sir, are supposed to talk to me."

Ethan smiled at me and then at my mom. "What would you like to know?"

"Tell me about your family." My mom pulled Ethan into the living room away from the rest of us. He threw me a funny face, and I smiled after him, knowing my mom had her memorized list questions. He'd be back in no time.

Mel giggled and shook her head. "Anthony, you remember when Mom did that to you, right?"

"Most terrifying experience of my life." He left the pot he was stirring to wrap an arm around my sister. "But not more terrifying than asking you out on that first date."

She gave him a little whack. I watched them out of the corner of my eye as I pulled glasses out from the cupboard. My sister's smile sparkled, but recently, I wasn't so sure about her boyfriend. There were moments. Maybe because I sometimes caught him staring at other girls or admiring me as I walked into a room. I shook my head. I didn't want to think that my sister had ended up with a guy like that.

"Oh, Jadyn." Mel's voice pulled me out of my thoughts. "I forgot to tell you that you got some mail yesterday from your apartment management. The envelope was stamped 'urgent.'"

My eyes flew to Mel's face. I tried to keep my expression calm and steadied my voice even before I opened my mouth to speak. "It's probably a notice about being able to return to my apartment soon."

The lie slipped off my tongue so quickly that it almost felt true. I cringed behind the refrigerator door that I had opened to shield myself from her gaze.

"Oh, really."

I froze, staring at the half empty milk carton. Her tone seemed even, but it hid a thread of anger that I recognized from our childhood days when she caught me playing with her favorite baby doll. Taking the milk and grape juice off the shelf, I lifted them to the counter.

She knew. The only way Mel could know the contents of the envelope was if she read it. I spun to stare at her and saw the answer in her face.

"You opened my mail." My furious whisper carried through the house because the voices in the living room quieted.

Anthony slid his gaze up from the pot in front of him.

I waved my finger. "How could you read my mail?"

"How could you lie?" My sister had crossed her arms. Her eyes speared me with her fury and she pulled out a hand, hitting the counter. "Only temporary, you said. For a month. It doesn't look like you'll be moving out any time soon!"

I wanted to throw up. My brain raced through all the different ways to handle this. The quiet in the house kept me from thinking clearly. It was bad enough that Mel knew now, but I didn't want everyone else to know. I raised my hands and tried to shush her. "Let's step outside."

"I don't think so." She planted her feet and stared me down. "Why didn't you tell me that you couldn't pay your rent? That you'd been evicted! Not the victim of some pest control problem."

Her words punched me in the gut, and my knees wobbled but I refused to sink. Her words kept coming.

"How could you lie to me like that! Sisters are supposed to be best friends and watch out for each other. How can I ever trust you again? If I were me, I'd kick you out now."

A soft tickle of tears filled the corners of my eyes. I'd been caught in the middle of a lie I'd had no intention to clear up or maybe ever tell anyone.

Words choked from my throat. "I thought I had it figured out."

"Well, you obviously didn't. What kind of person lies to their own family?" Her voice trumpeted, and I knew that Mom and Ethan had heard everything. Shame settled on me like a fog. I didn't want to face either of them. Anthony was doing his best not to move anything except the spoon in the pot. "And to be evicted! How could you let that happen to you?"

"Mel." Anthony held the pot off the stove. "Do you think this is done?"

My sister's gaze aimed at her boyfriend and the pot in his hands. "I'll go ask Mom."

As my sister left, I walked out the back door to the deck. Fresh air enveloped me, and I breathed deep. I needed space. I wanted to run and run and run some more until all of this was far away from me. But I knew that I couldn't run far enough to escape.

From inside the house, my mother's calm voice ushered everyone back into the kitchen. "Let's eat, kiddos. I've been looking forward to having you all at home for the entire month—a few of you have been gallivanting about rather than spending time with dear old mom."

I knew she was talking about me. I looked at my feet.

Ethan's hand slipped to my back as he joined me outside. He rubbed a circle across my lower back. He whispered into my ear, "You doing okay?"

Tears prickled my eyes again. I just wanted him to hold me while we cuddled on the couch, watching some silly movie that I would never remember. No accusation lined his voice; he seemed solely concerned about me. I gave a small nod.

Throughout the meal, Mom, Ethan, and Anthony carried the conversations. Nausea swept through me again at disappointing my sister. At what everyone else must be thinking. What would my mom tell all her friends?

Two hours later as Ethan and I drove back toward downtown Pittsburgh, I played with my earring, trying to keep my mind from imagining the conversations that my mom would have with her friends about her failure daughter who got evicted.

Ethan tapped my thigh. "It feels like some sort of apocalypse happened, but it didn't."

"I want her to be happy with me. And you. What do you think?"

"She did open your personal mail. That's a federal crime." He slowed to a stop at a red light.

"Right. All of this started because she opened my mail."

The light turned green. "I would have helped you out."

"I planned on telling everyone after I moved into my own place again. If I'm offered the promotion at work, I'd probably be able to pay the overdue rent and pay for a new apartment, too."

"Ah. Keeping people happy by not telling them what was actually going on in your life,"

I bit my lip. "My mom has been so proud of me for becoming a real adult these last couple of months."

"So that's a yes."

"Maybe."

"Jadyn, we'll figure this out. If you need a place to crash, I have a few female friends who would put you up for a night or two if things are too intense with your sister."

I found myself smiling. I loved that he would call in a favor on my behalf. Even though interacting with Mel the next couple of days smeared my world gray, it was nice to know that Ethan was in my corner.

I was feeling brave on Thursday, so I wore my teal paisley tights with my signature black dress. As my first day of teaching art classes, I wanted to look artistic. I'd need to avoid Victoria at work or get her to ignore me like Mel had done since our fight. Despite being in Chicago again for work, Ethan had texted or called every day to check in on me and the situation. I couldn't wish for a better boyfriend.

I checked my work email and discovered information from Chris about showing my artwork in his gallery. He wanted all ten pieces I had originally entered in the contest by the end of the week. He promised to help me set prices. Clients could offer their best bids, but Chris had warned that prices rarely topped one hundred dollars for new artists. My mind stepped way back from the dream of supporting myself through my artwork. Financially, it wasn't possible at the moment, but maybe in a few years it could be.

Lana tiptoed into my cubicle with her laptop balanced on her hand. "Good morning, Jadyn! What will we be doing today?"

Her chipper voice reminded me of those shrill bird songs in the early hours of morning. The ones that cause you to reach for the earplugs. Or a BB gun.

I pointed to a stack of files that I had not been able to go through for the past month due to the additional work that I'd been receiving from Max's campaign. "Keep going through those files. Check up on the accounts and update the spreadsheets. A few might need immediate attention. Run them past me before doing anything."

"Got it." Lana plopped in my extra chair with her computer on her lap and pulled out a few files to look at. The girl was efficient. She got through things faster than a cheetah racing across savannah.

My cell phone rang. I answered immediately when I saw Chris's name.

"Jadyn, do you think you can bring your paintings over today? One of my other artists backed out at the last second."

"Sure." I mentally calculated how I would manage to do this during my already crazy workday and then volunteering tonight. "I'll bring the paintings over tonight if that's okay."

"The sooner the better."

We both hung up, and I glanced up to see Lana staring at me. "Did I hear something about paintings?"

I grinned at her, deciding that I wanted to tell someone about my success. "An art gallery in the Strip is going to showcase a few of my pieces!"

"You aren't referring to m1x3d, are you? I love that gallery!"

"That's the one." I did a little happy dance, wanting to hug the entire world all of a sudden. How cool that someone else had heard of the gallery! Hope bloomed between my ribs. "I never thought I'd see my stuff in a gallery!"

"We should celebrate." Lana put her computer down on the floor and stood up. She grabbed my hand and twirled me around. I laughed, enjoying myself.

"What are we celebrating?" Victoria's voice froze the cubicle.

Lana pulled her hand from me as though I had shocked her and sat, picking up her computer. Like she hadn't been caught dancing around with me. I swallowed and tugged at my dress. Caught in teal paisley.

"I've just received news that some of my artwork will be shown in a gallery in town."

"That must be why you're wearing those hideous tights."

I took a deep breath and tried to smile.

"I need you to stay late on Thursdays to take notes on the weekly management meetings. Dinner is catered."

"What time would you need me till?" If they only needed me for an extra hour, I could still manage to teach the art classes.

"We're usually here till 9:00."

"I can't do it." I frowned, keeping my voice neutral. "I'm sorry. I have a commitment with a youth program downtown."

Victoria sniffed at me. "Well, then. Lana?"

"Oh, it would be my pleasure!" Lana practically leaped from her chair. For a moment, I thought she would salute.

I backed toward my desk and hit my leg on the cold metal. I moved my leg and felt a weird tug on my tights. I looked down. My beloved paisley tights had a deep snag across the calf.

Things were definitely unraveling.

Chapter Sixteen

That evening, I carried my art supplies and some examples to show the kids at the art class in the Carnegie Library in Oakland. I found the classroom easily and stashed my paints, brushes, and paper in the corner of the room. The Oakland branch of the Carnegie Library had a section of the building particularly for community classes. All surfaces boasted easy wiping, and since watercolor wasn't harsh, we were permitted to rinse our paintbrushes in the bathroom. Propping up a couple of copies of famous paintings against the dry erase board, I tried to quell my racing nerves. I took a deep breath. As I let it out, I paced the room, allowing a prayer to escape from the depths of my being. *Lord Jesus, help me.*

I glanced at the door to see a slight girl with honey-colored hair walking through the door. She clutched a sketch pad to her chest.

Smiling as normally as I could so as to not scare her off, I tucked some hair behind my ear and walked toward her. "Welcome! Are you here for the art class?"

She shrugged and tucked a hand in her jean pocket.

"Wonderful! Choose a place to sit and let's get you started on something." I hurried over to my art supplies, selecting some brushes and paint to fulfill an idea that had come to me. I carried the supplies to her. "If you would, paint a picture of your name that you feel describes who you are. We'll share them with the entire class later."

Fifteen minutes into class, all eleven of my students had arrived. I didn't know a single name yet. They all sat quietly as they worked on their name cards. I had taken a seat at the table, too, and worked on my own name. Early on, I had decided that I wanted them to call me by my first name, so I painted swirls and lines around the letters of my name. Through my eyelashes, I stared at my students, trying to gauge them and notice specific things about each one.

"I'll start." Heads bobbed up and I lifted my painting. "I chose these rigid lines dissecting the page to show how my life feels with all my different responsibilities. Do you see how these lines crunch on the edges? Life gets cramped. Meanwhile, the swirls of colors represent my desire to incorporate art throughout my life. Creativity follows me everywhere and doesn't fit into the borders of these lines. I'm Jadyn, and I'll be teaching this class."

I scanned the class and made eye contact with a couple of students who were looking up and listening well, including the honey-haired girl.

"Let's continue clockwise now. Explain a bit about your creation and tell us your name last. Meanwhile, I'll check you off on the roll sheet."

I checked off students' names as they shared, and I found myself impressed by the different levels of skill in the class. The creativity surprised me. Finally, the honey-haired girl held up her sheet. She'd chosen only to use shades of brown.

"These earthy tones reflect my life because I'm always dealing with all sorts of crap, but at least artwork can make those hard things beautiful. I'm Crystal." She gave a little shrug and set her paper face up on the table.

Something about her tugged on my heart. I wanted to take her out for some coffee and listen to her story. We could dress in browns and eat and drink only browns.

"I chose simple black and white to illustrate how I see the world." A boy with thick glasses frames and long hair pointed to his paper. "The skulls represent where we're headed in the end. I like to keep things in focus. I'm Bailey."

A girl with pink hair began to go through her piece and then another girl with a ton of ear piercings showed off her designs. Each showed something unique to them. I could practically see pieces of their souls.

As the last student explained his artwork, I checked the time. Class was nearly over, and we hadn't even begun the instruction yet. I opened the folder in front of me and removed the syllabi that had been approved by the board. "Thanks, everyone, for participating. It's a pleasure to meet all of you. We're almost out of time so I want to hand out these syllabi for this class. It will give you an idea about what we'll be doing weekly; however, I want you to know that I will sometimes deviate from this structure. I see it as a guideline, not so much as a rule. Also, please leave your name pictures. I'll bring them back every class for us, until we all know each other without the little aid."

I handed the stack of syllabi off to the student next to me and began to gather up my art supplies. The students still sat at the table, not talking, just watching me. I cocked my head, confused why they were still in the room. "You all are free to go now."

Immediately, chairs scraped the floor as the kids pushed back. As soon as they hit the hallway, I heard their voices. Placing the art supplies back into my bags, I startled when Crystal brought over a handful of clean paintbrushes.

"Sorry, Miss Jadyn, I thought I would scrub the brushes out for you."

"No, I definitely appreciate it. I thought that everyone had left." I took the paintbrushes and put them in the bag.

"Can I help with anything else?"

I checked Crystal's face to see if the question was actually sincere. When it seemed to be the case, I gestured to the table. "Yeah, could you grab the paintings that you all did?"

Once the classroom was back in order, we walked out of the library together, not speaking. I wanted to ask her all sorts of questions, but I didn't want to scare her off either. We parted ways as soon as we were outside. As I walked to my car, I realized that I could hardly wait for next week. I might not have made any money for the evening, but I was excited to know these kids.

I pulled out my cell phone and checked my messages. Travis had texted about hanging out this week. Mel wanted to know if we needed milk. She still seemed to be only talking to me about necessary things; she had yet to forgive me for lying. Ethan asked if I was free next Saturday night for a special dinner. My heart leaped. The more I discovered about this man, the more I wanted to spend time with him.

A few days later, I was still counting down to my date with Ethan. *Only four more days to go.* It had been a long workday so crashing in the apartment sounded amazing. My sister was supposed to be out with Anthony for their nine-month anniversary. I unlocked the door and walked in, flipping on lights as I walked through the quiet apartment. Mel had been spending as much time with Anthony as she could. When we were together, she usually refused to speak to me and even when I asked for advice, she wouldn't answer. I was starting to think that I should give up on trying to interact with my sister. Her hostility made life just plain uncomfortable.

The evening hours passed quickly as I planned my next art class, listened to music, worked on paperwork for my art gallery showing, and daydreamed about other paintings that I could create. I was careful to keep my creativity contained to a small part of the couch where I sat because Mel liked the apartment pristine and uncluttered—the antithesis of my own living style.

Hearing the key in the lock to the apartment alerted me to Mel's return. The door banged open and she fell through with a grin as wide as her face. "I can't believe it. Jadyn, we talked about marriage tonight! He brought it up."

Gasping, I sprang to my feet from where I was sitting on the couch. Even though I wasn't so keen on Anthony, I was thrilled that she was finally speaking to me about something other than laundry, cleaning up my mess, and groceries. "What! Sit and tell me more."

Mel collapsed on the couch next to me and leaned her head against the cushions. "Well, with my apartment lease coming to a close in two months, I was talking about whether to renew or find a new place. At first, Anthony suggested that I move in with him, but you know Mom. She'd have a canary if I did anything like that, and besides it goes against everything we learned growing up. So then, Anthony suggested that we talk about getting married!"

I let this information wash over me and tried to be excited for her, but I kept hearing in my head how Anthony had dared suggest that my sister move in with him before they were married. Perhaps I was too old-fashioned, but it bothered me.

"We're thinking of doing a simple courthouse wedding to make things official, and then, we'll have a big party later." Mel stared at the ceiling with a huge grin across her face.

My heart tugged. I remembered sharing our pink bedroom as little girls and dreaming about our weddings together. Her dream wedding had always been a large affair with a huge ceremony and larger reception. I couldn't help but feel that this courthouse idea didn't sound at all like her. "I thought you always wanted a big wedding ceremony."

Mel's gushy happiness immediately cooled. "Marriage is a two-person decision, which requires compromise. I'm sure you'll understand one day."

My sister's patronizing words kicked me like a cleat to the shins. Had my lie really damaged our relationship this much?

"I hope you're figuring out a new apartment situation because you will not be living with Anthony and me in two months and a day."

A knock at the door interrupted Mel. She marched over to the door and peeked through the peephole. My sister shrugged. "It's *your* friend."

She was in a mood.

Mel pulled the door open and I saw Travis standing on the other side. "Hey, girls. I figured that I didn't have anything to do so I would drop on over to hang out."

I fought the urge to groan and drop my head into my hands. I didn't know what to do. Travis didn't seem to be getting my cues of non-interest. I watched her spine stiffen. She kept her body in front of the door even as Travis tried to move around her. A part of me wanted to speak up and save Travis from the coming explosion, but then again, I didn't want him there either. Walking over to Mel, I placed a hand on her shoulder. "Travis, tonight's not a good night for hanging out."

"Aw, Jadyn, you're no fun." Travis pouted a little and then laughed. "I'll be no bother."

Mel shrugged my hand off her shoulder. "You're right because you can't stay. I want to know why you think it's okay to show up at a girl's apartment completely unannounced and then expect to be invited to spend the rest of the evening with her. What's wrong with you?"

I wanted to melt into the floor.

Travis's mouth hung open.

My sister stood with legs spread and shoulders back. She looked terrifying. She pointed her finger at Travis. "This is the last time you show up without receiving permission to visit. Do you understand me?"

Travis flushed. His eyes glazed over, and his neck was going blotchy. Sure signs of oncoming tears. His flight instinct would surely click into hyper drive.

Mel had no right to treat him that way, even though it was her apartment and we had known Travis forever. He was still my friend. I took a calming breath, deciding to try to make peace in this situation.

I slipped my hand through Mel's outstretched arm and pulled her gently away from the door. Mouthing "I'm sorry" to Travis, I shut the door.

Now I had one other thing to fix. My sister had a point, but Travis hadn't needed the full strength of her annoyance with me.

"Did you have to tear into him like that?"

A door slammed, and I looked over my shoulder. My sister had shut herself into her bedroom.

"Crap." I yanked my teal paisley tights off and tossed them toward the trashcan. I was preparing for my special Saturday night date with Ethan.

"What's going on?" my sister yelled from the living room. We had reached an uneasy truce for the moment.

"I forgot that my tights have a run in them. I was going to wear them for my date with Ethan."

"Good riddance is what I say." My sister had moved to stand in the doorway of my bedroom. "Those tights were too crazy."

"But I loved them."

"Wear some teal jewelry or something. It's still got that pop of color but lacks the insanity of paisley."

I smiled at Mel, loving that she'd finally given me some sort of advice. Things felt almost normal again, but then she frowned and walked back into the other room as though she had realized she'd broken a pact with herself.

A knock on the front door bounced through my thoughts, distracting me from all else except that

Ethan was here. I jumped to my feet, deciding that I could survive the chilly autumn evening bare-legged. I slipped on my shoes. I heard Mel opening the door and welcoming him in. I straightened my dress, grabbed my purse, and entered the living room. Feeling shy, knowing that I had dressed just for Ethan, I kept my eyes on my toes but finally brought my eyes up to smile at him. The warm look in his eyes sent fire through the core of me.

"Mel, I'll see you later!" I took my jacket off a hook from the door and wrapped my arm through Ethan's. As the apartment door shut on us, I threw a smile up at him. He smiled down at me.

"That dress is beautiful on you." Rather than speaking his compliment at normal volume, he had whispered it, sending chills down my spine.

"Thanks." I squeezed his arm. A few minutes later, we exited the building and climbed into Ethan's car.

"I have some exciting news." Ethan announced as he started the engine. "I don't know if I can wait till we're at the restaurant to tell you."

"Why wait?" I threw open my hands. "Now is a better time than any other."

"Davenport's Chicago office offered me a promotion—"

"That's great!"

"I'm going to take it. The pay is excellent, and I'll be more specialized there."

My heart dropped. I didn't want him to move all the way to Chicago just as things were coming together for the two of us. *Jesus, I'm trying to trust you on this, but what are you doing?*

Ethan continued. "I figured you'll end up there, too, since Victoria said you'd be getting a promotion when you finished the job with Max and she wants to move Lana into a consultant position."

I waited a minute before answering, quietly. "But it hasn't been offered yet." I frowned. I kind of wanted to pretend that it wasn't actually something I needed to make a decision about.

"Well, it would be cool if we both move to Chicago. We'd be close."

My heart tried to skip a beat but fell back into rhythm. I didn't want to disappoint Ethan with my uncertainty, so I decided on a congratulatory response. "I'm so excited for you!" I swallowed back my fears for our relationship and the upcoming decisions. "I think you made a good choice to take the promotion. Do you know when you'll be transferred?"

"No idea, but probably not in the next month or so."

Ethan parked outside a Spanish restaurant in the South Side, and I tried to ignore the sinking feeling in my stomach. What if Victoria didn't end up offering me the Chicago promotion? Without it, I would lose Ethan and my family's approval—not to mention still be in debt. I held back my deep sigh, not wanting to concern Ethan. I needed to win back my sister's approval most of all.

Chapter Seventeen

It had been almost two weeks since Mel had read my mail and found out about my eviction. I missed our sister heart-to-hearts. This truce of only asking me necessary things like, "Apples or bananas?" or "What did Mom say about Sunday?" or to tell me, "Anthony will be here soon," stretched me like chewing gum. The whole thing so exhausted me, I'd been thinking about couch surfing at work because I practically lived there already. And I might have emotionally ordered some clothing online that I needed to immediately return. Again.

Late one Saturday morning, I stretched across the couch in our living room, brainstorming with Ethan about ways to handle my money problem. A knock on the door interrupted us, and I leaped to answer it. On the ground in front of my feet sat a box addressed to me from a well-known clothing company.

"What's the box?"

"Nothing." I dragged the package into the apartment with my foot. When things got tough, I couldn't seem to stop myself from hitting the "order now" button.

"Why's your name on it?" Ethan stood next to me now.

Lies crowded my brain, but I shoved them away. "Do you want some coffee?"

He took my hand. "Hey."

I bit my lip. I didn't know what I would see on his face.

"You're serious about fixing your debt, aren't you?" His words burned through me, but his voice was gentle. I peeked up. His eyes crinkled at me, and I relaxed into his gaze. "Little decisions add up. Your daily weekday coffee that costs five dollars means twenty-five dollars a week and a hundred dollars a month. That's a lot of money you could be saving."

"I'm going to return the box."

"If worst comes to worst, your apartment building owner will take you to court for the money you owe." Ethan tugged me toward the couch and pulled me down beside him as he stretched on the floor at the foot of the couch. I studied his face, thinking how he'd be leaving for Chicago soon and imagining what it could be like to join him there.

"I don't want that." My brain raced. Something had to be done. "I've been really enjoying teaching art, but I wish it paid."

"I guess you'll have to start small."

"If you're talking about giving up coffee, I can't hear you." I stuck my fingers in my ears.

"Not completely. Just make them at home rather than buying from the shop." Ethan shifted so he could poke my foot; I wiggled my toes at him. He grabbed my foot and pulled me down to the floor beside him, where he wrapped his arms around me and squeezed. Our backs pressed against the couch.

"How about you call me instead of shopping or buying coffee next time?"

"I don't think you're prepared for that." I giggled and tried to wriggle from his arms.

"I think I'll be the judge of that." Ethan's arms tightened around me, but for the sake of the game, I kept struggling. I spun in his arms, trying to get more leverage to free myself; suddenly, I realized that his face was inches from my own. My breath caught somewhere between my lungs and throat in a little gasp. I pushed my hands between us, creating a little bit of distance between his chest and mine. I stopped moving. Ethan grinned at me and leaned forward while looking at my lips. A gentle kiss, almost requesting and testing my response. When I leaned in, the kiss deepened.

The apartment door handle jiggled, and we flew apart, trying to find some semblance of normalcy, though my heart beat rapidly. We created a space between the two of us even as we still sat on the floor with our backs to the couch. I knew my curls had to be standing on end. It wouldn't have been so bad to be caught kissing Ethan, but it seemed too soon for people to see that when I was just getting used to it myself. The bolt clicked, and the door swung open to reveal my sister with her boyfriend. I smiled at them, ready with my greeting, but they walked in without noticing us. Mel moved into the kitchen, pulling out glasses for both of them and filling them with water.

I decided to greet them, despite the fact that they were ignoring us; I tried to keep annoyance out of my voice. "Hey, Mel. Anthony. Did you have a good morning?"

Anthony gave a head bob as he sipped his water while Mel smiled.

I tried again. "What did you all do?"

"We looked at apartments together." Anthony shrugged at Mel as though saying, "Why shouldn't we tell her?"

My heart dropped. I knew my sister had been pissed at me, but I hadn't realized that she had been that serious about moving in with her boyfriend

216

any time soon. This would cramp my plans, especially as I needed time to make more money.

"Anthony!" Mel crossed her arms. "We weren't going to say anything."

"Babe. You were mad about Jadyn not telling you about her apartment news. Why would you turn around and do that same thing to her?" Anthony threw back the rest of his water and strode to the bathroom as though he could hardly wait to get away from my sister. Despite being frustrated with her myself, I didn't like the harsh tone of Anthony's voice.

"Fine." Mel lasered her dark eyes on me. "I might as well tell you now."

Ethan and I hadn't been touching when they'd walked in. His foot nudged mine and I drew strength from his nearness. Who knew such a small touch could be a quiet little cheer for the heart?

She walked into the living room and planted her feet, crossing her arms, as though protecting herself from something I might throw at her. "You'll need to move out in a month because I'll be moving in with Anthony…after our wedding. Besides, my lease ends soon."

I couldn't keep my eyebrows from rising. Mel had just thrown a punch to my gut, but even more than that, I still couldn't believe that my sister had given up her dreams of a big celebration for a courthouse wedding. People did change. I guess.

"Also, I shouldn't have read your mail." Her voice softened. Wow, two different people had addressed me in the last two seconds. Militant Mel and Penitent Mel. I didn't know what to make of it. I found my head tilting to study my sister. No matter how much she frustrated me, I still loved her so much that I'd keep her despite her quick mood changes.

Ethan's foot bumped against mine, so I moved my eyes to him. He tilted his head toward my sister. "Well, aren't you going to say something?"

"There's rumor that I might get a promotion at work for Chicago." I straightened my t-shirt. "I'm considering taking the job. Ethan's been promoted as well, and this could probably solve the whole apartment thing."

"What!" Mel clapped her hands in front of her. "Tell me more!"

"Victoria told me that when I finish one of my campaigns that I'll probably be promoted to the Chicago branch of the company, and I hope I can still pursue my art career on the side."

She plopped herself down on the couch near where I sat on the floor. When Anthony exited the bathroom, she patted the open seat next to her. "My little sister got a promotion!"

If I had known that my promotion held the key to my sister's good graces, maybe I'd have saved myself some discomfort. I exchanged a look with

Ethan. Mel grabbed my hand and clasped it between her two. I blinked at her sudden warmth.

"It's basically the same type of work that I'm doing now, but on a bigger scale." I explained as I worked my free fingers through the carpet. I smoothed, ruffled, re-smoothed.

"You're still moving out in a month, though, right?" Anthony's voice jarred my carpet-smoothing pattern, drawing me back to the present where three people stared at me. I wanted to snap back at him, but I held it in check.

"I had hoped to be in my own place by then, but with all the work I have, I haven't had the time or option to find a new place. I'll need more than a month." At my words, Mel released my hand. The logistics threatened to overwhelm me because Max's campaign wouldn't be done for another two and a half months at least. I might need to move back in with Mom if Mel kicked me out.

Anthony frowned at me. "Unfortunately, you don't have that option."

I found myself wondering if the universe had some kind of vendetta against my personal happiness.

Tuesday morning without coffee might as well have been another Monday.

"Good morning, Jadyn!" Lana swung into my cube with all the energy of a small child who'd eaten too much candy. "I checked your schedule for you. You have three different meetings with clients, including Max. He'll be here in about fifteen minutes, maybe earlier, knowing him."

I rubbed my forehead, wanting to rub my eyes but restraining myself since I needed my eye makeup in place for the rest of the day. I still hadn't figured out how Lana managed to do everything I told her and then some. She seemed inhuman. "Thanks. Do you want to meet with…"

Pulling my planner out of the stack that Lana had obviously neatened on my desk, I checked my client appointments.

"Silas?" Lana filled in the blank and I nearly gawked at her. She knew my schedule and clients better than I did. I wondered if I ought to let her handle this appointment when she could be moving in to take my job. *But does it matter? I'll be getting that promotion.*

Lana and I discussed the different facets of the Silas campaign while I tried to forget my coffee needs. Preparing tasks to keep Lana busy kept me busier than ever. Either I needed caffeine or a vacation. *Caffeine's cheaper.*

"Lana, what time was Max supposed to be here?" I reached for the schedule.

"9:30."

We both looked at the clock on my wall. It was almost ten. We shared a look. Max never showed up. What might be keeping him? "Oswald quit a few weeks ago. That's probably what happened."

Lana nodded as I reached for my cell phone, pulling up Max's number and dialing. The phone rang and rang but went to his voicemail. I dialed again. Max kept his phone on him at all times, so I figured I'd keep trying. Just when I thought the phone would click to the machine, Max's voice came across the line. "Louis speaking."

"Hey, Max." It was hard to gauge his mood from the two words. "I have you on my schedule for a meeting this morning at 9:30. Were you still planning on coming?"

"What time is it?" Max's voice seemed kind of far away.

I checked the clock on the wall. "It's 10:15."

Max groaned into the phone. "How did that happen? I don't understand how time is slipping away from me like this."

"I've also missed you at a few of the concert events for Sophia and Lionel recently. Are you doing all right?"

"No, things are way out of hand." He took a breath. "Give me a minute."

The connection ended, and I placed my cell on my desk. I really needed coffee.

My cell phone rang with the tinny tone of an old-fashioned phone. That meant it was a client. I answered, knowing it would be Max again.

"Jadyn, I can't do it. I'm done. I can't do this anymore."

I slowly released a breath and gathered my thoughts. What was he referring to? I pictured Victoria's face if I had to tell her that we'd lost Max's business. "Can you explain more about what you're referring to?"

"I had no idea how much work Oswald did to keep my life organized. Since he quit, I can't seem to make any appointments. Yesterday, I missed three big meetings with important investors. Men with this type of money dislike being stood up. And I have nothing to wear; Oswald used to schedule my shopping trips. Maybe it's time for me to take a sabbatical."

No! I needed Max. My job success was based on his happiness. *Besides, I like his quirky self.*

"What type of planner do you have?" It seemed like the natural question under the circumstances.

"My phone is connected to my Gmail account so I can get updates on my phone and computer; however, Oswald managed all of that."

"That's not so difficult to manage." My brain raced. This man sounded absolutely exhausted and almost burnt out, although I would never suggest that idea to him. In a chick flick, I would cue some sort of makeover or shopping spree, especially after the complaint of having nothing to wear. I kicked the thought out of my head, but then reconsidered.

"Max, can you check your schedule for me today? I think I might be able to help you out, but you'll need your wallet."

He was silent for a moment. "Free and clear. If I haven't forgotten anything."

"Get your driver to bring you to my office. Text when you're here." I hung up the phone.

Lana was staring at me with wide, blue eyes.

"My happiness depends on his," I said. "Most important rule for working with clients: cater to their emotional needs as well as their campaigns. Sometimes this means doing some extra work on the side."

In the next twenty minutes, I sent off emails and made a list of things that Lana could do with the rest of her workday. A sliver of worry wiggled through me as I thought of Lana handling all my work better than I could, but I shook the thought away. Max was my focus right now. Finally, I grabbed my purse, dropped my cell inside, and checked my schedule. "Do you need my planner for the rest of the day or can I take it?"

"I made myself a copy already." Lana held up a loose sheet of paper. For once, I was thankful that Lana tended to be over-prepared.

My cell phone beeped. "I'll see you later, but I might be out for the rest of the day."

Within minutes, I stood on the sidewalk looking for Max's sedan. Movement caught my eye and I saw a driver exiting a Lincoln. I walked across the pavement and entered the open car door. Max sat in the back seat, nursing a martini. I buckled myself in and then took the glass from him gently. "Here's the plan. No more alcohol, and on to the shopping spree."

He straightened in his seat.

"But first, coffee." I winked at the driver who had been listening and the car moved forward. I could feel in my gut that this would be a good time. And better yet, I could shop without my credit card being involved.

Over the next two hours, Max and I hit J. Crew, Nordstrom's, and every store that would make my wallet cry, to solve his clothing crisis for his upcoming events. He had bought enough expensive clothes to pay my overdue rent three times over. But Max seemed rejuvenated. In the meantime, I had been reorganizing his planner and updating it on his phone. One more store would give me enough time to finish his schedule. Although I loved my paper, I knew how to work digital.

He exited the changing room in a gold suit with black accents. He struck a pose, sticking a hand in a mini pocket. "I'm thinking this suit would be perfect for sports games here in da 'Burgh."

I squinted my eyes. "You'll be the star of the show; that's for sure!"

"Jadyn." Max crossed to where I sat on the long sofa and sat beside me. "Thank you for making me go on this shopping trip. You know how to cheer up a guy."

"You're too nice." I waved my hand at him. "Go try on another one of those outfits."

I finished programming his phone and sent myself some necessary information to be able to help him in the future. Plus, keeping Max happy meant a greater chance of the Chicago promotion.

"This is the one!" Max threw the curtain back to reveal a charcoal gray suit with navy vest and accessories. He admired himself in the three-paneled mirror. "This is what I'm going to wear for the next concert that we do for Sophia and Lionel. When is that concert?"

"Check yourself." I offered him his handheld.

He scooped up the device, navigating with seemingly no problem. "How do I check the concerts?"

I stood up and pointed over his shoulder. "If you hit 'concerts' in this column, it will show you all your upcoming concerts. Same with the other words like 'appointments.'"

"Okay. So the next concert is going to be next Friday." He stared hard at the screen, then chuckled. "Jadyn, I wish I could promote you."

I laughed. "Today I'll just settle for a ride home."

But $1,600 bonus would be nice. For now, I'll focus on keeping him happy...and keeping my promotion.

Chapter Eighteen

Chris had given me a hundred flyers about my art showing at m1x3d. A week later, I still hadn't passed any around.

I dropped the stack of them on my desk. But then I didn't want to leave them out for people to see so I opened my junk drawer and shoved the pile in, shutting the drawer. *Out of sight, out of mind.*

But *then* I kept thinking about it and how I wanted to share this moment with people. This was my art—my chance for success. I yanked the junk drawer back open, ripping a couple of the flyers in the process. I smoothed the wrinkled papers. I lifted a few sheets off the top and slid them between some folders to carry down to the break room with me.

Once in the break room, I checked to make sure it was empty and hurried over to the bulletin board where I tacked up the printout before grabbing a cup of coffee to take back to my desk. Armed with my coffee cup, I decided that I could give sheets to a couple of my coworkers.

During my lunch break, I tacked flyers to all the bulletin boards that I could find in coffee shops and telephone poles near the office. I even stopped at the Carnegie Library and asked if they'd keep a couple of sheets. I emailed my Thursday night art students, inviting them to attend. My stack of printouts had greatly decreased, but I could still hand them out to a few more people.

After work, Mel and I were meeting at the grocery store again to pick up the week's groceries. Somehow, it seemed easier to split the grocery bill in half when we were both present. Maybe I'd give her a flyer then?

I already had a cart and was wheeling through the produce section when I heard my sister's voice. She dropped her purse in the cart, spoke into her phone, and moved to look at the apples without so much as a nod in my direction. *Typical.*

I ran my finger across the edge of the art gallery invitation; I eyed her soft leather purse. Sliding a sheet from my bag, I slipped it into her purse, hoping she'd notice my name across the front of the paper before tossing it out.

Mel dropped a bag of apples into our metal cart, and I cringed, thinking of the bruises that would form on those apples. We'd been bruising each other without thinking about it recently, too.

My cell beeped, and I checked a message from Ethan. *I searched m1x3d online and it shows samples of your work! You're practically famous. Would you mind an escort on opening night?*

A hundred butterfly wings waltzed through my heart. Even with Ethan on another business trip to Chicago, he took the time to be a part of my life and he supported my art. I had to be the luckiest girl in the world. I grinned at my telephone, knowing that I probably looked ridiculous, but not caring. My fingers flew across the keyboard. *Only if you pick me up in a chariot pulled by white horses.* I added a winky face for good measure and then sent the text.

I had not even released my phone back into my purse when Ethan's response came in. *Your wish is my command.*

Lana cleared her throat before entering my cubicle Thursday morning. I smiled at her as she walked in and sat in her usual spot across from me. A small portion of my desk had somehow become her area, I supposed because it made things simpler as I tried to train her. But I wasn't sure. Her blonde hair lacked its usual bounce, and her eyes appeared darker than usual.

"Is everything all right?"

She jerked her head up. Her lips pinched together and then relaxed. "I received some interesting news from our reviewers for a couple of different advertisements, including Mr. Louis's."

I leaned forward while messing with the pens in the jar. "Mm-hmm?"

"Apparently, the "I am America" idea with Mr. Louis's campaign is not performing well with our test audience. Their results use words like 'un-relatable' and 'old-fashioned.' They're going to run the ads through a couple of other test groups before giving us the final report."

"The most important age group is the young professionals." I rolled my neck around slowly while shutting my eyes. Still messing with the pens with one hand, I accidentally flipped a pen onto my desk. I could not afford to have Max's campaign fail, especially after just getting him back on the bandwagon. "Keep me in the loop about the ads. We're getting to the point where it's too late to majorly change the design, but we still can reverse this."

"Is there anything else I can do to fix this?" Lana shuffled some papers in her corner of my desk. "I feel like I am responsible for this, too."

The unmistakable click of heels down the hallway interrupted the conversation and warned of Victoria's approach. I shoved the stray pen back into the jar. A moment later, she was standing in my cube, holding my m1x3d flyer in her hand. She'd probably gotten it from the break room. "What is this?"

"My artwork is being shown at the m1x3d Art Gallery." My fingers itched for the pen jar, but I tried to keep from squirming by standing up. The added height made me feel less like a small child getting reprimanded and more like an equal.

"You failed to get this approved by the board." Victoria waved the sheet at me and the office around me went quiet. This is when I wished for my own office with real walls instead of cubicles where everyone knew how everyone else was doing.

I tried to stand up tall. "I thought the community board didn't need any approval from management."

"The bulletin board doesn't. But you, showing your artwork at a gallery that uses our competitors for their advertisement, does require approval from the Davenport board." Victoria flattened the sheet of paper onto my desk while Lana skirted around her and left my cubicle. I fought the urge to follow Lana's escape route.

I decided to play the apologetic card. "I had no idea that I needed approval for my artwork to be shown with m1x3d."

"Well, you should have read your work contract more closely." Victoria stood with her hands on her hips. "I expect you to sever your connection with this art gallery immediately."

My cheeks flushed warm, matching the first flickers of anger in my gut. "What?"

"As a contracted employee of Davenport, you are required by agreement to seek approval for any art pursuit of your own such as showing your work in an art gallery, especially by galleries not partnered with us."

I dug my fingernails into my palm, wishing that I could wake up from this bad dream. This couldn't be legal, but as my boss, Victoria could demand it from me. Sigh. I finally catch a break in my artwork and suddenly it's being taken away from me! I longed to walk out the door while yelling, "I quit." *Can't do that.*

"I expect to hear by the end of the day that you've canceled that art showing." Victoria clicked out of my office and I collapsed into my desk chair. The art showing had been one of my few hopes for making up the rent, and it was making my dream into a reality. I rubbed my eyes and tried to hold back the tears that clogged my throat. A light tap on my cube brought my head up. Lana was back, holding an open file as she walked over to my desk. She pushed it toward me.

"I went and got a copy of the contract you signed so you can look at it yourself."

My mouth parted. I thought that Victoria had Lana in her back pocket, but here she was offering to help me look into my legal rights. Or was she? I gave her a smile, hoping. Opening the file folder, I flipped through the contract and started reading for the section that would keep me from showing my artwork.

I was supposed to have a coach and horses. *Where is my fairy godmother?*

As soon as I could steal some time away from the office in the afternoon, I slipped out to walk the sidewalk around the building. The cool temperature nipped at my heels, and the University of Pittsburgh students had returned. I dialed Ethan's phone. After ringing for a while, the voice mail clicked on. I just wanted to hear his voice. *Beep.* I opened my mouth to start leaving a message when another beep sounded in my ear. I checked the screen. Ethan was calling so I accepted his call.

"I have some bad news and I don't know what to do." The story tumbled forth. "Lana found a copy of the contract that I signed so we can find out if it's within my rights to show my artwork at a competing gallery. I found the clause."

"Have you thought about going over Victoria to the Board?"

I weaved through a small crowd of tourists. "I don't know if I'm prepared for the type of treatment that will open me up to from Victoria."

"Honestly, if you don't want to pull your art from the show yet, I would think the best idea is to go to the Board and explain the situation. That's what your contract says, right? Ask the board. Not Victoria. Even if they agree with her, they may allow you to complete the showing first."

Hope tickled my insides; then I nodded but remembered that Ethan couldn't see me. Standing at a crosswalk, I waited for the light to turn so I could cross. "I think you have something there. Thanks for listening to me go crazy." *Maybe the Board would somehow see my show as a corporate asset.*

"It's no problem. I wish I was there to give you a big hug and maybe a kiss or two."

"I'd like that." I smiled. "Now, I need to figure out how to get in contact with the board."

Back in my office, I pulled up the internal company page that clocked my hours, tracked birthdays, and localized important company announcements. I read through all the tabs, searching for something that would give me a clue who to talk to on the board that needed to okay my art show. Someone...sympathetic. The top tab bar showed nothing. I scrolled to the bottom of the page to locate the sitemap button.

Bingo.

I clicked, and my computer loaded a PowerPoint slideshow that recorded the hierarchy of the office. Flipping through the pages as quickly as I could, I finally found the section that showed the different company committees. The chair of the board was Michael Davenport, Victoria's uncle. The man was sharp like Victoria except older and sometimes kindlier. Yet, you never knew how a Davenport would swing at this company since they'd mostly kept it a family business even as it had grown. Victoria's father ran the larger Chicago branch.

Staring at Davenport's name on the screen, I couldn't help but pray. *Jesus, what can I say to this man so I'll find favor in his eyes for this art showing?*

I didn't want to go to his office. But only an hour remained till the end of the day. I knew I shouldn't put it off. My art show was meant to open in forty-eight hours, anyway. I at least had to try to smooth this over before the show opened. I couldn't afford to lose my job over this.

What will Victoria think?

I forced myself to stand up and walk out of my cubicle. As I navigated through the building to Mr. Davenport's corner office, I tried to focus on breathing and explaining my story to him. In the end, I chanted to myself over and over. *Help me, Jesus.*

I peeked into Mr. Davenport's office from the hallway; seeing no one in there but him, I took a deep breath and then knocked. His gray head came up, making eye contact with me. I opened the door, letting myself into his office.

"Miss Simon, how can I help you today?" Mr. Davenport moved his laptop away from him, shutting the top and then folding his hands in front of him.

I carried myself over to the chair in front of his desk and sat down, trying to steady my heartbeat. I ran my pointer finger over my fingernails, discovering a ragged edge. "Well, I came to speak to you about a situation involving work and my pursuit of art."

Glancing at Mr. Davenport and not seeing that he had anything to say, I pushed myself to continue. "You see, I'm an artist and I've been hoping to show my artwork for a long time. I recently had a big break and m1x3d art gallery in the Strip District will be showing my artwork this weekend. Victoria informed me this morning that it's against company policy to allow employees to show their work through a gallery that isn't partnered with our company. I checked my contract and saw what she meant. She did say that my show could happen if the board approved. I guess what I'm asking is if you might allow me to show my work at the gallery this weekend."

I wanted to keep building my case for Mr. Davenport, but I also knew I needed to stop talking and allow him to respond. I shut my mouth and waited, rubbing the jagged nail over and over with the pad of my finger.

Mr. Davenport leaned back in his chair. "My niece is protective of the company, but she is also right in this case. Although I don't personally agree with the policy, it was put in place at when the company was incorporated and it's important to uphold these rules. Will you be profiting from this art show?"

"Not initially." I shifted in my chair. My finger was beginning to chafe. *I need a nail file.* "But there is the possibility that my artwork could be purchased."

Mr. Davenport steepled his fingers in front of him and his eyebrows drew together as he thought deeply. "Have you signed any type of contract with this gallery?"

"I haven't."

"Miss Simon, I hate to stand in the way of your art career; however, this is something that the Board will have to consider. I understand that you don't have a lot of time before the showing. So I advise you to prepare to pull your artwork out if you want to keep your job here. I will give you a call in the morning after speaking to the rest of the Board."

"Thank you, Mr. Davenport. Also, it might be worth considering that my relationship with this art gallery might form a new partnership with our company as well." I tossed this idea out as I stood from the chair.

The desk phone rang. He picked up the receiver as I left his office. Someone had just filled my castle in the sky with cement blocks, crashing it to earth.

Could ripped dreams be glued together again? Not like new. Victoria's command to tell her that I had canceled my art showing by the end of the day echoed through my head. I had to talk to her before the day ended. My skin grew warm and sweat snaked down my back. I walked to Victoria's office, expecting to see her hunched over her desk or standing in front of her window. I glanced through her door. The light was off.

I scanned the office quickly and saw that her work bags were gone. Breath rushed out of my lungs. I'd have to face her the following day, but for now, I didn't have to explain that I had not canceled the art showing yet because I'd approached the chair of the board.

She, and I, would be there bright and early in the morning, though.

Chapter Nineteen

After hours of tossing in bed, I stared at the glowing clock on my nightstand. 5:00 a.m., Friday morning. A bit early to get up but I couldn't sleep anymore. My brain whirled in a million different directions, frantic to know what Mr. Davenport and the board would decide. I threw my feet over the side of the bed and slid to standing. I cracked the bedroom door and tiptoed to the kitchen to make some coffee. I still had a couple of hours until I needed to get ready for work, so a nice cup of coffee and some time alone would be calming.

The gurgle of the coffee maker soothed me as I leaned against the counter. *Will I have to pull my work from the show?* I hadn't told Chris about this yet. A part of me hoped that if I didn't say anything that my paintings would get to stay.

The rest of the morning passed quickly as I experimented with creating a homemade latte. A few more latte practices, and I could be a hire-in barista. But then, it was time to go to the office. Mel sent me off with another travel mug full of coffee for the road. "Anthony and I are looking forward to seeing your show tonight!"

I smiled, trying to hide my nerves. She saw them anyway, misreading them as nerves about the show, not the fact that the show might not happen. I hadn't told her about that anyway. Would she think that omission was another lie?

Lana showed up at exactly five past eight, as always. She was never a minute earlier or a minute later, but at least she was dependable. "Any news on the art show?"

I shook my head no, and I kept worrying that Victoria would show up before I heard from the board. Over the next two hours, we worked together to finish different tasks and to contact clients. Max's campaign was in its final stages with no more news of bumps, and he'd made all his most recent appointments as far as I knew.

Next week, we'd be presenting.

The click of stilettos alerted us to Victoria's approach. Each heel click made my stomach twist tighter. Lana shoved a bunch of papers together. Victoria entered, and at that cue, Lana left.

"I had to leave early yesterday and didn't have the chance to make sure that you canceled the art show." Victoria crossed her legs as she lowered herself into the chair that Lana had vacated. Her signature white pencil skirt wrapped around her while the pop of a red belt circled her thin waist. "I expect that you did."

I took a sip of cold coffee, hoping that the caffeine would inspire brilliance, but nothing came. So I started in with what I knew. "Victoria, I checked my contract and you were right, I needed board permission. So I spoke to Mr. Davenport yesterday afternoon about it."

Victoria's eyebrows arched high, etching a wrinkle across her forehead.

"I figured that I might still get the board to take the case into consideration, especially since Chris and his art galleries could potentially become our clients through our interactions with them. Every connection could be a possible networking opportunity." I repressed the urge to pat myself on the back. The caffeine had kicked in; I could feel it.

Victoria's eyes flashed. She opened her mouth just as my office phone rang.

"One moment." I picked up the phone. "Jadyn Simon speaking."

"Miss Simon, it's Michael Davenport. Would you please come down to my office?"

"Of course, Mr. Davenport. I'll be right there." I threw a look at Victoria and saw her eyes widen.

"Give me the phone," Victoria snapped at me.

"Mr. Davenport, Victoria is in my office right now and would like to speak to you if that's all right." Like a small child who answered the phone for her parent and then had to hand it off.

"Fine," Mr. Davenport grumbled into the phone.

I handed the phone to Victoria and then didn't know whether to leave or stay. She jerked her head toward the hallway and I realized that she was dismissing me from my own office. I stood, smoothing my skirt and giving her a nod. Then, I did what any girl would do. I headed right down to Mr. Davenport's office, even as I heard Victoria's voice slice through the office. "I was handling the situation. She did not get permission from the board; therefore, she needs to end..."

Rubbing my forehead, I walked into the hallway and could finally stop hearing Victoria's voice. She'd never champion my cause with her uncle, but it sounded as though they had been arguing, at least. When I arrived at Mr. Davenport's office, I peeked through the door window and saw that he was not on the phone. I tapped on the door and then opened it.

"Mr. Davenport?" I walked toward the desk. He was standing on the other side, not looking at me, but when he turned, his face looked haggard.

"Yes, please take a seat." I lowered myself into the chair across from his desk as he paced behind his desk. He folded his hands behind him and paced five steps forward and then five steps back. "Victoria is frustrated because she feels as though you went over her head; however, you did the right thing in approaching the board with this decision as that is what is required according to your work contract."

I tried not to wring my hands in my lap. I slid my hands under my thighs to keep them still as I listened to Mr. Davenport.

"After a discussion with the other board members, we've decided that we want to support the local art scene by allowing you to show your work with this gallery…"

Mr. Davenport was still speaking, but I found myself wanting to burst into a million pieces. I also wanted to collapse in a heap of relief that I wouldn't have to pull out at the last second. The local art community was small. To suddenly quit an art show could possibly ruin my reputation before it even began. My ears tuned back into Mr. Davenport's voice.

"Yet, we will need you to agree to enquire about some sort of partnership with the owner of the art galleries for advertising. And I look forward to seeing your work on Mr. Louis's campaign in a week."

My heart sank. For once, I just wanted to enjoy the success of my art, rather than having to sell my company's advertising skills again. But how could I refuse? Mr. Davenport was allowing me to have my art show. *And did I hear a threat in his voice when he mentioned Max's advertising?*

Leaving work an hour early had seemed like it would leave enough time, but that get-ready-for-art-show time had flown by and in thirty minutes, Ethan would be arriving. The apartment door slammed. Mel was home.

"Have you seen my black heels with the lattice toe?" I yelled from my bedroom.

I heard her bags hit the floor. "Sorry, I haven't, but you can check my closet if you want any of my shoes."

I blinked. Practically cordial. *She must have had a good day at work.*

Settling on a theme of black with silver accents, I ran through the apartment to look at Mel's shoes. I still needed to do my makeup, but if I didn't find a pair of shoes to wear then I would need to rework the entire outfit. Yes! A pair of plain black heels and sparkling silver heels. I grabbed the silver heels and held them against the silver belt that encircled my waist over my LBD. Perfect.

As I passed my sister in the living room, I held up the shoes. "Is it okay if I borrow these?"

"Totally fine. But lose the belt." She hurried around the apartment, tidying things up. "What should I wear tonight?"

"Wear what you've got on. Maybe unbutton the jacket and you'll be just right, especially to represent your artist sister!" I glanced over her, taking in the navy business suit with white pumps, as I unhooked my belt. "You don't need to clean up. Ethan's seen it worse."

Mel shot me a glare. "This is *my* apartment, and it matters to *me*."

Her words struck me, reminding me that I was only an unwanted visitor. Ducking back into my room to deposit the shoes near my purse, toss the belt, and to shake off my sister's words, I spun into the bathroom to complete my look with a French twist and some red lipstick. A knock sounded on the apartment door.

"I got it," Mel called. I heard the door open and then Ethan's deep voice sent chills down my spine. Somehow, even after months of dating, his voice still affected me.

"Is our artist ready?" he asked my sister. I dabbed my lips on a tissue, analyzing the lines along my lips, hoping they were straight enough. I wanted to walk out of the bathroom like a sophisticated lady, but my nerves were so tight and the excitement so keen that I skipped out instead and did a little twirl even though my black dress wouldn't move.

"Here I am!" I struck a pose, placing a hand on my waist. I peeped up through my eyelashes at Ethan, and my stomach cartwheeled. He wore a black suit, white button-up, and black skinny tie pinned with a silver jewel. In his hand, he held a bouquet of red roses. *He must be a mind reader.* My hands flew to my mouth as I crossed the rest of the room to him. "You look so good."

"And you look like a successful artist and muse." He offered the roses to me with a slight bow. "When you're ready, your carriage awaits."

I accepted the roses, drawing the flowers to my nose. "My carriage?"

"You'll have to come out and see." He grinned at me, not giving away another clue.

Mel scooted in and took the roses from me. "Here, I'll take those and put them in a vase while you finish getting ready."

I suddenly wanted to kiss my sister. Instead, I whirled back to my room to grab a few last things. I slipped on her silver heels and knew that I cut a glamorous figure. Ethan stood by the door, messing with his phone as I came from my room. As soon as my heel hit the kitchen floor, his head jerked up. His look of appreciation made my toes squirm, but I kept my head high. He swung the apartment door open for me as I yelled over my shoulder. "I'll see you later!"

Ethan offered his arm to me as we walked through the building and then onto the sidewalk. I scanned the street for a carriage with white horses. All I saw were cars.

"They were completely out of horse carriages, so I opted for something a bit different." As he spoke, he waved his arm toward the street.

I couldn't tell what he was referring to, but then a white antique car pulled to the curb. A man in a white suit jumped from the driver's side, ran around to the sidewalk side of the car, and opened the back door.

My mouth fell open.

"Your ride awaits." He walked me to the car and helped me through the door and then followed the driver to the other side of the car where Ethan got in. The antique had been completely renovated, but the shape and design seemed to be true to its originals. I stroked the seat that I sat on.

"It's beautiful!" I slid my arm through his. "This is truly unique!"

"I wanted the leading lady to arrive in style for her premiere art show."

My grin reached to my ears, and I had to look away from his face.

When we pulled up in front of the art gallery, Ethan jumped out to open the door for me. I pinched my hand as I stepped from the car, just to make sure that all of this was truly real life and not a dream. Ethan leaned in and told the driver that he could park and come in if he wanted. Then, he straightened and offered his arm to me again. I squeezed his arm and smiled up at him.

"I want to be the perfect arm candy," he whispered down to me.

"Oh, you're far more than just arm candy." I laughed. As soon as we entered the doors, I saw my paintings hanging on the walls. Happiness welled up in my eyes, but I held the tears back. My mascara belonged on my eyelashes, not my cheeks. A moment later, Chris and Rosa stepped up to me.

"Ah!" Chris stuck out his right hand to me. "Our star artist is here!"

Star artist? Star artist! I shook hands with him and smiled at Rosa. I hadn't yet figured out if their relationship extended past employer and employee, but the fact that one of Chris's art galleries was named after Rosa was not lost on me. "I am so pleased to see how it all looks. You've done a lovely job of displaying the pieces! I'm sorry I couldn't make it over at all to help finalize the look."

"Oh, no. We understand that you're busy." Rosa replied in a soft voice that rolled her Rs.

"Now, you must look around and feel free to mingle with artists and patrons alike. I may snag you to introduce you to a few myself, if I may." Chris looked to Ethan for permission.

Ethan smiled, and I realized that I needed to introduce the two men. "Chris, this is Ethan. And this is Rosa."

Ethan released my arm to shake hands with Chris and then with Rosa. I smiled at them all and then I saw a flash of white behind them.

It couldn't be.

I squinted my eyes. Victoria, at my art show! My knees grew a bit weak, and Mr. Davenport's words came back to me. I needed to broach the subject of advertising. I squeezed my eyes shut, not wanting to bring it up.

"Well, we'll leave you two for now." Chris and Rosa moved away. Like a rowboat without oars, I floated, but then Ethan's hand engulfed my hand. He lifted my hand to his elbow and drew my arm through. Tingles shot through me.

"Look." I stood on tiptoe so my whisper would reach Ethan's ear. "Victoria's here."

Ethan raised his eyebrows, and I slid my eyes in the direction where I had last seen Victoria. She still stood there in front of my painting of "Inner War."

"Let's go say 'hi.'" He began walking toward Victoria. I wanted to run in the other direction, but I gave in to Ethan's pull, knowing that his presence would keep things civil, at least. I imagined that she would probably still be frustrated about me going to the board over her. We stepped beside her, and I broke the silence.

"Victoria, I'm so glad that you were able to make it."

She sniffed. "My father always says that it was part of the job to support our employees in their endeavors. However wrongheaded they may be."

I forced myself to ignore her chilly voice. "It's an honor to have you present."

Silence. I wanted to tug on Ethan's arm to leave and I almost did when Victoria opened her mouth again. Her voice had lost its rigid quality. "What inspired this piece?"

I glanced at "Inner War" and recalled my turbulent emotions as I had allowed the painting to shape itself before my brush even touched the canvas. I suspected Wassily Kandinsky would have liked it since it mimicked a bit of the abstract style he had pioneered, capturing emotions and sounds with color and shapes. Letting go of Ethan's arm, I stepped up to the picture and pointed to the reds and then the blues. "To me, it's a depiction of inner conflict when you feel a certain way but know you ought to act in opposition to it. This represents the point where you don't know which side will win."

Victoria nodded her head, and she looked as though she might say something. But then, a new voice cut through the conversation. "Here's where I find the star of the night!"

I turned to find Travis behind me with a bouquet of daisies. He handed them to me.

"Thank you, Travis." I didn't want to accept his flowers in front of Ethan, but no one was nearby to hand the flowers off to, so I tucked them into my arm.

"I know they are your favorite so I wanted to make sure you got some." Travis shot a look at Ethan.

Frowning, I tilted my head at Travis.

I needed to get rid of the flowers. Fast. "I'll be right back. I'm going to go find somewhere to put these flowers."

Moving away from Ethan and Travis, I scanned the crowd for Rosa, guessing that she'd know what to do with my flowers. Suddenly, she appeared at my side, lifting the bouquet from my hands. "I'll vase these and put them by your paintings. Hand off any other flowers to me, if they come."

"You're a gem!" Then I looked for Ethan. He and Travis seemed locked in a heated conversation of some sort. Victoria had moved to another section of art. Nervous, I strode through the room to get back to them, but a hand on my arm stopped me. I pasted a smile on my face and turned.

"Darling! I'm so proud of you!" Mom pulled me into her arms. I saw my sister and her boyfriend; she grinned at me. Anthony was holding Mel's hand, but his eyes shot in the opposite direction. I followed his gaze and realized he was ogling Victoria, who was dressed in her usual tight skirt. My nose crinkled in disgust. Mom squeezed me, reminding me that I was still in her arms, and then let go. "I never thought you'd make anything out of your artwork, but you have!"

"Thanks, Mom." I didn't have time to deal with her shin-kick comment. Ethan and Travis still stood in deep conversation, and judging by Ethan's stiff stance, I worried over what they might be talking about. I smiled at my family again. "You guys should take a look around. I think there are some refreshments near the back."

Other artists mingled through the crowd. I could recognize any fellow artist simply by the look of quiet pride radiating from their faces; however, the simple silver name tags that Chris had supplied for each of us also helped. I ran a finger over my silver tag. I wanted to dance around the room and do-si-do with every elbow that jutted toward me. I was here. Not to represent other artists or show someone else's work. I was here for me. *A real artist.*

As I tried to make my way back to Ethan, coworkers and friends stopped me every few steps to congratulate me or ask me a question. A few people that I didn't recognize stopped me to ask about different pieces that I had painted. I saw a few students from my art class amongst the crowd.

Crystal, clad all in browns, sent me a little wave and then slid her hand into that of a nearby boy's.

Finally, only a few steps kept me from Ethan and Travis. My heels clicked across the floor, muffled due to the noise of the gallery. Travis was pointing at Ethan's chest and I heard him over the noise. "You don't know her like I do."

Oh. It sounded like things had gone too far. I stepped up to them and slid my arm through Ethan's, pretending that I hadn't heard anything. "Sorry, guys. I dropped off the flowers but then stopped to talk with some people along the way."

Ethan was stiff under my fingertips, and Travis shoved fists into his pockets—his jaw jutted out, like he'd been caught doing something wrong. Neither one would look at me. I shifted my gaze between the two of them, hoping for a clue as to what had just been said. When Travis slunk away, I leaned into Ethan. "Do you want to go find the food?"

"No." He dropped my arm and strode away. I staggered forward, regaining my balance, and watched his back move away from me. I stood there with my mouth hanging open. Something had happened while I was gone and now neither man wanted to be near me.

Where is that fairy godmother?

Chapter Twenty

I found Ethan outside the art gallery about twenty minutes later, after I'd worked through artist introductions and answered questions about my artwork. His hands stuffed in pockets and his shoulders hunched, he looked pretty miserable. I walked over to him and placed my hand on his elbow.

He shifted away. Travis had said something to him and I had no idea how to handle what was going on.

"I wish you had told me." Ethan broke the silence, but he wouldn't look at me. He studied the sidewalk as though analyzing a detailed masterpiece. "I thought we had something special. But Travis?"

"What about Travis?" I tried to keep my voice neutral, but I struggled against the accusation in Ethan's voice.

"How can I trust you tell me the truth when I know that you would lie to your own family?"

His statement smacked me across the face, and I had to steady myself. I hadn't imagined that such a lie would even touch this relationship. "Ethan, I was wrong about lying then, but what's this really about?"

"I think I need some space from us, to think about all of this." His words cut me. "I didn't realize I was being two-timed. Again."

"Two timing?" *Space.* My legs trembled, and I stepped backward toward the gallery. I needed to find Travis now. This had to end. I stumbled through the doors, shocked that Ethan would accuse me of cheating on him, but then fire pumped through my veins. Where was Travis? My eyes scanned the crowd still thick with bodies weaving through the small art space.

There he was. Travis stood with my mother, gesturing away. I took no notice of the people that I pushed through to get to Travis. In my peripheral vision, I saw Max sparkling in a sequin-embellished suit. Only he could get away with that look, but just barely.

"Mom, would you mind grabbing me a drink?" I interrupted their conversation. Anger clipped my words short.

She did a double take, studying my face on the second look.

"I need to talk to Travis."

Her lips parted, but I held my hand up. Mom hustled to the drink bar. She'd be back soon to try to save Travis. I set my sights on him. I let my anger seep out as he stared mildly at me through his blonde eyelashes.

His smug face made me want to throw up; instead, I spit out my words. "What. Did. You. Say?"

Travis raised his eyebrows. "What are you talking about?"

"Pickled cucumbers, Travis. What did you say to Ethan tonight?" Less a question, it was pure demand and Travis acted far too calm about it. His smile widened over his teeth.

"I simply told him that you are mine, that you and I belong together."

Confusion ricocheted through me, clashing with my anger. I studied Travis's face, checking to see if he was being honest with me, but I saw none of the telltale signs of a lie. He honestly believed what he'd just said.

"Ethan's my boyfriend."

"Boyfriends change." Travis checked his phone screen, then slid the phone into his pocket, looking at me with a gaze that held no real expression except boredom.

I eyed Travis. I was missing something.

"Oh, my lovely Miss Simon!" Max's voice bubbled through my thoughts as he maneuvered through the crowd.

"You and I are not done, Travis," I muttered. I spun around and accepted Max's hug.

"What a success of a night! Have you seen the guest book? Quite a turnout and many admirers of your work. I expect you'll be famous soon." He stepped back from me, looked between me and Travis, and saw the tears forming in my eyes.

"What!" He brushed a teardrop from my cheekbone. "I hope these are happy tears, my dear!"

I shook my head and sniffled. Travis stood there with one corner of his mouth quirked up. I resisted the urge to smack him, but Max must have seen the flash of passion in my eyes because he hooked his hand around my waist and dragged me through the crowd. "Let's get you some fresh air."

We crossed the threshold, and cool night air tiptoed across my skin. Ethan leaned against the building. Max bee-lined for him, pulling me behind him and depositing me in front of Ethan. "I think you lost something of great value, sir."

My eyes widened. He'd said that about me. Then he gripped Ethan's arm, tugging him from the wall. He tucked my arm through Ethan's. "I believe your lady artist needs you still."

Ethan walked like a toy soldier, but he allowed Max to lead us back into the gallery for more mingling. While I tried hard to speak with as many of the people present as possible, Ethan kept my hand in his elbow and interacted with those who spoke to him. How could we be so physically close but so far all at once? *Robotic arm candy.*

Waking up the next morning, I longed to pull the blankets back over my head and never come out, especially because the first thing I remembered was the weirdness with Ethan and then with Travis, not the art show success. I squeezed my eyes shut, wishing the bad away. Not being able to, I climbed out of bed and headed to the kitchen. Mel already sat at the kitchen table, looking worse than I felt. Her curls flopped like a lopsided beehive and the skin around her eyes puffed red. She sniffled a good morning to me and handed me a mug of coffee that she'd already poured.

"Anthony and I had a fight." Her voice cracked. "I caught him staring at a girl's butt last night. The worst part is that I went to the bathroom and when I came out, I saw him not only talking to her, but he squeezed her butt."

"He what?" I barely managed not to spit out my coffee.

A sickly green hue hinted around her cheeks. "I know. I want to pretend it didn't happen, but I watched it with my own eyes. He swears that it's never happened before, but how am I supposed to know?"

"Well, you're in good company." I leaned heavily against the counter, thinking of my own boy problems. "Ethan and I had a misunderstanding because of some conversation he had with Travis."

"This is the guy I want to marry." She shook her head. "At least, I thought I was going to, but now, I'm not so sure."

"Speaking of that, Mom okayed me moving in with her when your lease is up." I'd called her the other day and she'd given me permission as long as I paid rent and looked for a new place to live. As much as she loved us, I guessed she was loving her independence, too. "This is a terrible Saturday."

"Let's order some delicious breakfast. I'll pay." Mel reached for her phone. "I could use a sugary pick-me-up and a chick flick. You in?"

I took a deep breath and slowly released it. "Nothing could be better at this moment."

Ethan was in Chicago again, and our communications were stilted, even though I had tried to explain what had happened with Travis, but the week sped by in a flurry of activity as Lana and I worked together to prepare for the presentation— I'd be presenting it on Friday to Max, Victoria, Mr. Davenport, Sophia, and Lionel. Lana proved to be a huge help as she could work on projects with other clients as I finalized his campaign.

My cell phone buzzed as I worked through a stack of papers, detailing the updated performance results of Max's advertisements. I slid the code across the cell phone screen and unlocked the text. Travis wrote, *You and Ethan still having difficulties? Want to get together to talk about it?*

"The last thing I want to do is talk to you." I spoke aloud before I had time to realize it. I glanced up at Lana who was looking at me with wide eyes. "Sorry, I didn't mean to speak aloud. I've been having some men problems recently."

Lana shook her head. "The worst. Work-wise, have you found anything new on the performance results?"

I shuffled through the papers in front of me, thinking about Travis's text and how to respond. A sheet caught my eye. "Here it is."

My stomach sank as I read through the comments. Not again. Lana stood and came to my side of the desk to look at the paper with me. Reading the feedback made me want to ignore the world, to cuddle up on the couch with Ethan and a good movie.

"The graphics don't jive with the message."

"The American Dream is overused."

"This would be better if you only used text."

"What's with the cello and the piano piled on each other?"

I set the paper down. "How does this keep happening?"

"We don't have time to fix this before the presentation tomorrow morning." Lana rubbed her hand across her forehead as she, too, scanned the comments.

"You're right. Under the circumstances, I think we're just going to have to present what we have and hope for the best." I held up one last comment sheet, trying to muster some sort of humor. "At least this person liked the font that we chose."

The conference room filled quickly the next morning. Lana had kindly picked up coffee and donuts to sweeten up the crowd. Once everyone had seated themselves, I stood. My abdomen was in knots.

"Thank you, everyone, for making it here this morning to view the unveiling of "Music Collaboration." We'll be walking through the creation process to the final advertisements. Feel free to help yourself to donuts and coffee whenever you need." I moved to the front of the room and sent Lana a look.

Together, we flipped through the slideshow, allowing different contributing departments to share their portion of the project. Things were moving smoothly. Lionel and Sophia still seemed interested in what was happening while Max glowed with excitement. Victoria bounced her foot through the presentation and took notes occasionally. Mr. Davenport seemed bored.

As we drew closer to the slide about the views of the test audiences, my insides crumpled. Things could go badly here. Lana had volunteered to share the slide even though I believed it was my responsibility to share any bad news, but she had been adamant. As she shared the results, I checked faces and reactions. Victoria's foot stopped kicking, and Mr. Davenport turned to stone. Max started turning red.

No one said a thing when Lana finished. I stood and switched places with Lana. "Finally, we'll take a look at the advertisements that we've created to specifically represent the work of Lionel and Sophia."

The images came on screen. I had seen these advertisements so much that I was more interested in the people viewing them. I scanned the faces around the conference room. The social media people were exchanging concerned looks. Max's face had gone from red to white. Victoria's feet were firmly planted on the ground and her lips were pursed. Mr. Davenport hadn't moved. I didn't want to ask what I needed to next, but this was how these types of meetings went. "Do any of you have any feedback to give on this campaign?"

Lionel put up his hand. "I love what you've done with my and Sophie's ideas! You took them into consideration and incorporated them. I appreciate that."

"I particularly like the American Dream spread." Sophia uncrossed her arms and leaned forward.

I was pleased to hear that the artists were happy, but the other faces around the room didn't agree with this positive feedback.

"It's terrible." Victoria spoke through white lips. "Haphazard and cluttered."

"Can you explain that statement in more depth?" Why hadn't she mentioned this before when she'd looked over the project a few days ago? My insides cramped, making it hard to breathe. I tried to focus, but another cramp hit. Had I just gotten my period?

"To me, it looks that you tried to have too many things going on at once. Collaboration is important, but the art shouldn't overwhelm your selling point."

Why does she hate me? But as I eyed the projected images, I began to see what had gone wrong with the designs.

I shot a glance at Max. I couldn't read his face. He seemed lost between opinions, and for a moment, I wished for Oswald to help guide his response.

"I don't know who or what to believe anymore. I thought it was good, but now I'm not so sure. And I can't be anything but certain, or it doesn't work for me." Max stood, straightening his suit. "I think we're done here. It's been a pleasure, and I definitely like Jadyn, but this is *business* and I think I may have to consider taking our *business* elsewhere."

My heart flew to my throat, and my insides seized up, cramping ricocheted all the way to my back. I needed painkillers immediately, but first to fix this situation. Victoria was on her feet. "Mr. Louis, I'm sure you don't mean that. Jadyn is one of our star consultants and she has not yet let down one client."

I tried to keep from shaking. She'd done a quick turnaround. I'd never heard Victoria say a good word about me and now she'd said more than one.

"There's a first time for everything." Max strode toward the door. This seemed so out of character for the man I knew. Lionel and Sophia had jumped up and were scurrying to catch up to him as though they were small children.

Victoria threw a look at me that would have made puppies whimper. I tried to think through the pain in my uterus and quickly followed him. "Mr. Louis, please give me one more chance to meet your expectations on this campaign. I'm certain that it can be fixed."

Max crossed his arms and stared hard at me. I kept myself from shifting my weight or fidgeting because I could sense he was judging my sincerity. He dipped his chin. "I'll be back on Monday at nine. You'll either have it or you won't."

He spun on his heel and left.

No one spoke after my client's dramatic exit. Everyone filed out quietly. A funereal vibe hung over the whole atmosphere. *Did my career just die?*

"You lose this account, you lose your job." Victoria clicked past me to the hallway. I was right. She hated me.

"Miss Simon, we have high expectations for you." Mr. Davenport stopped beside me and put a hand on my arm. "If you display half the creativity that I saw in your artwork last week, I think you can succeed at this."

I tried to smile in response. Lana bustled around, tidying and organizing the now-empty room. I had seventy-two hours.

If I lost this job, it meant no promotion, no place to live, not being close to Ethan. But what did it matter, anyway? I already didn't have any of those things. But I wanted all those things. Didn't I? At least, I still had my art.

But first, pain medication. For my heart and my period.

Chapter Twenty One

My steps echoed though the night's silence as I walked the last block to Mel's. The darkness pressed on me almost as much as Victoria's last words. I let myself into the apartment, kicking off my shoes even before I crossed the threshold in order to keep from waking my sister. At eleven, she'd already be in bed. Or she should be. But…the television still chattered.

And there she was, curled up on the couch, eyes open, a tissue box clutched in her arm and a pile of crumpled tissues on the floor next to her. I couldn't help but think she'd never let *me* fall to pieces in her apartment. But it was her place. I pushed the mean thought away.

I set my shoes beside the door, dropped my bag, and walked quietly to the couch where I sat on the edge of the cushion, close by her feet. She didn't look at me, just kept watching *I Love Lucy*. Mel only watched this show when she wanted to be comforted or couldn't sleep. I ran my hand along her calf. "Hey, sis. You okay?"

My question jerked her eyes to me and I saw new tears forming. She grabbed another tissue as tears streamed down her face. What could have happened? She hadn't texted me. I moved behind Mel and wound my arms around her. Sometimes, hugs accomplished more than words. She shook in my arms.

"I had an awful day, too." I spoke because she didn't seem ready to speak. "My biggest campaign of all time fell flat. I have till Monday morning to create a whole new design. If I fail, I lose my job."

She giggled through her tears. "What a pair we make."

Laughing and speaking. Both good signs.

Wiggling my fingers through her hair, I started to give her a head rub. "So are you going to tell me about your bad day? I don't think it can beat mine. After all, I came so close to losing my career."

"My day beats yours." Mel sniffled and snagged another tissue from the box. "I broke up with Anthony today. Or maybe he broke up with me. Whatever happened, the marriage is off."

The words barely escaped before another torrent of tears struck. I tightened my hug around her and scratched her back with one hand. I wanted to make her laugh again, but I didn't want to discount her grief. "I am so sorry, Mel. I award you "The Very Worst Day" certificate."

I swiped a tissue from the box and handed it to her for good measure. I heard her chuckle even as she blew her nose into the "certificate."

"On top of that"—she cleared her throat—"I hadn't renewed the lease for this apartment because I was going to move in with Anthony. Now I'm afraid that I won't be able to renew it, so I won't have anywhere to live!"

"Two peas in a pod. Want to move back to Mom's with me?"

Mel elbowed me in the side. "No way. I'm not going back to Mom's."

"Do you want to have a sleepover in the living room tonight?" I changed the subject. When we were little girls, living room sleepovers fixed everything. We'd keep the television on all night with reruns of *Dick Van Dyke* and *I Love Lucy*. Nothing could beat that time for the two of us. My body ached for my own bed, but my sister needed me, and I didn't want to leave her alone.

She snuggled deeper into my arms and nodded.

Saturday morning, I walked into the Eat 'n Park, a Pittsburgh classic. Smiley cookies winked at me from the dessert display cases near the cash register; Lana leaned against the case. She wore jeans and a pink sweatshirt with a huge purse slung over her shoulder. I'd never seen her so relaxed, but then again, I was dressed pretty similarly, minus the pink.

"Two?" The hostess didn't look up as she counted out menus.

"We might be expecting two more," I answered as I slid my phone from my purse and checked the screen. I hoped that Ted from Social Media and Isbeth from Design would make it, but they had made no promises. After all, it was Saturday.

The hostess led us to a table for four and handed out the menus. Once settled, I spoke to Lana. "I'm not sure where to begin to fix the problem in the campaign. Nothing like this has ever happened to me."

I kept thinking of Victoria. Words tumbled out of my mouth before I could stop them. "And is it just me, or does Victoria hate me?"

"Honey, these things happen." Lana opened her menu. "Bosses hate all their employees because they're threatened."

"Victoria—threatened by me? I bombed the campaign."

"Yes, but you successfully bypassed her authority with the art show, and Max did give you a second chance. People like you." Lana turned a page in her menu, keeping her eyes on the page "But let's figure out what we want to order before we dive into solving this campaign."

The restaurant seemed quiet for a Saturday morning, but it was eight thirty. Things probably wouldn't speed up for another hour or so. My brain churned over Lana's insight. Was she right? It did make sense. I finally settled on pancakes with bacon and eggs just as our waitress arrived with waters. "You girls want to order or wait on the rest of your party?"

I glanced at Lana. "I think we'll order."

With ordering out of the way, Lana pulled a notebook from her giant purse. She opened to a page already filled with notes. "I took the notes from yesterday and reorganized them to help us out as we try to brainstorm what went wrong and how to mend this issue."

"I'm still trying to figure out what went wrong. Everyone seemed to love it until yesterday." I tried to keep the despair out of my voice. I had one weekend to figure out a new campaign plan—without the help of most of the planning team. I still couldn't believe that Lana had agreed to show up and I couldn't help but feel that she was worthy of a consultant's job. She had an eye for details that I didn't, like taking notes from the meeting to utilize in replanning. "Lana, you've surprised me at every turn with your efficiency, your thoughtfulness, and support throughout the last month or so. I couldn't have done this without you."

"Thank you." Lana smiled at me, and her voice stayed quiet. "Based on the meeting feedback yesterday, the sell point was lost in the clutter."

I groaned and fought the urge to bang my head against the table. My head already pounded from the late night before and my back ached from either my period or sleeping on the couch with Mel. I'd left her sleeping this morning when I'd slipped out to meet Lana. "A lot of those ideas were patched together from Lionel, Sophia, and Max. I wanted to tailor the campaign to please them."

"Which might have sacrificed the integrity of the design and message that we originally wanted to send out to their potential audience."

I looked at Lana with fresh appreciation. She'd make a killer consultant with that type of intuition. Pride bloomed in my chest. I'd helped her become that.

"Hello, ladies!" Isbeth marched up to our table, wearing a patterned dress and boots. "I didn't mean to run late, but things got a little out of hand with the kids."

Isbeth settled into a chair, opened a menu, scanned quickly, and then closed it. I was glad to have her here. She had a sharp eye for imagery and she was never afraid of being blunt but always shared with good intentions.

"Isbeth, we were just pinpointing areas that need improvement," I explained as the waitress approached and then took Isbeth's order.

"Lovely! I had been thinking for a while that the design was all wrong for Mr. Louis and his artists. Honestly, it reminded me of my five-year-old twins' messy bedroom. Can't find a thing." She reached for Lana's glass of water and nearly took a sip before she stopped to ask, "Do you mind?"

Lana shook her head and Isbeth sipped her water. Meanwhile, I was trying to grasp what Isbeth had just. Why hadn't she spoken up sooner? I forced myself to let her I-told-you-so attitude roll off my back. We needed to get down to business.

"Jadyn," Lana's voice broke through my thoughts and I looked up to see her worried eyes on me. "A simple salvage would be to change all the images and backgrounds for these. The question is, what would we supplement with? Right now, the artwork varies but in too wide a range."

That's what I loved about Lana—she was able to see right to the root problem.

At that moment, our food arrived. Lana and I both had monstrous plates of food while Isbeth had ordered yogurt and granola with fruit. I tried not to feel judged next to Isbeth's conservative Saturday morning breakfast. I stuffed a wedge of pancake in my mouth and enjoyed the mingle of butter, syrup, and pancake. This almost made up for the crazy weekend ahead of me. Someone in my peripheral caught my eye. Turning my head, my eyes met those of Crystal. She sat with a group of teenagers clad in rumpled hoodies slumping over coffee mugs. She wiggled from her booth and walked toward me. As usual, she wore all shades of brown. I finished chewing and swallowing just as Crystal slid into the empty chair next to me at our table. She gave me a side hug.

"Hi, Miss J, I was wondering how your big work thing went on Friday." She worked a corner of her brown sweater. "I remember how nervous you were about it at class last week."

"That's actually why I'm here this morning." I glanced at my coworkers across the table. Both focused on their breakfast. "My boss hated the campaign design and our client gave us until Monday morning to rework it."

"Kind of like a make-up test or maybe repainting a canvas." Crystal tore at the napkin on the clean pair of silverware in front of her. "What are you going to do now?"

"What we just figured is that we need to change the imagery behind the text." I speared a piece of pancake and put it in my mouth.

"So what's the theme?" Crystal asked me as I chewed. I gestured to Lana, wondering if she could answer while I worked on this mouthful.

Lana explained, "Arts and music collaboration."

"It's like what you said last week about art being a community effort." Crystal threw a look over her shoulder at her friends. I peeked, too, and noticed that the teenagers didn't even seem to notice that Crystal wasn't there anymore. She gave a little shrug and then stood up. "Well, good luck, Miss J. I'll see you at class."

An idea bubbled in my head. "Hey, do you want to grab ice cream after class on Thursday?"

"Yeah, maybe." She turned for a moment and grinned at me before resuming her retreat back to her peers.

"What a funny teenager," Isbeth commented around a spoonful of yogurt speckled with granola.

She definitely isn't your average teenager. I nodded, thinking about my art class and the students that were growing on me. I hadn't expected to like them so much. Crystal's words sat on the edge of my brain, almost an idea but not quite fully formed yet. I frowned, trying to force this thought to come out. Suddenly, I knew.

The project still needed to uphold the ideals of collaboration. By definition, collaboration meant people working together toward a common goal. I had art and music. But a defined goal? Not really.

Midafternoon, when I finally returned to the apartment with my mind set on a nap, I pushed through the door to find my sister exactly where I'd left her. She was sitting up now, but the mound of tissues had grown. She'd moved on from *I Love Lucy* to *Friends*. Her cell phone sat next to her on the arm of the couch.

"Have you eaten?" My gaze traveled to the kitchen where I saw a used mug and a dirty coffee maker. She'd at least had coffee. Bad news when Mel left things dirty. A part of me could hardly wait to move so I could leave messes in my living space again.

"I didn't feel like it."

"You have to take care of yourself." I moved into the kitchen and rinsed out the coffee pot. "What do you want?"

"Nothing."

"You have to eat." I opened the fridge and stared at the contents. What would tempt her to eat? Eggs, cheese, leftovers? Ice cream was usually the best remedy for a broken heart, but she needed real food first. A pizza coupon caught my eye. "How about some pizza?"

"Only if we get garlic sticks."

"Done." I let the fridge door slam as I reached for the pizza coupon and retrieved my phone. In moments, I'd ordered pizza and garlic sticks.

I stalked to the couch and bounced onto the same cushion as Mel, causing her to rise slightly in the air.

"I called management this morning to find out if I can extend my lease." Her voice held no emotion.

"Mel, don't you think you might be moving too fast? You and Anthony could get back together." I laced my arm through hers.

She heaved a sob. "That's the thing. We're not going to."

"You don't know that." I rubbed her arm, trying to soothe her even as she began to cry harder.

"But I do." Mel sniffled. "I want a man who knows how to keep his eyes and his hands to himself. He has a few online dating profiles, and a couple of months ago, I discovered some texts on his phone from a girl. I just ignored it. But I can't do that anymore. If he doesn't respect me in those small ways now, what will keep him from worse down the road?"

I bit my lip. She had a point, and I had become less and less impressed with Anthony the more that I had seen him. But still, I wanted my sister to be happy. "People can change."

"Anthony can't change soon enough for our relationship."

"Don't negate what God can do in him."

"But that takes someone who's willing to choose God's standard of living first. I don't see him doing that." My sister wiped her eyes on her already mascara-stained sleeping t-shirt. "So I called management and they've allowed me to extend my lease for another year. They're going to charge me two hundred dollars for the added inconvenience."

Mel grew quieter. "And I know I've been terrible to you recently, but I was wondering if you might consider staying here for a while."

She wouldn't look at me. Her shoulders slumped, and she pulled her knees into her chest, hugging them. I wanted pump her spunk back into her veins again and make her stand tall. But she was right. Living with her the last month had been one of the hardest things I'd ever done, and I wasn't sure if extending our time together might mean the end of the new warmth between us. Of course, if I got the promotion, I'd be moving to Chicago anyway, so a month or two couldn't kill it, could it? Staying there would be better than the hour commute from Mom's. I hugged my sister, already listing all the reasons in my head why this would be a bad idea.

"I'll think about it."

Chapter Twenty Two

The conference room—filled with the same faces as Friday—felt all too familiar. A lot of things were different: the presentation, everyone's clothing, and a new sense of doubt. Maybe I was the only one feeling the grumpiness of the crowd and the uncertainty that this campaign could be fixed in only a weekend. I hoped so.

"Let's skip the preamble." I quieted the butterflies in my tummy, which were better than Friday's cramps, and walked the length of the room. "We're all here to see the new plan, and to start off, we have a new name: *Collaborative City of Bridges*."

Lana flipped the power point slide and all heads swiveled to the screen. "These are the designs in place before the weekend."

A few people muffled groans.

The slide flipped. "We've decided not to throw out all of the ideas, but rather to tweak them for CCB. The issues were primarily with the backgrounds and images. No actual unifying theme. Therefore, since Sophia and Lionel are Pittsburgh artists, we want to unify this collaborative effort with the concrete theme of Pittsburgh, explored through the eyes of artists."

Lana began to flip through the slides with a steady rhythm.

"You are seeing pieces I have created that match the text. Streamlined, consistent—boring. We need to brand ourselves as fresh and community-focused. Incorporate artwork from others and expand our community, building a larger platform for the musical artistry that Sophia and Lionel will share with us. Pittsburgh artists supporting other Pittsburgh artists.

"For example, we could exhibit a couple standing on the Roberto Clemente Bridge holding hands— that would be the image to accompany one of the ballads. For upbeat music, we can choose artwork that shows the "T," and other transportation in motion—like bikers, buses, cars moving past in a blur of motion. And yes, painters can capture vehicles in motion. One of my students recently did an earth-toned piece that would fit well with some of the more ethnic songs."

Lana flipped to our final slide that showed a sampling of our new ideas. The mood around the table had lightened as though someone had pulled a curtain aside, allowing sunshine in. A couple people whispered between themselves, and there were no solid frowns. "May I answer any questions?"

"What's your timeline for finishing this campaign if we see it through?" Victoria leaned forward, holding herself with perfect posture.

I paused. I hadn't foreseen this question, so I glanced at Lana, hoping she'd could send me an idea through brain wavelengths. She wasn't looking at me. I settled quickly on a random time span. "One month. Long enough to flesh out the idea. Short enough to not hamper Mr. Louis's greater plan in relation to his artists but long enough for us to contact, and coordinate with, potential collaborators."

"How will you find artists to collaborate on such short notice?" Lionel gripped a paper cup in his hands. Nine in the morning didn't look like it sat well with him.

"As an artist in Pittsburgh, I do have some connections with local artists here. A gallery. Plus, I teach an art class with some exceptionally talented student artists."

"I love it!" Max stood from his chair. "In a month, let's see what you have, Miss Simon."

Air rushed from my lungs and I realized that I had bought myself more time—that I wasn't losing my job yet and this could be fixed. *Chicago, here I come!*

I needed to move and feel the wind. Exercising wasn't my thing but sometimes, the mood just hit. I threw on my workout clothes. Headphones in. Music loud. I ran to the park where I chased the trails through the trees and skirted other exercisers. As my feet thumped across the ground, my brain scaled mountains of thoughts, considering the future and the present. My mind landed on Ethan and stayed there. I hated being far away from him—especially emotionally. I longed to speak with him face to face because telephone conversations and texting just couldn't cut it when it came to working out hurts.

Could they even be worked out?

My muscles burned with effort and breath rushed in and out of my lungs. I wanted to yell from the tops of the hills that I was alive and life was good and God had done it again. Instead, I released a deep sigh of breath, praising Him in the quiet of my heart, and I took the route that would carry me home.

Once in Mel's building, I ran the stairs to get a tiny bit more workout. On her floor, I stretched my legs out as I walked the hallway to our door. I fished my keys out of my pants and dropped the keys in surprise.

Travis sat on the floor next to our door. I scooped up the fallen keys and eyed him. "What are you doing here?"

"Waiting for you. I saw you run by a while ago, so I figured I'd come wait for you. I didn't knock because Mel can be pretty scary."

I checked the time on my phone. She wouldn't be home for at least another thirty minutes, but I knew she wouldn't appreciate a guy in our space right now. After breakups, she tended to be pretty anti-male.

"Travis, it's good to see you, but it's not a good time for you to be popping in." I jingled the keys in my hand, not wanting to meet his eyes. "I've been meaning—"

Travis stood and wrapped his hand around mine, silencing the keys in my fingers. He stood close— too close. "Have you heard that when a woman messes with her keys outside of her apartment that she wants to be kissed?"

My head jerked up to Travis's face. Only inches separated our faces.

He leaned in, and I stepped backwards, but his hand on mine held me near as his other arm came around me. *Pink potatoes, this has to end.*

"Travis, stop."

He pulled me close, pressing his hand against my sweaty lower back.

This is not romantic.

"Travis." I placed my free hand on his chest to buffer myself against him. "You've been a friend for years but right now, you're not acting like a friend. You always want something from me. Usually, I'm happy to help you out. But this time, I'm not."

I pushed from his arms, and he loosened his grip. I took in his face and saw a range of emotions flit across his face. First, surprise. Then, anger. But it settled on sadness, as though he knew I'd respond best to that. He cleared his throat and blinked. "You're my best friend. I feel like I've been losing you to Ethan."

His plea sent a prickle through my heart, but I couldn't be what he so wanted me to be. *That doesn't excuse his behavior.*

"My relationship with Ethan won't cost you my friendship, but your lack of boundaries and tampering with my relationship will."

"What are you saying?" Travis worked his fingers through his hair until it was standing on end. "A good friend doesn't set boundaries for a friendship."

"Wrong." I called him on that lie before my bravery failed me and my runner's high faded. "A true friend sets healthy boundaries."

Travis crossed his arms and frowned at me. "Then don't expect me to ever be your friend again."

His statement rang in my ears, reminding me of his childhood declarations, using almost the exact same threat. It hadn't scared me then, and I wouldn't let it scare me now. "I'd hate for you to carry out that threat, Travis, but I won't stop you. I appreciate your friendship, but things can't continue like this."

"I see how it is. If it wasn't for Ethan, you wouldn't be telling me this. I have lost you." Travis threw the words out like throwing knives. What he didn't realize was that each one missed its mark.

I watched him stalk away before I let myself into the apartment and locked the door after me.

Ethan arrived home from Chicago in the middle of that week, and I could hardly wait to see him. We'd been texting back and forth a lot and I'd found it so hard not to invite myself over, but I didn't want to push myself into the space he seemed to need.

My cell vibrated on the desk. A call from Ethan! I grabbed the phone and walked out of my cube. My heart pounded and a part of me feared that this might be a "breakup" call. I found an unassigned office and shut myself inside.

"Jadyn, can you take the afternoon off from work today?"

I shivered with delight. *Not a breakup yet.* We still needed to work through the art gallery moment more in person, but judging by his voice, he seemed to be doing okay.

I weighed the consequences of his request. All of me wanted to skip out of work right away, but with so much work to complete for the Collaborative City of Bridges, I didn't have the time. "Oh, I want to. I have so much to do. But I can probably leave an hour early. Would that work?"

"Sure. Want to meet at my place at 4:30?"

"I'll be there."

I spent the afternoon doing all the necessary work, but a part of me kept counting the minutes until I'd be with Ethan again. I wanted closure for the art gallery disagreement and to explain that Travis would only ever be a friend, if that.

I barely noticed the commute to Ethan's before I was at his apartment. I knocked, and the door swung open immediately. He held it open for me and I stepped over the threshold with a big grin on my face. I set my purse down and gave him a hug. "I missed you."

Ethan squeezed me tightly and then released me. "Come into the kitchen. I want to order some Italian takeout, but I wanted to make sure that I got something you'd love."

"I like it all!" I accepted the menu that Ethan handed me. He'd circled a couple of different things.

I handed the menu back. "I love food, but I'm more interested in being with you than eating."

Ethan grinned and pulled his cell from his pocket. He ordered and then hung up. "I've been thinking a lot about why I acted the way that I did at the art gallery."

I nodded, wanting to encourage Ethan to continue. He walked toward the kitchen table, pulled out a chair for me, and then settled himself across from me. Then he was standing again, grabbing a glass of water for each of us.

"It goes back to my old girlfriend. The short story is that she was dating me and another guy at the same time. When I first caught her with the other guy, she lied to me, saying he was just a friend. She'd lied to everyone else, too."

I gasped. At what that kind of romantic treachery might do to a person, and because I wanted to chase this girl down and cram her into the next shuttle to Pluto. She didn't deserve an actual planet. My fingers reached out to Ethan's hand that lay across the table. He flipped his hand and captured mine in a soft handhold.

"I guess that's why Travis got such a good reaction out of me. I can't stand the thought of being two-timed again."

I squeezed his hand. "Ethan, that's not me. I'd never do that to you. I'd never do that to anyone. I respect you and me too much to play games like that."

"I know." He shifted in his seat. "I've gotten to know you and I should know you're not that girl. But fear messes with minds. You seemed so different from anyone I'd ever met, and I'd let my guard down."

"Travis has been in my life for a long time, but he's not a man I could date. You are. I can trust your friendship and support even when you're thinking I did you wrong." I gazed into Ethan's eyes with all the seriousness that I could muster. I wanted him to feel the weight of belief behind my words, but the expression in his eyes as he looked back at me made my breath catch in my throat. His eyes held such tenderness.

"I'm sorry for even thinking that you might cheat on me."

"To me, "cheating" implies that we are exclusive?"

"Yes, I think I'd like us to be." He grinned at me. "Would you be okay with that?"

My world spun. Surprise must have shown on my face.

"Maybe a hug will help you think it out." He stood and tugged me by my hand. With a quick pull, Ethan had me in his arms with his hands around my waist. I rested my cheek against his shoulder as though all the world's problems had just drifted away.

I wanted to stay there forever. Or in Chicago, together.

Chapter Twenty Three

Friday night, three days after Ethan and I had decided to be serious, he texted and asked me to join him for dinner at his favorite sandwich place downtown. I jumped at the chance to spend more time with him. After we had our wraps made, Ethan paid and then we sat in a corner table.

"I'll be moving to Chicago in a month." He unwrapped his sandwich and scooped it up to take a bite, but some of the filling tumbled out. "I wanted you to be one of the first to know so we could discuss logistics. Would you like to go with me some weekend to look at apartments?"

I pulled back the paper around one end of my sandwich, keeping most of the sandwich cocooned. "I'd love to be your wing woman for apartment hunting, but I don't think that would be such a good idea with Max's campaign hanging on by a thread."

"Lana's a great assistant. I bet she could handle it just fine, and…I want you to like whatever apartment I end up with." Ethan took another bite of his sandwich and a bunch of insides fell through his fingers. I took a nibble of my own dinner, considering his words. Although originally, I hadn't liked the idea of training Lana, she'd been a wonderful asset and she really was ready to become a full-fledged consultant.

"I would love to come, Ethan, but I just don't think I can. The campaign is my responsibility, not Lana's." I reached for my drink to take a sip.

"I should have kept my sandwich wrapped up like you did." He eyed my neat side of the table, then his own space.

I lifted my wrap, proud of my eating methods. "Yep. It's kind of like a diaper. Keeps all the filling wrapped up tight inside."

My eyes widened. I had just said that out loud, comparing food to poop. Giggles tried to mask my embarrassment even as my cheeks flamed, and I briefly considered ducking under the table to hide.

"You'd make a great spokeswoman for sandwich diapers." Ethan grinned at me with eyes alight with laughter. His words made me laugh harder. I needed a minute before I could recover enough to finish my own sandwich.

His leaving for Chicago made my chest ache, but I comforted myself with the thought that I would soon follow.

Family dinner on Sunday night was a smaller affair than usual—just the girls. I washed my hands at the sink and then carried a bowl of mango to the dining room table. Mel still looked as though she'd been hit by a train. She hadn't done anything with her curls other than to pile them on her head, and her dress code recently had consisted of sweat pants and a big pull-over. No makeup.

"You need to pull yourself together and not let Anthony ruin your life." My mother stood behind Mel's chair with her hands on my sister's shoulders. "You've got to show him that he's the one missing out, not you."

"Mom. I broke up with the man that I thought I was going to marry. Aren't I allowed to be sad over it?" Mel rested her elbow on the table and dropped her head into her hand.

"Sure, baby, but you can't stay like this forever."

I returned to the kitchen to grab the salad dressing from the table and tried to push away my feeling of relief that my mother was focused on my sister instead of me. I walked back in and set the dressing down. Sitting in my chair, I viewed my family. Even if we were messed up, I was glad to have us. "Are you two ready to eat?"

Mom situated herself, extending her hands to each of us. She prayed. "Heavenly Father, thank you for my girls and all the wonderful things that they are capable of. Please prepare Jadyn for her Chicago promotion and provide a wonderful husband for Mel."

I peeked through my eyelashes at my sister and saw her cringe. Mom had no sense of timing. I squeezed Mel's fingertips, trying to encourage her not to take our mother's words to heart. She pressed her lips together, an understanding of Mom's high expectations between us. Mom still prayed, but I no longer heard her words as I reveled in this renewed feeling of camaraderie with my sister. And then, Mom released our hands, so we started to pass the salad fixings around the table.

"There are just so few good men in the world anymore." Mom piled lettuce on her plate. "I thought your father was a good man, but he up and left. I thought Anthony was good, but he's got wandering eyes and hands. I sure hope Ethan turns out to be a good man."

I kept my mouth shut. My mom didn't really want me to respond.

"Good ones are all taken or they die young," Mom continued. "I've dated some good men since your father left, but you just can't trust appearances and I'm so happy that I didn't end up with any of them."

Mel squirmed and set the salad bowl down heavily on the table. "So, Jadyn, have you come to any sort of conclusion about staying with me longer?"

Topic change. But I wasn't sure this topic suited me so well either. I dropped mango pieces on top of my salad, buying me a minute or two to think through my words. "Maybe we should talk about this later."

"I thought it would be easier to get it situated here since you *were* going to move home with Mom, right?" She stabbed a chunk of carrot with her fork.

"Jadyn! You did not tell me that your sister offered to let you stay with her now." Mom's eyebrows reached toward her hairline. "You know I don't have room for you here if there's another option."

The house boasted extra bedrooms, but Mom had converted them into an office, sitting room, and craft room.

"Mel just offered." I tried to keep my voice level. "I think it would be better if we waited to discuss this."

"No, let's talk about it now." Mel had her intense face on.

I honestly just didn't want to make her feel worse, but living with her had been like trying to get the attention of a giraffe. If she treated me as less than equal again, it would ruin our relationship. I didn't want to fight in front of my mom. It would save both of us embarrassment if we just waited until the drive home. Mom would surely have an opinion, too. But Mel was having none of it, so I plunged ahead.

"Here's the thing. You've opened my mail, ignored me, and then planned to kick me out. You've failed to treat me with any equality these last two months. It's your home, not mine."

I risked a look at my sister and saw that her mouth hung open, her fork suspended in front of it. Shock seemed like the right word to describe the expression on her face. She lowered the fork. "Well. You lied to me."

"Girls. Two wrongs do not make a right."

Mel and I stared at each other, and I wondered if I had accidentally entered myself into a staring contest. I fought the urge to shut my eyes.

I blinked. "It was wrong for me to lie to you, and that lie has caused problems, even with with Ethan. I regret that. But you also overstepped yourself. I can't have a roommate, even a beloved sister, who treats me like that."

Mel shoveled a huge bite into her mouth and rearranged her salad on her plate. I decided I could eat as well.

Mom reached for her water glass. I tried to keep my face still because whatever my sister thought, she wasn't sharing, but Mom began talking.

"And Jadyn, didn't you say that Ethan received that promotion to Chicago? It's like a match made in heaven."

I winced over that last phrase. Her pride in me always seemed so misplaced. "Ethan will be moving this month."

"If we establish some ground rules for living together, will you think about living with me till you leave for Chicago?" Mel's voice barely whispered, softer and pleading and somehow, more mature. I looked at her quickly; she seemed sad rather than angry. The loss of Anthony had altered my strong, unapologetic sister. She seemed more vulnerable. I wanted to give in to her offer, but I also couldn't forget how stressful living with her had been. The desire to soften tugged at me. But was this new Mel here to stay?

Tightening Max's *Collaborative City of Bridges* campaign in a month created an extremely hectic schedule for myself and Lana. Each day required that we hit the ground running to keep everything moving forward smoothly. But in our heels.

"Who was that artist at your art show with the silver-tipped hair?" Lana leaned over a list of artists we were considering for our campaign.

"I knew I was forgetting something. I can contact Chris for the list of artists that he's shown. We might be able to work with a couple of them." I reached for my cell phone just as I heard the telltale click of heels on the hallway floor.

When Victoria showed up in my cubicle on that Wednesday afternoon, she and Lana shared a look that sent Lana hurrying out of the cube.

"Victoria, it's a pleasure to see you. How's it going?" I tried to steady myself. What was that look between them?

"After looking over your work for Mr. Louis' campaign, I've decided that Davenport Cities Consulting can officially offer you a promotion to our Chicago branch."

Shock slipped through my veins. But a question poked me. Why were we having this conversation in my cubicle where anyone could pass by and hear what she was saying to me?

"The downside is that I need to know now if you'll take the promotion." Victoria lowered her voice as if she suddenly realized that people might hear her. "You see, your job here will be eliminated after you complete Mr. Louis's campaign at the end of the month."

This announcement shouldn't have bothered me, but she'd broken the two-inch heels off my shoes and expected me to still walk in them. I had no money. No other job options. "What do you mean, my job will be eliminated?"

"We have plans to promote another employee to a consultant position. This is a win-win situation for you both with better pay and a better position."

Her cheery voice paired with the strange news clawed me like a feral cat. Victoria wanted to get me out of the way. My mind scrambled through the people that she could mean, and it didn't take me too long to figure it out. I'd always just thought I'd take the Chicago promotion—that's what everyone expected of me and it would be the easiest course of action, but suddenly, I wasn't so sure that I wanted to play so easily into Victoria's plan, even if I did like Lana. But I had no choice because I needed a job, and of course, Ethan would be in Chicago. "I'll take it."

Victoria crossed her arms. "Excellent. We'll start moving the paperwork forward to transfer you to Chicago, probably within the next two to three months."

I opened my mouth to speak only to see her back as she exited my cubicle. My head spun. I heard a tap on the cubicle wall. Lana. Other than Victoria, she was the last person that I wanted to see at the moment. I waved her in, but then stood and grabbed my purse. "I'll be out for an hour."

My feet carried me straight to Daisy's coffeehouse before I realized where I was walking. I really shouldn't splurge on coffee, but I needed space from the office. I stepped through the door, and the artistic environment and eclectic decoration blew fresh air through me.

"What can I get for you today, Miss Jadyn?" The dreadlocked barista set a wipe cloth aside and met me across from the cash register.

His use of my name made me look at him again. He read the expression of my face and smiled at me. "I make a point to remember names."

"But you see so many customers throughout the day!"

Gavin, his nametag read. How had I missed that?

He shrugged at me. "Now, what may I get for you on this chilly afternoon? We have all the fall favorites, but my personal choice is an Earl Grey latte with a shot of vanilla flavor."

"I'll go with your personal favorite. A small." I pulled out my wallet and waited for the price.

Gavin waved his hand at my wallet. "Today, it's on me."

"You don't have to do that." I argued. "I am perfectly capable of paying."

"I know you are but indulge me in this." He smiled. "It brings me joy. Go find yourself a seat. I'll bring it out to you when it's ready."

Humbled by this man's generosity, I wandered over to the community bulletin board, and my eyes took in all the pieces of papers announcing yoga, music lessons, and so much more. My flyer sandwiched between concert tickets and a babysitting flyer. I stared at it. Could I do art in Chicago? I wondered what it would be like to take the promotion there. My mom would be pleased. Mel would be happy for me. Ethan could hardly wait for me to join him there. And I wanted to make them all happy, but a small part of me whispered doubt.

Do *you* want to go?

One thing I did know was that gallery flyer had to come down because that dream ended when I had agreed to the promotion. Maybe I was being melodramatic since the art show would last for a month in total, but I wanted to face reality. I reached up and unpinned the flyer gently. I held the paper in my hands as though a sheet of gold, precious and priceless. Stepping toward the garbage can, I bent to toss the paper in, but a throat cleared behind me.

"Here's your drink, Miss Jadyn." Gavin held the mug out to me and then pointed at the paper in my hands. "I wasn't able to make your grand opening, but I visited your artwork after and I purchased a small piece for the shop."

"I'm honored that you'd want something of mine for Daisy's!" My heart swelled. I tucked the paper into my purse, forgetting the trash can for the moment, and accepted my drink from Gavin.

"You should leave that sheet up until the show's over. It could generate you some more interested patrons." Gavin gestured to his community board.

"I just took a promotion in Chicago that I'm not even sure that I want. So it just felt right to take the sheet down early."

"Let's sit." Gavin led me to a table in a quiet corner of the shop, and we relaxed into the chairs. Across from me, he fiddled with a worn friendship bracelet encircling his wrist. The threads were softened light green and grey. Only time faded colors like that.

I wondered how long he'd had the bracelet.

"Life often feels option-less, but we do always have some sort of choice."

I pulled my tea in closer to myself and blew on it, trying to force it to drinkable temperature. A part of me had grown tired of basing all my decisions off other people's advice, like Mel. But Gavin wasn't Mel.

He tugged on his bracelet, running his fingers along its length. "I lost my daughter, Daisy, in a house fire five years ago. My wife left me soon after. When I think about it all, I'm filled with the regret of not having loved my daughter and wife better when they were both in my life. I pursued a lot of good things but didn't care well for the most precious people in my life."

Through Gavin's confession, my hand had crept to my throat as I imagined the pain of his loss.

"It was the most painful thing that I've ever dealt with. It changed the way that I live my life—changed the way that I view success." He ran his fingers across the bracelet again. "Before my house burned, society would have called my life successful, but I was missing out on what really mattered. If you don't want to leave, then don't."

"Dreams are expensive. And I won't have a job in a month."

Gavin stood, and nodded. "I'd be happy to give you some work here if you end up needing that."

I churned over his words.

Chapter Twenty Four

Two more weeks before the final presentation. Thursday night's art class came faster than I was ready for, but I welcomed the happy distraction. As I walked from my car to the library, loaded down with art supplies, I cranked through all the different ideas for this week's topic: landscape. My cell phone rang its normal cello ringtone, so I had no idea who was calling me. I shifted bags from hand to hand until I could grab the ringing phone. m1x3d art gallery.

"Jadyn Simon speaking." I stopped on the stairs to the library.

"Jadyn, it's Chris! I'm calling because I wanted you to know that you can pick up the check for your sold paintings. Overall, you've sold more than any of our new artists, so I was wondering: Could you supply me with a new selection of pieces?"

Could this be enough to solve my money problems? A million thoughts raced through my head. But one kept repeating over and over and over again. *I'm an artist!*

The next moment, I remembered that I didn't have space in Mel's apartment, nor did I have any time to create new pieces with the campaign hanging over my head. Plus, taking the job in Chicago deeply complicated my ability to partner with any type of art gallery here in Pittsburgh. All of this closed in on me and suddenly, I had to fight for breath. I caught sight of one my art students on the sidewalk and gave him a little wave. I needed to go.

"This is so great to hear!" I lowered my voice, not wanting to be overheard by any students who might be arriving. "Unfortunately, I don't think I'll be able to show with you any longer because of my workload, and I've accepted a promotion in Chicago. But may I get back to you on that later?"

"Sure. Let me know when you come in to pick up your check. I'll talk to you later." The connection ended. His voice had sounded clipped and disappointed. *I hate disappointed.*

When I walked into the classroom, Crystal already had her personal art supplies set up at her portion of the table. Her hair, piled on top of her head, made her appear taller. She wore long dangling earrings that touched the tops of her shoulder and her lips were smeared with an odd deep brown lipstick. She jumped up when she caught sight of me with all my bags and hurried to take a few from me.

"What are in these?" She pretended to stumble under their weight.

I laughed at her antics as I lowered the bags I carried to the side table. "Don't look because you'll see soon enough. So, do you want to grab ice cream after class today?"

"That'd be great. I'll just text my mom to make sure it's okay." Crystal didn't try to hide the excitement on her face as she scurried to retrieve her cell phone and send off a text.

Other students began to arrive. Ashland had changed the color of his hair again and I was beginning to see that it was a weekly thing for him. His poor, dried-out, violet hair. Bailey wore the same skull shirt as he had last week. Nicole arrived toting her violin, probably having just come from some sort of lesson or practice. I wanted to memorize each and every one of them with their silly and sweet quirks.

"Since most of you are here, let's begin." I paced the classroom. "I'm sure you've noticed that as people, we are constantly looking to achieve success, whether in academics, extracurricular activities, or relationships. But as artists, we need to set a new standard of success for ourselves. Does anyone have an idea of how we can do that?"

As usual, the silence seemed to stretch forever, but I didn't allow it to bother me. I moved to the bags that I had brought and began to empty them on the table before me. Knickknacks of all sizes, shapes, and designs spilled out. Household items mixed with more eccentric items like balloons and crazy wire decorations.

"Start simple, like 'success is when I spend some time painting every day.'"

Ashland bobbed his violet head. "Or doing your own thing."

"That's it exactly!" I found my hands coming together in a happy clap, which brought a grin to Ashland's face. A ball rolled off the table and I scrambled to catch it up before it rolled across the classroom.

"Maybe, first, we should think about what we think success is?" one of the girls suggested.

Crystal spoke up. ""Right! The art industry is super tough, though. So maybe we can count success as simply entering one of our pieces into a contest. Even if we didn't win, we did something for our work."

"Having our own code of success helps on the days when others don't understand what we're doing." I turned to the table behind me, placing the runaway ball amongst the pile of junk, like a mini garage sale. "I want to you all to think about that while creating a city scape with these pieces."

I enjoyed watching what each student chose. Nicole asked to incorporate her violin bow into her landscape while Bailey surprised me by choosing a silk daisy rather than something depressing like a skull. One girl arranged chopsticks amidst a plastic apple and a bouncy ball. They set up the area and then photographed it with my camera and their cell phones as well. As usual, the hour-long class sped by with most students staying almost thirty minutes later. With no class after us, most stayed until I stopped teaching, and nothing inspired me more than watching fellow artists grow. The only other time I felt this alive was when I was painting. After all the students had left, Crystal packed up her things. "Good news! My mom said it's fine for me to go for ice cream."

"Sweet! How do you feel about frozen yogurt? We can leave the stuff in my car here and walk there. It's only a couple blocks down, and it's not too cold yet."

Crystal helped me throw all the items back into the bags. She carried a couple out for me and then we headed to the frozen yogurt place.

I didn't want to ask her all the normal questions that teenagers get about school and such, but my words seemed to tangle, so quiet stretched.

"I think it's cool that you showed your art at m1x3d." Crystal scuffed her shoe against the sidewalk as we waited for the signal to cross the street.

"Honestly, I never thought I'd ever show any of my art. It happened by accident —I entered some of my work in a Hispanic-themed art contest, but the owner of that art gallery owned m1x3d, too."

We entered the frozen yogurt shop and we both assembled our desserts. Mine heavy on the fruit while Crystal's was loaded with chocolate and cookie dough. I paid, then we sat.

She scooped a chunk of cookie dough. "I daydream about showing my artwork in a gallery someday."

Crystal's words made me think of Chris's offer and then of Max's campaign.

"How would you feel about having your artwork potentially used in an advertising campaign?"

"What do you mean?" Crystal asked around a bite of cookie dough and brownie.

I quickly explained what I had been thinking.

"This is the campaign that you were talking about when I saw you last week at the restaurant?" She'd set her spoon down and was leaning forward, warm caramel eyes bright and lips tipping up.

"Exactly the one. Do you think the other students in the class would be interested? I can't promise that everyone's would make it, but we're looking for a lot of different and specific artwork."

"They'd be dumb not to! I mean, just me, I want to get my art out into the world even if my name wouldn't be plastered everywhere. Or could I have my name on it somewhere? Can I bring my mom?"

"I don't see why the works couldn't be signed." I scraped a mango bit from the bottom of my cup and scooped it up with a lump of tart frozen yogurt.

The teenager across from me chewed on her spoon but then placed it in the empty bowl. She stared across the restaurant. I could be comfortable with silence, but my mind flipped through potential conversation topics. Not one seemed quite right. The silence seemed to stretch too long, and I stacked Crystal's bowl into mine.

Her attention snapped back to our table. "May I ask you a question?"

I smiled, thankful that she had some conversation topic to bring up since all of mine had struck out even before I'd voiced them.

"Why did you start teaching the art class?" Crystal's eyes were wide, and she had crossed her arms as though to protect herself from my answer.

I smiled wider, hoping it would soften her stance. "I took the art class because I love art, but also because I know how tough being a teenager can be and art was always a good outlet for me."

"But why do you sit with us and then ask me for ice cream?"

I tugged at the hem of my shirt, buying myself some time to consider my response and word it just right. "I'm still learning myself and I don't have a lot of time to devote to artwork and improving my own abilities. Sitting with you all helps me to do that. And I asked you to have ice cream because I think you're an awesome student. If you're uncomfortable, I'm sorry. I didn't mean to make you feel singled out."

Crystal leaned back further in her chair and uncrossed her arms. "I'm just not used to adults acting like they actually care."

Her words settled into my heart and expanded there. The thought of moving to Chicago poked me from the inside, but I pushed it deeper inside. I didn't want thoughts of leaving to poison this moment. Guilt tagged me. I wondered if it would be possible to fly to Pittsburgh once a week for this class, but the cost would be too much. Good kids still needed people to care about them, and it seemed like very few had that.

Things between my sister and me had been good since she and Anthony had broken up. It made me wonder how much their relationship might have messed with our sister relationship, but sisters were forever. She even had offered to make dinner a couple of nights a week for the two of us, and she'd told me that Ethan could come sometimes. I was even beginning to like having a roommate.

"Jadyn, can you grab the salt from the table?" My sister stood in the kitchen, looking into a bowl that she'd just pulled from the cupboard. I jumped up from the couch to grab the saltshaker from the tiny dining room table and carried it over to her. "How do you feel about pancakes for dinner?"

"People are going to think the only thing we ever eat is pancakes." I stretched my back before I wandered to the couch. I waited for Mel to exclaim over not caring what other people might think, but she just pulled out the pancake mix and combined the ingredients. Shrugging, I settled in front of my laptop to search for art inspiration.

"So I've been thinking about what you said at Mom's the other night." Mel poured batter into the frying pan. She wiped the extra off the lip of the bowl. "I truly want to make living together something that you'd want to do. With your success at the art gallery—did you pick up your check?"

"Not yet." I wasn't ready to sever my relationship with m1x3d or Chris or art.

"I've been thinking about how you need a space to create art, especially since your art showing. How would you feel if we set aside a portion of the apartment for a studio?"

My eyebrows rose, and my jaw slowly fell open. She had always been pretty supportive, but she must want me to stay very much if she was offering to give me more space in her apartment. I studied her from across the room. "Are you serious? Where would that be?"

I took stock of the apartment, noting the available space that we had. A two-bedroom apartment with living, dining, and kitchen space. We didn't have an extra room.

"What if we made the dining room your art space or, if that's too open, you could use my walk-in closet—that is, after we move my clothes out."

"You'd let me use your closet?" I couldn't believe she'd offer that to me, but I was honored that she was willing to put my art career above her wardrobe. She had an impeccable taste in fashion. Of course, the lighting was terrible in there.

Mel gave a little shrug. "It's not my favorite option, but I want you to be happy and to feel as though this is actually your place, too, if you decide to stay. Or you could move some of your things into the walk-in and set up your art space in the living room."

"Jumping giraffes. You'd allow me to use part of your closet space *and* some of the dining room?" I set my laptop aside and stood with my sister in the kitchen so I could see her face. "You know good lighting is imperative, so the corner by the window would be the best place for me."

Her hands flew together in a silent clap and her face lit up. "Wait! Does that mean you'll stay till you head to Chicago?"

"Yes, but we need to establish a couple of ground rules. Number one being that we don't open mail without permission from the other person first. Number two, I'd like to move some more of my personal items here so it feels like this is my apartment, too, not just yours. What rules do you need?"

Mel had been nodding, but her head stopped as she considered my question. "I think it would be good if we always give notice when we're bringing a guy home to hang out."

"I can do that. Just don't get used to me being around because I'll be leaving as soon as I finish Max's campaign."

If only I could have a job, my art hobby, my art classes, my man, and my sister all in the same city!

But the truth was, you couldn't have it all.

Chapter Twenty Five

"Please tell me you're taking the promotion." Ethan and I walked toward Point Park. He'd grabbed me for a walk mid-morning in the workday, and I'd loved when he'd held my hand. Even now, his thumb drew circles on the back of my hand, making thinking more difficult than usual, but I managed to piece my thoughts together.

"How could I turn it down?"

Ethan squeezed my hand and swung our arms. "I can hardly wait to explore Chicago with you; we can visit all the art museums, fancy restaurants, and The Bean!"

"The Bean—what is that?" I smiled, even though a part of me couldn't seem to join in his excitement. Isn't that what an adult did—accept the promotion? And then be excited about it? I'd accepted the job, so why wasn't I happy? I tried to push my mother's nagging voice away and focused on listening to Ethan talking about Chicago's wonders.

"The Bean is a giant, reflective bean-shaped structure that tourists love to take pictures at. I bet you can even show at an art gallery there, too. You're so talented that they'd have to want your work—maybe Chris can refer you someplace?"

Ethan's thoughts of my art career warmed my heart even as a cool fall zephyr brushed at the scarf around my neck. The sky above fit my mood—gray. Wind whirled bits of paper around our ankles, creating its own special rain dance, and I wondered how long we would have before lightning and thunder crashed onto this fall morning scene.

He tugged on my hand and I realized that my walk had slowed in comparison with his, so I picked up my pace.

"I've been looking into apartment complexes in Chicago, and I found one that's pretty nice. Do you have any ideas about where you're going to live?" Ethan glanced at me and stopped walking. "Are you okay?"

His concern surprised me, and I wondered if I *was* doing okay. I bit my lip. "Should I feel happy over this promotion? Because I don't feel happy. I'm confused."

"The promotion means a raise, a new city, no more Victoria out to get you, and a larger client base for your artwork. Besides, I'll be in Chicago." Ethan squeezed my hand and tugged me to himself, wrapping his other arm around my shoulders.

I breathed in the cool autumn scent mixed with his spicy cologne. Mmhmm. Happy. And this would be in Chicago. I tightened my arm around him.

"And…a job. Your job here is ending, right?" Ethan mumbled into my hair. And I pulled back from the hug but held on to his hand.

"I just keep thinking about my art. And the opportunities that have just opened up here."

"You can teach in Chicago, I'm sure." He guided us back toward our building. "What does Pittsburgh have that Chicago doesn't?"

"I did agree to teach the art classes for a year, and you know how much I hate to disappoint people." Admitting that aloud reminded me of Chris and his offer. I pressed my lips together. "Speaking of disappointing people, I had to turn down an opportunity to show more of my artwork with Chris because I just don't have time to create it right now, especially with Max's campaign being in its last half, and because of taking the promotion."

"Don't you have old stuff you could show?"

"Yeah, but it's not the quality that I want to give to Chris."

"Old stuff will disappoint Chris?"

"I want to create quality pieces. And you know the Chicago promotion comes with more responsibility and so longer hours. I'm not going to have time."

"That promotion is a big deal, too. Don't worry about disappointing Chris. I'm sure he can fill that space in his gallery."

I winced and hated the thought of losing my space in Chris's gallery. He'd "found" me. I made myself breathe, knowing that Ethan hadn't meant to hurt me with his observation. Being an artist was my dearest dream. "It's more like I'm disappointing me."

"You're so busy always pleasing others that you never have time to do the things that you like."

"That's exactly it."

I wanted to be able to do it all, but something had to give, and my job provided my livelihood. *God, is there any way to have all these things?*

With only a week to go before the final presentation, Lana and I had our hands full. Neither one of us had actually taken our usual lunch break in the last week, and I had discovered that Lana was extremely gifted in handling the details while I exercised my artist's eye on the visual side of things. Perhaps Victoria had asked me to train Lana in hopes that it would hamper my work, but instead,

Lana had been a huge asset. We actually made a great team. *Maybe we could remain a team? Hmm.*

"It's been awhile since you've told me about any of the guys you've dated." I shuffled through the papers in my desk inbox. So far, everything was lining up right for this campaign, mostly due to Lana, in my opinion. "Any new stories?"

Lana looked up from her laptop that she had balanced on the corner of my desk. It was only a matter of time till she had her own cubicle and clients. "I told you about Speechless, right? And then there was Touchy Guy."

"You haven't seen anyone since those two?"

I studied Lana. Her once whimsical sense of style had tailored down to sleek, professional lines with only a few surprising accents. She'd kept the flavor of herself, but somehow managed to conform to the more rigid, silent rules of being a consultant at Davenport.

"Actually, no. And it's not that guys haven't asked, but I'm tired of dating right now. It doesn't seem to get me anywhere except a temporary adrenaline rush and then back to square one again. Speaking of which, aren't you nervous for Ethan to be heading out to Chicago—and a whole new pool of girls? I'd be nervous."

My hands stopped their paper organization. Should I worry over all the girls that Ethan would be working with in Chicago? Good thing I would be there soon after him so he wouldn't forget me. "I hadn't thought about it."

Lana's laptop beeped, signaling the arrival of a new email; her eyes zeroed in on the email. "We just got acknowledgment that the first prints are complete. I'll go grab them."

When Lana returned with the prints, we set them up against the cubicle wall. Using the artwork of local artists seemed to be paying off, especially in creating the right tone for two new musical artists in Pittsburgh. If Sophia and Lionel could capture the scene in Pittsburgh, they'd surely be able to take other cities by storm; of course, Pittsburgh couldn't compare to New York City or Nashville, but never underestimate an underdog. And, of course, other cities would have other hometown artists to collaborate with, giving them a local boost.

"Lana, we definitely have something here. I think Max will like it."

A few days later, on my way home from work, I realized that I still hadn't stopped to see Chris at the gallery. I didn't want to go. I had been putting it off because I so longed to be able to keep my work in his gallery, but I couldn't keep him hanging like that anymore.

The door charms jangled over my head as I entered m1x3d. Rosa stood behind the counter, and she gave me a little wave. "Rosa, I came in to pick up my check. Is Chris here by chance?"

"No problem." Rosa opened a drawer in the counter and pulled out an envelope that she slid across to me. "He isn't, but he told me that you won't be showing with us anymore?"

I chewed my lip; hearing the disappointment in Rosa's voice went straight to the sadness in me. "I accepted a promotion in Chicago. Do you know when I should come in to pick up the pieces that weren't sold?"

"One moment. I will check the schedule." She hurried into the back room while I stood and surveyed the walls. All of the artwork still hung on the walls from my show. I meandered over to my pieces and admired them on the wall of this suave little gallery. Some of the pieces bore "sold" stickers, and pride swelled in my chest. I had wanted to be an artist and there I was, doing exactly that.

"Jadyn?"

She couldn't see me around the middle partition so I moved back to the counter. "I was just glancing at the work again."

"You can pick up your work the day after this show ends—so in two weeks."

"Perfect. I just assumed since Chris had asked me to supply him with more artwork that you'd be needing me to clear out these old pieces." I crossed my arms, playing with the sleeves of my favorite fall sweater. "Thanks for the check."

Knowing that a door had closed with m1x3d, I plodded out of the art gallery. I needed to dwell on the good. My work would be displayed for two more weeks, and in my hand, I held my first earnings for my paintings. But my heart still hung heavy. I slid into my car and opened the envelope. Five hundred and fifty dollars. Half what I needed for the remaining overdue rent money, but still, that would be so helpful. I'd make a copy of the check later, for my mom to hang on her wall.

I wanted to celebrate. I sent a text off to Ethan, telling him that I had made my first money as an artist, but I knew he was busy with work so I didn't expect a response. Checking the clock, I realized that Mel was off work and probably headed home. I dialed her number. "I just received my check for my paintings! Can we celebrate?"

"Yes!" Mel's excitement matched my own. "Do you want to eat out or do you want take out?"

"I think this calls for dinner out. We haven't done a sister date in ages. How about you meet me at Pasta Too?"

"You mean that Italian place in the suburbs?" She seemed a bit surprised over my choice.

"Do you remember the food there? It's worth it, but I'm still in the Strip District so it'll be a while before I arrive."

"No worries. I'll leave now, but I'll probably only get there fifteen minutes before you." Mel hung up. One thing I could count on with my sister is that she was almost always ready to celebrate any little thing that happened in my life. Of course, success—even minor success—should be acknowledged.

The commute lasted much longer than I would have preferred, but by the time I had arrived at Pasta Too, my sister had been seated in a cozy little corner. Italian bread crowned the table with a small saucer of oils with spices. My mouth watered. I settled into the chair across from her.

"So let's see the check!" She took a sip from her water while I rummaged in my purse and pulled out the little sliver of paper. My sister grabbed it from my hands. She held it up to the light and admired it.

"Sister, you're famous!" She handed the check back to me. "So are you going to use it on a shopping spree?"

"I wish I could, but it needs to be used for that overdue rent or credit card payments. And to pay for dinner tonight." I selected a piece of bread and dipped it into the oil. The flavors burst through my senses, matching my mood of happiness. Mel grinned at me with a slight twinkle in her eye that piqued my curiosity. She was up to something.

Mel reached into her giant purse and pulled a small gift bag from inside. "I thought this might be the perfect gift in light of your new status as an artist."

She pushed the bag toward me, and I tried not to choke on the bread. The little bag in front of me was silver with pink tissue paper. It didn't look big enough to hold anything of consequence; maybe she'd purchased some earrings for me or a new key chain. I scooped up the bag and pulled out the tissue paper, looking into the bottom of the bag. A scarf, maybe? Reaching my hand into the bag, my fingertips touched silky smooth. I drew out the soft fabric in my hand. The restaurant lights illuminated a teal paisley print, and I realized that I held a new pair of teal paisley tights in my hands. My mouth open, I stared at Mel. "I thought you hated my tights!"

"I did—I do." She shrugged. "But I know you love them. Every artist should be allowed to express herself however makes her most happy."

I jumped up from my chair and ran around the table to fold my sister into a hug. "Thank you so much! I love them, and I've been missing having a pair."

The waitress arrived at that moment and sped through her greeting, finishing with the specials. "Ladies, tonight we can add our special wine sauce to your entrees, but it's by request only. Are either of you interested?"

By request only. Mel and I glanced at each other, grinned, then ordered our entrees with the special wine sauce. Once the waitress left, Mel reached into her purse again and pulled out a few envelopes. "I stopped at home and grabbed the mail as I was leaving. I didn't open any of them."

I accepted the packet and flipped through them quickly before shoving them into my purse. I couldn't help but appreciate that she was taking my mail request seriously.

My mind recalled the Chicago promotion, and I missed this restaurant and my sister already. It seemed silly to be missing something when I was still present.

"Mel, can I ask you something?"

"Sure, but my advice is now by request only," she joked and jabbed her finger toward the kitchen where our waitress had just walked.

I pondered her words and my question and realized that I did want her opinion. "I'd like your advice on something then."

Her eyes widened, and she held up her hands. "Hold on. I want to relish this moment."

I rolled my eyes. "I decided to take the promotion because it seemed like the sensible thing to do, but I'm wondering what you think I should have done. And I just found out the workload is heavier than what I'm working now, so good-bye, art."

My sister crossed her arms and leaned her elbows against the table. "From a career standpoint, you should accept the promotion. On the other hand, you need to ask yourself what your priorities are and will this promotion fit into those plans?"

"So what do you think I should have done?" I reached for another slice of bread, thinking at the same time that I should save room for my dinner.

"Honestly, it's up to you and I shouldn't sway your decision on this, despite the fact that I will miss you when you move to Chicago. I'll support you in whatever you do."

"Even if you don't agree?" I wanted to squash the tremor in my voice, but it stayed there, showing how much Mel's opinion mattered to me. Which, in the end, was maybe okay. She'd wanted to please me, too. This was a new revelation.

"Definitely," she said.

Chapter Twenty Six

It had arrived: the morning of the final campaign presentation. As the previous night's dreams faded, one idea lingered: what about coffee and community all in one place? The meeting wasn't until ten. Would Gavin let me present at Daisy's? It seemed a bit insane to change the location of the meeting so abruptly…or maybe not insane. Creative. I checked my cell phone. Lana would be up, so I dialed her number and waited. When she picked up, her voice lacked the usual cheery tones.

"Lana, I hope I didn't wake you." I kept my voice in a lower decibel, hoping not to offend her ears at six in the morning. "I've just had an idea that I wanted to run past you for the presentation today." I filled her in quickly. "Well, what do you think?"

"It's definitely a gamble." She paused, and I guessed that she'd muffled a yawn. "But considering this is the second attempt at this campaign, it might be better to push the idea of art collaboration than to shy away from doing something out of the ordinary. After all, the point is to wow the audience and bring them back for more."

"So I'm thinking I should stop in and see the owner of Daisy's this morning."

"Why not? We can all have specialty coffees if we want. Caffeine makes people happy."

"Perfect. See you in two hours." I hung up and bounced into the living room to find Mel standing over our coffee pot. Happy couldn't start too soon.

"I think it's broken." Mel's hair poofed around her head and her big t-shirt sagged off her shoulder. An urge to hug her came over me so I went and slipped my arms around her.

"I know a hug is not the same as caffeine in the morning, but maybe it will help?" I tucked my head under her chin even though we matched in height, meaning my butt stuck out. My sister wrapped her arms around me and squeezed my shoulders.

"You have your big presentation today! How are you feeling about it?" Mel released me from the hug and moved to pull our back-up microwave coffee from the cabinet.

"Surprisingly, not so bad. Victoria seemed to think what we have is spot on for Max's campaign." I selected two mugs and set them on the counter. "Do you want cream and sugar?"

She measured portions into each of our cups. "And what about the whole promotion thing?"

I swallowed. That was something that I hadn't wanted to think about. It filled my stomach with dread. Ethan would be moving to Chicago in a matter of weeks, and I kept thinking of my art students, and how I would tell them that I would be leaving. I liked the idea of being a stable part of their lives. Art had the power to change and heal people. This, I knew firsthand. "Well, I guess I'd better tackle this campaign and then I can think about the promotion more seriously."

I wandered back to my bedroom and pulled on the paisley tights, slipping my feet into slippers afterward. The microwave dinged. "Do we have any flavored creamers?"

"Nope, I haven't been shopping yet this week." Mel held her mug close to her heart, but then she set it down and moved in a circle around me. She stared at my legs and I fought the urge to tug my t-shirt down farther over my thighs.

I clutched my coffee cup in my hand and eyed my sister, waiting for words of dislike for the tights that she'd given me. But she surprised me.

"I'm glad you're wearing those tights. You've come a long way since that first pair. You've shown your artwork in a gallery, and you're training new artists once a week. I'd say that you're most definitely coming into your own, and you should do the things that you want, even if I think it's a terrible fashion choice. It's you."

My heart jumped. She might not agree with my love for teal paisley tights, but she accepted *me*. I grinned.

"Just promise me you won't wear them with a red dress. That would murder any belief I have in your artist's eye." Mel headed toward her bedroom with her own mug as I groaned at the mental image. Shuddering, I crossed to my bedroom to ready for the day.

By 8:00 a.m., both Lana and I had already completed the final details that couldn't be done the night before. We'd each arrived thirty minutes early without having discussed it, and I was pleased to see her devotion to this project.

"Did you stop by Daisy's?" Lana slid the artwork originals into a canvas bag. "Also, did you see that card on your desk?"

"I stopped by on my way in. Talked to Gavin. He said that he'd create a space for us—apparently he has some partitions that he uses for groups wanting some privacy." I turned to my desk and spotted a card in all shades of brown. Only one girl would make a card in shades of brown. Lifting the card and flipping it open, I read Crystal's short message: "We city kids stick together." And she'd signed her name in cursive. She saw me as one of them; here I was choosing to leave them when we'd barely accepted each other. *Leaving my art too.*

But what can I do? I swallowed. Lana's voice drew me back to my cubicle again.

"Daisy's will definitely be a change of scenery. How do you want to manage getting all the right people down there?" Lana moved toward another stack of paintings, then put them in another canvas bag while I straightened the freshly printed posters of the artwork with text. I unzipped the flat board bag we used for transporting large prints. "Also, I got an email from m1x3d's most prominent artist. He said he wanted to hear more about the campaign. We could still use him later on."

I grinned at Lana, and we fist bumped before returning to our previous conversation. "I was thinking we'll have everyone meet in the conference room and then walk over there together. I could even draw the comparison about how we can't stay in a sterile white environment when we're trying to engage an audience surrounded by noise and media all the time."

"I like that." Lana lined up the bags by the door of the cubicle. "I'm going to grab some interns to help me carry these down to the coffee shop. Do you want us to go ahead and set them up?"

"Please! I'll head down there soon myself. Meanwhile, I think I need to talk to Victoria." I wasn't totally sure how I was going to bring this subject up with her, but after Crystal's card, I knew I needed to. First, I settled into my computer chair to check my email. I scanned through the subject lines and senders, looking for anything that seemed important. Just at that moment, a new email arrived. Ethan Alvey. Subject Line: *Good Luck*. Immediately, I clicked it open.

Dear Jadyn,

Good luck with the presentation today. I wish that your presentation didn't coincide with this Chicago trip, but such is life and it won't be long until you are here! I also have a surprise for you, but I'm going to wait until I'm back in town to tell you what I've done. Show them what you've got and kill that campaign!

Yours,

Ethan

Yours. He'd called himself mine? My mind whirled from his closing words to his promise of a surprise. My stomach dropped. Suddenly, I wasn't sure about talking with Victoria. Torn between Ethan and my art—what was I to do? And what was his surprise? It almost sounded ominous, but surely a surprise was a good thing. Right? I didn't have time to wonder over what Ethan had done. I clicked my computer into power save mode and headed toward Victoria's office. She'd be arriving soon, and I'd better do it before I backed away.

I arrived at Victoria's office just as she did, hoping she wouldn't say anything about my paisley tights. "Good morning, Victoria. I was wondering if you had a minute."

"You'll have many of my minutes later this morning. Can it wait till then?" She didn't look at me as she moved to her desk and put down her bags.

Yikes. I hoped her mood would improve by the time of the presentation. "I know you said that my job position was going to close after I left for Chicago, but what do you think about keeping Lana and myself on as a team? I think that you'll see with Max's campaign that we're quite a dream team."

Victoria didn't even move from staring out the window at the city. Her voice was monotone when she answered me. "Not an option. I don't have money enough to keep you both."

And Lana, apparently, has taken the prize. My heart dropped, and I returned to my cubicle without speaking another word to my boss, grabbing my purse before heading down to Daisy's to help Lana finish the setup. As I walked toward the coffee shop, I ran my conversation with Victoria through my head again. Why not move to Chicago and Ethan? I obviously wasn't wanted here. The promotion would solve my money problems and advance both my career and my romantic relationship. I should be happy.

Then I remembered Crystal's card and her face from our ice cream date flashed in my mind, how she was opening up to me. She would be fine if I moved, but would I? These kids represented my art to me, and they were the ones that the Lord wanted me to be loving and pouring into. I knew it deep inside. Every city had kids, but they wouldn't be my Pittsburgh kids.

But my Pittsburgh man would now be in Chicago with a bevy of Midwest beauties.

And a surprise.

I set the thought aside for a moment as my feet carried me across the threshold into Daisy's. The layered scents of coffee permeated the air; my mouth watered, and my muscles relaxed. I observed the small space and saw that partitions had been set up, separating a large portion of tables from two or three near the door. Gavin bustled from around the counter, bringing a couple of easels with him. "Come see what Lana has been doing."

I followed Gavin and took in the sight of original canvases propped along bookshelves with their coinciding posters. The effect was eye-catching, reminiscent of a community patchwork quilt, deliberate and designed. Beautiful and full of love.

"This is great, Lana." My junior consultant stood back, eyeing her organization, only to step forward to adjust the spacing between pictures. I hadn't needed to come down because Lana and Gavin clearly had it all under control.

At 10:05 a.m., everyone who was anyone who needed to be at the *Collaborative City of Bridges* campaign presentation sat around the conference table. They either talked quietly between themselves or checked their smart phones. Victoria clicked into the room a minute later, gazed around the room, and then waved me toward herself. I nodded at her. "Ladies and gentleman, we'll be starting in a moment."

In the hallway, Victoria stood with her arms crossed in front of her chest. Her eyes squinted at me and I fought the urge to tug at my dress as her gaze lowered to look at my teal paisley legs. She shook her head and frowned. "Jadyn, I wanted you to understand that if this second attempt at a campaign for Mr. Louis fails, you will lose your promotion with Davenport Cities Consulting and will forego severance pay."

My hands went cold. *What a terrible thing to say to an employee right before she presents!*

"Also, I thought I told you never to wear those tights again. They're hardly professional." Victoria spun on her heel to re-enter the conference room.

"They fit the tone of this campaign." My voice came out stronger than I thought it would, but if Victoria had heard, she pretended not to. I followed her into the conference room and most heads pivoted toward the two of us. It was time to move the meeting forward. "If you would all pick up your belongings and follow me, we'll be relocating."

No one moved from their chairs. A couple of people turned to Victoria, perhaps trying to figure out if she was the one behind this surprise move. Max stood. He wore a deep purple suit with gold cufflinks. "You heard her. Let's go."

Lionel and Sophia shot to their feet at Max's words, and the rest of the room began to shuffle belongings together. "Please follow me. We'll be walking about two blocks, just so you know, and bring your sense of adventure!"

I couldn't help but feel that everyone was a bit frustrated to be moving from the conference room and then the building, but I forced myself to keep a cheerful mood. Little did they know that at the end of this sidewalk were multiple mugs of steaming black drinks. As we rounded the corner and Daisy's came into view, I felt a tug on my elbow. Lionel walked slightly behind me.

"Isn't that the place you had me meet all my music inspirations?"

"Exactly the place." I smiled at him. "I thought it would make a good example of what you and Sophia want to do with your careers as professional-but-community artists."

Lionel grabbed the door for me. I led the way behind the partition to a large cluster of little tables shoved together with chairs winding along the perimeter. A large ceramic pot steamed in the center of the tables with a collection of mugs crowding in beside it. Pleasure filled me as I saw that Lana had covered all the paintings and posters with white sheets. *That girl has an eye for detail.*

Confidence blossomed under my rib cage. Everything would be okay. I would mess up many times in life, for certain. However, there would always be moments where I knew I had done something right and this was one of those times.

Once everyone had situated themselves, I made eye contact with Lana. In light of her training with me, we had decided that she should present the first part of the campaign with all the different logistics that she had orchestrated. I relaxed, relishing the chance to be able to listen rather than present, and I was proud of her. She'd gone from secretary to consultant material in mere months, and that had been no easy feat. I watched Victoria as Lana presented and noticed that she almost seemed to be smiling. I didn't know that my boss had the correct facial muscles to smile. Isbeth nodded as she reached for her mug. Max listened with his hands folded on the table in front of him. Things seemed to be going well.

"Finally, I want to draw your attention to the test results received from our focus groups from this campaign. Eighty-five percent expressed that the ad images made them interested in finding out more information about the product; the other fifteen percent thought they'd probably check it out if the information was easily accessible. Over all, the advertisements were well-received. Some even asked for more information as they left their focus groups."

Isbeth started to clap and a few others joined her, but Victoria's quick look quieted the sporadic clapping. Was it possible that Isbeth hadn't spoken up about the first campaign design faux paux because Victoria wanted me to fail? No, that couldn't be. When a consultant failed, the entire company failed.

"And now, Jadyn will share more about the images and the process that we walked through to find the results that we have today." Lana gestured toward me as I walked to where she was standing.

How could I even follow her up? We might have worked as a team early on, but now, she'd obviously pulled way ahead. And Victoria had a clear favorite.

Chapter Twenty Seven

I took a deep breath, pushing my insecure thoughts aside. "Thanks, Lana, for taking the time to share that information. Lana has been a wonderful asset these last weeks as she's been training as a consultant with me. She specialized in the nitty gritty details of the campaign, freeing me to focus on the artistic side of things." I paused to send Lana a smile before turning to the task at hand. At the end of this meeting, I'd either have a job or I wouldn't, but I was truly happy to know that Lana would. I tugged a sheet off the nearest couple of canvases and their corresponding poster. "What we have here is the original painting done by a teenage art student and with it is the poster created by our design department. Notice how the words are supported by the artwork and vice versa.

Lana, could you help me unveil the rest of the works?"

Together, we quickly pulled the remaining sheets off the paintings and posters. I worked my way around the room, explaining the decisions behind each collaboration, and outlining how the images could be used across social media and even on the streets. "Finally, these posters can easily be distributed among the local coffee shops because many, including this one, have community bulletin boards where these types of communications are welcomed."

I took a slow breath and scanned the faces around the room. Isbeth's face danced with excitement, and I relaxed a bit. Maybe I had been wrong to think that her silence during the first campaign had been a sabotage. As usual, Victoria was frowning at me, but mostly, I wondered what Max was thinking. Since he was the client, his opinion would be the deciding factor.

The normal sounds of customers selecting drinks and then the whir of the steamer and clanking of mugs filled the air. A staccato beat of hands clapping drew me back to this side of the partition, and I turned to see Max standing as he clapped his hands. Lionel and Sophia followed his lead and a few others, including Isbeth, stood and clapped as well. This was a new experience!

"Miss Simon, I am impressed with your gumption and creativity in rethinking this advertising campaign. As long as Lionel and Sophia agree, we shall be using this *Collaborative City of Bridges*." Max saluted me and then seated himself.

"Thank you. I couldn't have done it without Lana."

"And I could never have done any of this without Jadyn." Lana jumped into the discussion. "She's trained me in everything that I know, and she's taught me how to think outside the box."

With that, the meeting ended. My heart expanded sizes as I considered Lana's words of praise. A few people excused themselves and left while others lingered over their coffees to ask questions and catch up with each other while looking at the images still leaning on easels. This was what I loved about coffee shops. Somehow, they created a safe place for relaxing and interacting. A throat cleared nearby.

Victoria stood a foot from me with a frown. She jerked her chin up and then began walking. In Victoria code, this meant follow. My heart caught. Max had liked my campaign; that meant I wouldn't lose my promotion, so why was Victoria pulling me aside again?

I paused for a moment, resistant to Victoria's demand, and enjoyed all the artwork for the campaign. My eyes settled on Crystal's canvas. Her first work that used a range of colors and not just browns. Something shifted in me.

I took a deep breath and trailed Victoria outside.

She stood with her arms crossed in front of her chest and her toe tapping the pavement. "Since you've successfully completed Mr. Louis's campaign, you'll be leaving next month to take the promotion in the Chicago branch of the company. Congratulations."

I never thought I'd hear those words, especially after my first mess up of the campaign. Ethan would flip. But I didn't feel happy. If anything, my stomach churned. My mouth opened before I knew what I was doing. "Victoria, I can't take it."

Her eyebrows arched. "That's an impractical decision."

I bit the inside of my lip and took a deep breath; saying those words had released a tight band that had been constricting me the past few days. "It might not make sense for this career, but Pittsburgh is home and it's important to me to stay here right now."

"That's unfortunate. I must remind you that your current job is no longer available at the Pittsburgh branch." Victoria lacked any emotion as she said that. She didn't even look sorry to be telling me.

Her words weren't a surprise; she'd told me that would be the case, but it was still hard to grasp after the campaign's success. I put my hand to my head, trying to steady the cyclone of noise inside it. I said. "Are you sure that you can't keep Lana and I on as a team? Maybe I could freelance?"

"Stay and lose your job. Go and accept a promotion."

In that moment, I wondered if Victoria had a heart underneath her pristine exterior. She'd been given everything by virtue of being a Davenport, but she seemed less than human sometimes. I stared at her as she checked her perfectly manicured fingernails and saw her look up at me through her eyelashes. *Jesus, I don't understand how it's supposed to work out now.*

"I'll give you a day to rethink. One day." Victoria walked back toward the office with her slender hips swinging over her high heels.

I sat down on the sidewalk, not caring what pedestrians thought of me and making Daisy's customers walk around me as they stepped out the door. Cold seeped through my clothes from the chilled cement and I rubbed my teal paisley legs, wishing for a genie to appear and fix my job situation, solve my money problem, help my art dreams.

How could I stay in Pittsburgh without a job?

And my heart broke a little. What about Ethan?

I lay in bed, staring at the ceiling and then the wall and then the clock. Seven hours until I would be at work again, expected by Victoria to take the promotion. Who in their right mind turned down a job promotion like this one? More money, sure, but more hours, too.

The room was too hot. I padded from my bedroom to the kitchen to pour myself a glass of water from the fridge. What was I going to do? My mom had been so proud when she'd heard about the promotion, and Mel—she was hands-off this decision. Obviously, Victoria wanted me to take it, but I suspected she wanted me out of the picture because the board had sided with me. Even Lana thought that.

Then there was Crystal. She didn't even know that I was thinking of leaving Pittsburgh and the art classes; but her opinion mattered to me. And my art. That job would be great, but the hours promised to keep me from pursuing my fledgling art dreams. Here, Chris had asked for me to partner with his art gallery again, perhaps more than once or twice. I wanted to show my art at other galleries in my hometown. None of that mattered, though, if I did not have a job.

Finally, there was Ethan, already planning our Chicago adventures. My stomach twisted, and nausea settled in. I moved toward the bathroom. Making everyone happy was making me sick.

Cuddling into the couch, I stared at the end table, not really seeing as my brain roamed through my options. Shouldn't my decision hinge on more than my job? As I stared at the end table, the Bible sitting on the edge came into focus. I didn't have to figure this out by myself.

I switched on the light and pulled the Bible onto my lap, flipping through it. I didn't know what to read, but I needed guidance. I stopped at Hebrews 11, the list of those in the Faith Hall of Fame. Something about this list always soothed me, perhaps the rhythmic repetition of "By faith." The words flew off the page at me. Life after life of men and women who had lived lives of faith in God's plan. My eyes caught on a section of Bible verses about Enoch. Hadn't I heard something about him recently? I reread verses 5 and 6:

By faith, Enoch was taken up so that he should not see death, and he was not found, because God had taken him. Now before he was taken *he was commended as having pleased God. And without faith it is impossible to please him*, for whoever would draw near to God must believe that he exists and that he rewards those who seek him.

So. Yeah. Enoch. Enoch pleased God, and it was impossible to please God without faith. I sat deeper into the cushions, churning the words over in my head again. Was there some secret message in there for me? Maybe it wasn't so secret. I shut my eyes and trailed my fingers over the Bible page. *Jesus, more than anyone else, I want to please you. I don't know what would please you most—taking this promotion or not.*

Crystal's face came to mind, and then the faces of Ashland, Bailey, and Nicole cycled through. These kids needed someone to care about them. I did care. A lot of these kids didn't have a dad in their lives, and I knew what that was like. Painting helped me work through difficult times. It could help these kids, too. Besides, I had committed to teaching a full academic year. How could I abandon them for a job that would not even allow me to pursue my own art? I knew the crazy hours already, and I hadn't even been promoted yet.

What would please Jesus?

On my way into work, I stopped at Daisy's. Gavin stood behind the counter, and when he saw me coming through the door, he was already working on my drink. It was nice to be known. "A while back you offered me a job here if I ever needed one. Does that offer still stand because I'm about to be out of a job."

"After the success of the campaign?"

I sighed, and he thought for a moment.

"I would be honored to have you on my staff, part time or full time." Gavin pushed my drink across the counter to me as I handed him cash. "But I'll still need you to fill out all the usual paperwork."

"Of course, and thank you. I'll be back if not today, then tomorrow." I grinned at him and then exited the shop, feeling a bit lighter. Being a barista with Gavin and working with coffee would be fun and would help the money situation.

I skipped my cubicle completely and strode to Victoria's office before I lost my nerve, gripping my coffee cup for support. She stood at the window and I couldn't help but wonder if the reason she always stood there was because it highlighted the length of her body. I tapped at the doorframe. Victoria didn't move. "Come in."

The frigidity in the room threatened to silence me. But I walked up to a chair across from her desk and gripped it. "I've made my final decision." I swallowed hard and continued. "I've decided to decline the promotion."

"I am surprised at you." Victoria's eyes pierced me like lasers. "You have a promising career ahead of you at this company."

"I'll be packing up my office today." I clung to my cup, trying hard not to distrust Victoria's sugary words. It was time to go. On my way back to the cubicle, I stopped in the break room and copier room to grab a couple of extra cardboard boxes. Lana sat in my cubicle when I walked in, a small box of her own by her feet. She eyed the boxes that I had in my hands. Her face bloomed into a smile, and she jumped to her feet, hugging me awkwardly around the boxes.

"Congratulations!" Lana stepped back and took a box from me. "Can I help you pack up your office?"

I smiled, but it must have been a sad smile because she stopped what she was doing.

Lana stood still, watching me.

"I didn't take the promotion."

"You didn't? Why not? Then why the boxes?" The questions tumbled from her mouth, and she thumped down into her seat. She used her foot to shove her little box farther under her chair. "You should sit and explain."

So I recounted all my thoughts; it took nearly five minutes.

"Finally," I concluded, "I want my life to please God, and when I'm working on my art or teaching my art students, I feel alive in a way that I haven't in a long time—like I was created to do it!"

"When you find something like that, you need to hang on to it." Lana picked up a box and started to put my things into it. In that moment, I couldn't be mad at her for being ready to move into my office even before I left.

My only worry now was telling Ethan.

Chapter Twenty Eight

A week after I'd declined my promotion and subsequently quit my job, I was scheduled to begin training with Gavin. And I still hadn't told Ethan. On the phone, I hinted that I had some bad news, but I justified not saying anything because I wanted to tell him in person. Ethan planned to arrive in Pittsburgh within the hour and spend the afternoon with me. I checked my cell phone with a paint-splattered finger to see if Ethan might have texted. Nothing. Most of his work had already been transferred to Chicago so he was only back to pack up his apartment and move. A knock reverberated on the apartment door. I stood from my easel, swishing my paintbrush in the water before setting it on the table, and headed to the door. I unlocked it and swung it open.

"Hello, beautiful soul." Ethan took me in from head to toe. I pictured what he was probably seeing: a light-brown-skinned, paint-splattered, curly-haired girl. He stepped into the room and slid his arms around my waist, squeezing me tight to his chest.

"You'll get paint on you!" I worried.

"I don't care. It would be an honor to be paint-speckled by you," he rumbled, and I could hear his voice through both his chest and his mouth. His heart beat against my ear, and our breathing began to synchronize. Ethan moved a hand to my head and stroked my hair away from my face. "Before we get to my surprise, I want to hear about this bad news you have."

Heartbeat slamming in my ears, I tried to remember the words that I had recited in the shower when I was thinking of this conversation earlier in the day. I kept my face resting on Ethan's chest, breathing in his spicy scent.

I tightened my arms around him and then released a little bit to lean back so I could see his face. "I've left Davenport because, after careful thought and prayer, I realized that I need to pursue my art and I don't want to leave my art students. The worst part of this is that I won't be moving to Chicago, so I won't be near you anymore." I squeezed back the tears, but one escaped anyway.

His face froze, and his eyes searched mine. He pulled me back into a hug and placed his nose in my hair. Ethan took a deep breath. "I wonder how I never heard anything about this sooner."

"I didn't want to ruin your excitement." Even as I gave this excuse, I tasted the familiar bitterness of disappointing someone. Yet I knew deep down that this was the decision I needed to stand by.

"In the end, it is your decision." He squeezed me tight. "But I won't let it dampen my surprise."

He moved his hand to his pocket and pulled an envelope out, handing it to me.

"What's this?" I asked as I took it from him and began to rip it open. A thin piece of rectangular paper. A check. My eyes bugged out. One thousand, two hundred dollars! I read the memo as my mouth fell open. *Overdue rent*. I jerked my face toward Ethan and tried to work out what to say.

His face shone with excitement and happiness, with just a tinge of concern.

"You didn't have to do this."

"I wanted to commission a piece of art from my favorite artist for my apartment in Chicago. Will that cover the costs?" Ethan reached for my hands, taking the envelope and check and setting them on the table so he could have both my hands free. "Jadyn, you've stretched me a lot these past few months and shown me how hung up I was on always being perfect—never taking any true risks.

You challenge me to try new things despite the chance of failure, even with a long-distance relationship."

Words stuck in my throat. A part of me had worried that with so much distance between us, Ethan would want to call off our relationship, but he'd commissioned a painting from me, meaning he wanted me around for longer. His check would cover the rest of the overdue rent. I moved my hands from his and wrapped my arms around him again. My heart thudded.

Footsteps in the hallway reminded me that Ethan and I still stood in the doorway with the door open. A guy walking past mumbled, "Get a room."

My cheeks burned, and I wiggled from Ethan's arms to shut the door. When I spun around, he was looking at me with his hands resting on his slim hips. "Thank you so much, Ethan. I don't know what to say. It feels too generous."

"It's nothing. Besides, by commissioning you, you'll have to come visit me once or twice. To figure out the space, and the light, and what kind of art might go well."

I studied the man standing before me, and I couldn't believe that he'd want to keep me in his life, even long distance. He acted like it was a no brainer. "Is it okay if I come more than that? And for other reasons?"

"I'd be crushed if you didn't."

I'd never known a long-distance relationship that had worked out. This could, maybe, be the first.

Ethan tugged me into his arms again, and I rested my cheek against his chest, trusting that we could figure out this long-distance thing.

"So here's what I was thinking," Mel wiped the kitchen counter of our apartment that evening. "Since you have a low-paying job right now, you can pay a quarter portion of rent, and how about you do all the cleaning and cooking?"

"I see what you're doing—trying to get out of chores!" Her rent offer did seem generous, but at the same time, I didn't want her to start acting like I was not an equal partner in this living situation. "That's nice of you, but I can use my savings."

"What savings? If you had savings, you'd have been able to pay your overdue rent with it."

I frowned. She was right. "I'm afraid that you're going to start acting like when I first moved in, and we've barely settled into such a good thing."

"I won't." She wrung out the washcloth and draped it across the sink faucet. "The thing is that it would be helpful if you did those chores because I hardly have time between my job, working out, and volunteer commitments."

I couldn't help but roll my eyes at Mel. "How about we try it for a month and reconvene to see if it's working for everyone?"

My cell phone buzzed from across the room and then erupted in rings. A client call? It had been so long since I heard that ringtone that I wasn't sure what to make of it. I crossed the room and picked up the phone. "Jadyn Simon speaking."

"I go into Davenport Cities Consulting on Tuesday and find your cubicle occupied by someone else. That is no way to treat an employee that has just earned my business!" Max's voice came through the phone in light tones despite what he was saying. "Anyway, I'm outside your building. May I take you for coffee?"

I peeked at the clock. But then again, why was I worried about the hour? I had nowhere to be in the morning, although I did have barista training tomorrow afternoon.

"Um. Sure." I let my eyes trail down my body. Sweatpants and sweatshirt would not fly. I ducked into my bedroom and grabbed a pair of jeans. "I'll be out in five minutes."

Minutes later, my heels and I clicked out onto the sidewalk in front of my building, looking for Max. His gold Cadillac sat purring by the edge of the pavement; Max changed cars like some people changed clothes. The chauffeur leaped from the driver's side and hurried around to open the door for me. I slid into the backseat.

"I love a lady in heels and jeans." Max winked at me and I thanked my sister silently for having suggested the heels at the last moment. "I want to cut right to the chase if you don't mind."

I leaned toward him so I could see his face in the streetlights as we drove through Pittsburgh.

"I'd like to offer you a position as my assistant." He folded his hands and waited, allowing silence to blossom.

My hand flew to my throat, and my mouth opened. I hadn't seen this coming. I pictured someone smooth and sophisticated like Oswald, and I wondered if I was up to the task of working so closely with Max. "I don't know what to say."

"Pay is negotiable and so are hours, although I expect you to attend events with me on most occasions. You would start immediately. I already know you are more than qualified."

I gulped in some air, suddenly feeling hot despite the chilly temperatures of the recent days. My mind raced. I remembered all the moments that Max had been off-the-wall crazy and I wondered again if I could handle that. I liked the idea of choosing my own hours. But then I recalled how he had seemed like he was going to fire me over my first campaign slip-up. I needed job security. The Cadillac stopped outside of Daisy's, and the chauffeur hurried to open the door for us.

Daisy's assistant manager, Ben, ran the shop in the evening hours, and he teased me for not being able to stay away. I kidded him for his Pittsburgh "yinz." After ordering coffees and sitting down, Max looked at me expectantly. He folded his hands on the table and I noticed his nails were glossy clear. "So, Jadyn, what do you say?"

"Your offer is tremendous; however, I'm concerned that you might fire me one day because I made some sort of error." I reminded him of the first pass on his campaign. "I'm human and I'll make mistakes." I voiced this almost in a whisper.

Ben carried our drinks over and set them down in front of us. "Always a pleasure to have yinz here."

I rolled my eyes at Ben.

"You want job security?" Max pulled me back to the conversation.

I bobbed my head up and down. "If you can promise me some sort of job security, I would be happy to work for you once the details are worked out."

"I'll have my lawyer draw up a contract that you can look over tomorrow." He grabbed his smart phone and dialed. The call lasted less than a minute, and I marveled that such a successful man would want me in his employ. Sometimes, I thought I should still be wearing pigtails—too young to be an adult, responsible for myself and for others.

But I knew without a doubt that I could do it.

My art students packed up their supplies after another Thursday night class. More and more of them were staying late to walk to a coffee shop together afterwards. With Thanksgiving almost here, warm drinks tempted more than frozen yogurt. The first couple of weeks that we had done this, the students had been quiet. But more recently, they chattered all the way there, including me in their conversations as well.

"Miss J, I heard you lost your job at that consulting place. That sucks." Bailey pushed his glasses up his nose.

"You lost your job?" Nicole dropped back closer to us. "When that happens in my family, things get tough."

"I did lose my job, but God provided for me with a part-time job at a coffee shop. I'm sharing an apartment with my sister, and an old client has offered me a position with him, and my overdue rent was paid." I grinned, thankfulness swelling in my chest.

The coffee shop came into view. Ashland held the door for all of us, and I thumped him on the shoulder as I walked past. "Thanks, dude."

I scanned the shop, looking for a space big enough to hold the bunch of us. From a small table in the back, a hand waved. Chris. *I should have called him.*

"You going to get something?" Crystal asked me as I began to move toward Chris.

"Yeah, in a minute." I jerked my thumb toward Chris. "I need to talk to that guy first. You all go ahead."

I strode to Chris's table and pulled out the empty seat across from him. "I owe you an apology for not calling you back about showing my paintings. It was highly unprofessional of me, and if you'd care to hear my excuses, I have them."

Chris pushed the screen of his laptop down. "I must admit that I was disappointed. You're a talented artist, but you can't allow your art to slide into the background."

I had blown my art connection. I filled my lungs with new air. "Thanks, Chris, for all you've done for me. I appreciate it. Circumstances have changed since then—I thought I was moving to Chicago, but I've decided to stay in Pittsburgh to work on my art."

Chris steepled his fingers, narrowing his eyes at me.

I fought the urge to look away.

"What an opportune turn of events!" he said.

I forced myself to wait while Chris allowed silence to stretch between us.

"I could really use another reoccurring artist. My clients responded well to your artwork, making a decent profit for the both of us—five percent more than the average new artist. Would you be interested?"

I pressed my fingers to my mouth. This couldn't be true. I mumbled through my hands. "Pink potatoes. Are you sure this isn't a dream?"

Chris grinned at me. "Not a dream. You create beautiful pieces that match the tone of m1x3d."

I stood and caught sight of the teenagers on the other side of the shop. "I would love it—and look forward to working out these details with you."

He nodded his agreement and I walked over to the empty counter to order my drink. The girl behind the counter asked, "What can I get for you?"

For once, contentment coursed through me and I didn't need the coffee. But I knew it would make me happy. "I'll have black coffee with two shots of vanilla."

Three weeks after turning down the job promotion with Davenport Cities Consulting, I walked into Daisy's with my apron and hat in hand. 5:00 a.m. I didn't mind the early hour, especially knowing I could have as much coffee as I wanted. Gavin stood behind the counter as always, but today, he held a mug in front of him that I hadn't seen before. That's one thing I loved about Daisy's—most of the mugs were one of a kind.

"Hey, Gavin. How's it going?" I looped the apron over my head and tied a bow behind my back. Gavin's dreads were pulled up in a colorful hat today, and he kind of reminded me of that one famous Jamaican.

"A young man came in looking for you yesterday, leaving this." Gavin pulled a waffle cone from behind the counter and handed it to me. I flipped it over in my hands and found a paper wedged inside the cone. I pulled it out.

I read the message out loud. "Ice cream date after work? No trucks allowed."

I would know that hand writing anywhere. It was sweet that Ethan had done something so creative rather than text or call me. I grinned at Gavin.

He smiled back. "I'm glad you've joined the team here." He lifted the mug from the counter. "And here, this is the Jadyn mug, purchased in honor of your bravery in pursuing your art while working at Daisy's and with Mr. Louis." He handed me a teal mug filled with dark, steaming liquid. "Within the cup is what I've dubbed No Regrets."

I blew across the surface of the coffee and took a sip. The flavor was a kick of bitter with a smooth, sweet undertone, almost like dark chocolate. Delicious.

"Gavin! This is divine and definitely aptly named." I took another sip of the dark brew. Dark moments and the sweet—like so much of my life. I'd finally figured out the right blend. "Living the life. No regret

Barbara Brutt

About the Author

Barbara Brutt is a 20-something hope-in-progress who's called three countries home, but she currently traipses around Pittsburgh, PA. Barbara plunked down hard into a smattering of jobs from shop girl to project manager with a healthy dose of nanny and house cleaner. Flying to new adventures is her favorite, especially when on an airplane or aerial silk, but it is words that pluck story-songs through her imagination. Barbara adores ice cream and only buys purses that provide room for a book or two.

Acknowledgements

In 2017, I determined that I would submit my manuscript to every opportunity that strolled near me. Thanks to Vinspire Publishing and a one-day unagented author submission event, *Teal Paisley Tights* suddenly found a home in the book world. Yes, I cried. I'm so grateful to Dawn Carrington and the Vinspire Publishing team for taking a chance on this story and me.

Backtrack to 2010, two college students sprawled between homework assignments and strung Jadyn Simon's story together. Alysha Jackson, my go-to brainstorm girl, caused some of the mayhem you see in these pages. Without her and my sister Deborah Brutt, Jadyn would not be the character she is today. And without my brother Jonathan Brutt, my website wouldn't be what it is.

Kim Peterson, who was the first person to suggest I write a novel and witnessed the birth of this story, invited me to join WAN, and this Writers Accountability Network continually makes me feel like a writer even when I'm not writing. And once Jaci Miller, another WAN-er, completed her edit of this story, I had the guts to release it into the hands of my publisher.

From a favorite author to amazing coach to wonderful friend, Sandra Byrd continues to be instrumental in my author journey. I will always remember asking her, "Do you think I have what it takes?" and she replied, "I don't know if you have what it takes, but I know your story does." In that moment, I determined that I would not let my story down.

My parents championed my book author dream even when others slid sideways glances like I was crazy for hoping. If it wasn't for those weekly trips to the library (thanks, Dad!) and the years of being homeschooled, I wouldn't be the reader and writer I am today. My mom still laughs over the reason I wanted to return to being homeschooled after one year at private school: "I don't have enough time to read."

I get tripped up when I try to acknowledge how my true grounding in life and in writing comes from my relationship with God. He gave me this word-joy. And despite the pockmarks of life and my creaky faith, I keep choosing Him.

Friends, new and old, who have celebrated this book with me, taking time to be curious about the process, asking me how I was doing, and talking me off the edge when I got scared—thank you. And also to you, the reader, who chose to pick up this book and be a part of the story. After all, a story is only half-formed until you read it into existence.

To all the bowls of ice cream that ushered me through every high and low, you were creamy, melty deliciousness.

Dear Reader,

If you enjoyed reading *Teal Paisley Tights*, I would appreciate it if you would help others enjoy this book, too. Here are some of the ways you can help spread the word:

Lend it. This book is lending enabled so please share it with a friend.

Recommend it. Help other readers find this book by recommending it to friends, readers' groups, book clubs, and discussion forums.

Share it. Let other readers know you've read the book by positing a note to your social media account and/or your Goodreads account.

Review it. Please tell others why you liked this book by reviewing it on your favorite ebook site.

Everything you do to help others learn about my book is greatly appreciated!

Barbara Brutt

Plan Your Next Escape!

What's Your Reading Pleasure?

Whether it's captivating historical romance, intriguing mysteries, young adult romance, illustrated children's books, or uplifting love stories, Vinspire Publishing has the adventure for you!

For a complete listing of books available, visit our website at www.vinspirepublishing.com.

Like us on Facebook at www.facebook.com/VinspirePublishing

Follow us on Twitter at www.twitter.com/vinspire2004

and follow our blog for details of our upcoming releases, giveaways, author insights, and more!

www.vinspirepublishingblog.com.

We are your travel guide to your next adventure!